"Wh

my lord?

Meredith questioned.

"Here." Brice touched a hand to a spot on his chest.

"But you were not wounded there." As she reached up he caught her hand and pressed it to his heart.

"Can you feel it?" His voice was low, hushed.

"Feel what?"

"The way my heart thunders when you touch me?"

"My lord . . ."

As she tried to pull away, he caught her hand and held it, palm flat against his chest. Though he held her as tenderly as a fragile flower, she could feel the carefully controlled power in his grip. His words were softly seductive. "You said that should I desire anything, I need only call. . . ."

Dear Reader:

We appreciate the feedback you've been giving us on Harlequin Historicals. It's nice to hear that so many of you share our enthusiasm.

During the long winter months, everyone looks forward to spring; and coming in April and May we'll have a wonderful surprise for you. In an unprecedented publishing venture, acclaimed Western romance writer Dorothy Garlock, writing here as Dorothy Glenn, joins forces with popular Kristin James to produce companion historical romances. *The Gentleman* and *The Hell Raiser* tell the stories of two Montana brothers who were separated as children, raised in entirely different life-styles and reunited as adults—only to clash bitterly and fall in love with each other's woman! Each book stands alone—together they're sensational. To celebrate the occasion, the heroes will be featured on the covers. Look for both books this spring from Harlequin Historicals.

As always, we look forward to your comments and suggestions. After all, these books are for you; so keep those letters coming. Meanwhile, enjoy!

The Editors
Harlequin Historicals
P.O. Box 7372
Grand Central Station
New York, NY 10017

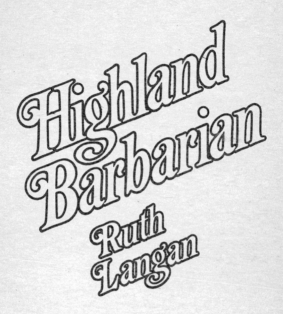

Highland Barbarian

Ruth Langan

Harlequin Books

TORONTO • NEW YORK • LONDON
AMSTERDAM • PARIS • SYDNEY • HAMBURG
STOCKHOLM • ATHENS • TOKYO • MILAN

To my mother, Anna Beatrice Curley Ryan,
In case I've forgotten to tell you lately
how much I love you

And, of course, to Tom.
Always to Tom

Harlequin Historical first edition March 1990

ISBN 0-373-28641-4

Books by Ruth Langan

Harlequin Historical

Mistress of the Seas #10
Texas Heart #31
Highland Barbarian #41

RUTH LANGAN

traces her ancestry to Scotland and Ireland. It is no
surprise then that she feels a kinship with the charac-
ters in her historical novels.

Married to her childhood sweetheart, she has raised
five children and lives in Michigan, the state where she
was born and raised.

Chapter One

Scotland
1561

The line of mourners stretched as far as the eye could see.
The men, women and children of the MacAlpin clan waited
patiently to pay their respects to their fallen laird, Alastair
MacAlpin. Dressed in simple peasant garments of rough
wool, their hands callused from lifetimes of hard labor, they
had left their fields and herds and trudged for miles to the
manor house of their chief.

Seventeen-year-old Meredith, his eldest daughter, sat beside his body to greet her people. Her thick dark hair, the
color of mahogany, had been brushed into silken waves that
fell to her waist. Her green eyes occasionally misted with
tears that were quickly blinked away.

Beside her sat the younger ones, sixteen-year-old Brenna,
with hair the color of a raven's wing and eyes that rivaled the
heather that bloomed on the hill, and fourteen-year-old
Megan, whose copper hair and gold-flecked eyes gave her a
glowing radiance that shamed even the sun. Though it was
Brenna's nature to be serene in the eye of the storm, it was

the first time Meredith had ever known her youngest sister, Megan, to be so subdued.

One by one the people paused to offer their condolences and to pledge their loyalty to Meredith, the new clan chieftain.

"You had a fine teacher, lass." The gnarled old man, Duncan MacAlpin, wiped a tear from the corner of his eye and placed a bony hand on the girl's shoulder. "You've learned your lessons well. You'll do the MacAlpin proud."

"Thank you, Duncan." Meredith steeled herself against the pain. There would be no public display of weakness. What her people, and especially her younger sisters, needed to see now was strength, dignity, hope. Later, when she was alone with her grief, she would give in to the overwhelming need to weep.

The clatter of horses' hooves sent the chickens squawking and clucking in the courtyard. The door to the manor house was opened to admit Gareth MacKenzie and a dozen of his men. The MacKenzie land adjoined the MacAlpin land to the north, then stretched for miles until it met the river Tweed.

"My condolences, Lady Meredith." Gareth MacKenzie bent low over her hand, then turned to study the still form of the MacAlpin. "You know, of course, who murdered your father?"

"Aye. Cowards. Highwaymen who struck under cover of darkness and hid behind masks. Duncan here said there were more than a dozen."

"You saw them?" Gareth turned a piercing gaze on the withered old man.

"I was bringing Mary back from a birthing at our nephew's farm. By the time I realized what was happening, they were gone. And the MacAlpin was drenched in his own blood." The old man choked back a sob before adding,

"Mary and I brought him here in our wagon. But even my Mary's medicines could not save him."

"Did you get a good look at any of their horses?" Gareth's hand hovered inches above his sword, and Meredith was touched by the vehemence in his tone. Though their lands had been adjoining for generations, she had never before been witness to Gareth's concern for her father's welfare.

"Nay." The old man's voice broke. "It was too dark, and my eyes are growing dim. But my arms are still strong enough to wield a broadsword with the best of them. A few minutes sooner and the MacAlpin would still be alive." He touched a hand to Meredith's shoulder and added softly, "Or I'd have died alongside him where I've always been."

"Don't dwell on it, Duncan." Meredith stood and wrapped her arms around the man who had been her father's right hand since they were lads. "You and Mary did all you could."

"Those were no highwaymen," Gareth said in a voice loud enough for all to hear.

A murmur went up among the crowd.

"What are you saying?" Meredith turned to study him while keeping an arm around Duncan's shoulders.

"It was the Highland Barbarian, Brice Campbell."

Meredith stiffened. The very name Brice Campbell sent terror through the hearts of all who heard it. He was a Highlander, and rumored to be the most feared warrior in all of Scotland. The Lowlanders, and especially the Borderers, found themselves under attack by both the English and their own neighbors in the Highlands.

"Everyone knows he and his men come down from the Highlands and strike, then disappear into the hills before anyone can catch them."

"But why would the Campbell attack Alastair Mac-Alpin?"

"The land." Gareth noted the hush that had descended over the crowd. "How many times have your borders been attacked in night raids in the past year?"

It was common knowledge that MacAlpin land had been attacked half a dozen times. Eight men had been killed and two boys under the age of ten. Crops had been destroyed, cattle stolen. And each time the looters had disappeared without a trace.

"'Twas the English. Everyone knows they are the ones who loot and pillage."

Meredith frowned. "My father never mentioned the Campbell."

"Not to you, perhaps. But he said as much to me."

She was stung by his words. For as long as she could remember, she and her father had shared everything. With the death of her mother and then the murder of her little brother, Brendan, father and daughter had forged a bond of love and trust. Why would he have kept such a thing from her?

As if reading her mind Gareth said, "You're young, lass. Alastair thought it too much of a burden to place on your shoulders. And so he confided in me and suggested that if anything should happen to him, he wanted to be assured that the MacKenzie clan would look out for you."

"I can look out for myself." She drew herself to her full height and turned away, dismissing him.

"I would not presume to intrude on your grief unless I thought it of the utmost importance." Gareth touched her shoulder and drew her around to face him, knowing that the crowd of onlookers overheard everything. "But those under the protection of the MacAlpin must be assured that they will have a strong leader. If it is indeed Brice Campbell who killed your father he will not be deterred by a lone woman. Your father would expect you to form a strong union immediately.''

He saw her eyes narrow fractionally as she gave him a withering look. "You would speak to me of marriage before my father is even in the ground?"

As she started to turn away he said, "I speak of a merger of our two lands, our two clans, in order to fight the common enemy. It is a small sacrifice to pay for the safety of those who depend upon you."

Meredith saw the looks that passed from Duncan to Mary, from one villager to another. Though no one spoke she could sense the fear that had suddenly taken hold. A seed had been planted. A seed of fear and rebellion. And she felt powerless to stop it.

"I am not suggesting that you marry me," Gareth said, pressing his advantage. "Though as the eldest, it would be my right." He saw her shiver and knew that he had touched a nerve. From the time they were children Meredith had sensed something unsettling about Gareth that she could not name.

Gareth dropped an arm about a young man's shoulders and thrust him forward. The two were the same height, and the same coloring, with golden hair and tawny skin. "My younger brother, Desmond, has always been a friend to you. As husband, he would pledge the strength of the entire MacKenzie clan to your protection."

Meredith saw the way the young man blushed. Desmond, dear, sweet Desmond, hated being made the center of attention. But he had always deferred to his older brother's wishes.

"As my husband, Desmond would also acquire all the MacAlpin land." Her voice was low, challenging.

Desmond always stammered when he was agitated. "Think...think you that the MacKenzies need your land?"

Meredith felt a wave of shame. It was well-known that the MacKenzie holdings were so vast that only Campbell land could compare. Still, the MacKenzie ambition was well-known. If not Desmond's, then at least Gareth's.

"I will speak of this no more until after my father has had a proper burial."

Gareth smiled and stepped forward to lift her hand to his lips. "That is as it should be. On the morrow we will return with a marriage offer that will bring peace and prosperity to our borders."

He seemed pleased when Desmond followed his lead and lifted Meredith's hand to his lips. Moving smartly, he marshaled his men from the house. With a clatter of hooves they left the mourners to whisper and gossip among themselves.

"Stand still, lass. A bride should be calm and serene on her wedding day." Morna, the old woman who had been with Meredith since her birth, fussed with the hem of the gown.

"Serenity is for Brenna."

"Aye. You've always preferred to be in the thick of battle." The old woman stood back to admire her handiwork. "Oh, lass. Your father would have been so proud."

At the mention of Alastair MacAlpin, Meredith's eyes clouded. Oh, Father, she prayed, looking out over the crowd that was hastily assembling, is this what you would have wanted? Am I to give myself to a man I do not love, in order to protect those I do?

She thought of Duncan, who along with his aged wife, Mary, had privately urged her to accept the MacKenzie offer. "Not for myself, lass," he had said fervently, "but for my children and grandchildren. There's been enough fighting among the clans. 'Tis the English we must fear. With enough strength we can stand up to their raids. If the MacKenzies can promise us peace and prosperity, we ought to at least consider it.''

There were others. They came in clusters of two and three to speak confidentially to their new chieftain, hoping to persuade her that there should be no more death and destruction. It was the look in the eyes of the old women that finally convinced Meredith. They had buried husbands and sons. Must they be condemned to bury grandsons as well?

The mere thought of giving herself to a man who did not hold her heart was appalling. But Meredith MacAlpin, whose ancestors could be traced to Kenneth MacAlpin, the first King of Scots, had been trained from infancy to put the needs of others above her own. This day she was determined to make the supreme sacrifice. She would marry Desmond MacKenzie. And she would find a way to love the sweet boy who had been her childhood friend.

She glanced at her two sisters, dressed in identical gowns of palest pink. She would do this for them, so that they could, for a little while longer, be young and carefree. So that the young men they fancied could grow to manhood and give them the lives they dreamed of.

''It is time.'' As the strains of the harp lifted on the spring breeze, Gareth MacKenzie slipped his mantle from his shoulders and fastened it about his brother. ''Wear the plaid with pride, Desmond.''

The two brothers embraced, then Gareth strode to the back of the church toward Meredith, a smile of supreme confidence lighting his features. ''I would be honored to walk with you to my brother's side.''

''I fear that honor is reserved for my father's dearest friend,'' Meredith said softly.

Ignoring Gareth's outstretched hand she placed her fingers lightly on Duncan's sleeve. The old man beamed with pride as Morna thrust a bouquet of heather and wildflowers into Meredith's arms.

Brenna and Megan walked slowly, tossing flower petals along the floor of the cathedral.

As the music swelled, the old man and the beautiful young woman began the long walk up the aisle toward the young man who stood waiting at the altar.

The ancient stone cathedral stood in a green meadow. The nearby loch was swollen from spring rains. The sun was just rising above hills still silvery with dew. To the east, the Lowlands were smooth, with only an occasional hill marring the vast expanse of green. To the west, the Highlands rose up, stark and wild and primitive. More than a million years ago the ice age dragged glaciers across the land, forming sharp hills and steep valleys. Only the hardiest of souls dared to live in such a harsh environment.

As the strains of the harp echoed in the morning mist, eerie figures formed a ring around the cathedral. Some led horses, others were on foot. All carried longbows. One, obviously their leader, tossed a rope to the highest point of the spire. Testing its strength, he slung the longbow over his shoulder and began climbing. When he reached the high open window, he pulled himself silently inside and stood on the stone ledge.

The bishop intoned the words of the service, then turned to face the young couple. Lifting his arms in prayer and supplication, he gazed heavenward. The words died on his lips as he let out a gasp.

An arrow sang through the air. The young bridegroom seemed to stiffen for a moment, then fell forward. With a shriek Meredith fell to her knees beside him and watched in horror as an ever-widening circle of blood stained his mantle.

As the crowd came to its feet a deep voice rang out. "Any man who reaches for his sword shall die."

Meredith turned and felt a dagger of fear pierce her heart. The man on the ledge above them was taller than any man she had ever seen, with shoulders wider than a longbow. He wore a saffron shirt beneath a rough tunic and, like a savage, was bare legged to the knees. His feet were encased in brogues and there was a mantle of dark homespun tossed rakishly across his shoulders. His dark hair was thick and shaggy.

Dozens of men dressed in similar fashion stepped into the cathedral. All of them held bows and arrows at the ready.

"I am Brice Campbell," their leader said, and she was certain he smiled at the fearful murmur that erupted. His name was known throughout all of Scotland and beyond. Only rarely was he referred to by the name Brice Campbell. Those who feared him called him the Highland Barbarian.

"I have come to avenge the blot on my good name inflicted by Gareth MacKenzie. It is not I who raided your lands and slew your sons and brothers. And now that I have silenced the liar's tongue, I declare this feud ended."

Meredith gave a little gasp as she realized that Brice Campbell thought he had killed Gareth. As she touched a hand to Desmond's throat and found no pulsebeat, she saw a movement from the corner of her eye. Turning, she watched Gareth duck behind a wooden pew and shamelessly pull Brenna in front of him as a shield.

Meredith's heart leaped to her throat. Her beloved younger sister was the only thing standing between Gareth MacKenzie and certain death.

"So that you will all remember that Brice Campbell is a just man," the voice from above intoned, "I will spare the life of Gareth MacKenzie's bride."

As the menacing Campbell turned to take his leave, an arrow sang through the air, fired from the protection of the pew. It narrowly missed its mark, sailing through the open window mere inches from the man's head. Instantly Brice Campbell's men unleashed a barrage of arrows, which brought down more than a dozen men on both sides of the aisle. MacKenzie and MacAlpin clanswomen became widows in the blink of an eye.

Meredith's gaze searched wildly about the sanctuary until she spied both her sisters unharmed. Megan had taken refuge behind the altar, where she was frantically searching for a weapon. Brenna lay on the floor, where she had been roughly pushed aside by Gareth MacKenzie.

"Fool!" the man at the window ledge shouted. "This feud was to have ended. But one among you has seen fit to carry it on. Now shall you all rue the day you crossed Brice Campbell. The lady's blood is on your hands."

Before Meredith could move, the man soared through the air, dangling from a rope, and caught her up with one arm.

Looking into her face, Brice Campbell felt for a moment as if all the air had been crushed from his lungs. Her hair, lush and dark, intertwined with ivy and wildflowers, fell to below her waist. The scent of wildflowers surrounded her like a spring meadow. Her skin was as flawless as fine porcelain. Her lips were pursed as if to issue a protest. Her eyes, as green as the Highland hills, were wide with fear. She blinked, and he watched them darken with sudden fury.

He stared at her heaving breasts, modestly covered by a gown of pristine white. The cloth was so soft, so fragile, it could have been spun by angels. His fingers tingled as he pulled her to him.

Meredith felt hands as strong as iron lift her as effortlessly as if she were a leaf. Cradled against his massive chest she felt his muscles strain as he pulled both their weights against the rope. Together they swung through the air and landed on the stone window ledge. As he set her on her feet she felt herself slipping. Her hands reached out for him, clutching blindly at his mantle. But before she could utter a cry he was holding her firmly against him.

"Touch one weapon and you shall watch the lady die by my hand," he called to the assembly.

Meredith felt the anger ripple through him, though he strove to control it. Through narrowed lids he studied the crowd below until, content that no one would offer further resistance, he turned. Still clutching her to him Brice grasped the rope and leaped through the open window. He landed on the ground and in one swift movement scooped Meredith up into his arms and climbed onto the broad back of a horse.

His men backed from the cathedral, then scrambled onto their horses. Before the people inside could even begin to get to their feet, the horses were galloping toward the hills. Once there, they disappeared into the rising mists, into the forests, into the feared Highlands.

Held in Brice Campbell's arms, Meredith felt her heartbeat keeping time to the pounding rhythm of the horses' hooves.

The man who held her captive was the strongest, most fearsome man she had ever seen. In the morning light his skin was ruddy. His hair held the hint of sun in the dark, burnished curls that kissed his wide, unwrinkled brow. The muscles of his arms were as thick and hard as twisted ropes. She stared, fascinated, as he urged his mount forward, holding her against his chest as effortlessly as a child holds a kitten. But it was his eyes that captured her gaze. Dark, piercing eyes that fastened on hers and held her gaze when she yearned to turn away.

"So, my lady. It seems you've been made a widow before you were even given the chance to savor the MacKenzie charm. A pity that you'll spend your wedding night in a hovel in the Highlands."

Meredith bit her lip and lowered her head so that this barbarian would not see her terror. She had just been stolen by a savage. A Highland savage. And if even half the stories she'd heard about the Campbells were true, she would never see her beloved Borderland or countrymen again.

Chapter Two

A faint rosy glow spread across the horizon. The hills were washed with pale light.

All through the day and night they had ridden, and when darkness cloaked the hills and forests, Meredith had sensed the change in the landscape. They had been climbing steadily from the beginning of their journey. The terrain was littered with rocky crags and steep pinnacles and frigid waters. The surefooted animals picked their way over the obstacles with the skill of those born in the Highlands.

Now, with the dawn light breaking through the mist, Meredith had her first glimpse of the Highlands. Though close to exhaustion she could not fail to be moved by the glens and fells, the rushing streams and waterfalls. The wild, primitive beauty of the land thrilled and terrified her. Like the man who held her, mile after mile, in his arms. Splendid. Frightening.

After his first murmured phrases, he had spoken not a word to her. At times he had called out to his men in the darkness. They had shouted their responses. Some of the men cursed. More than a few curses had come from his own lips when his mount stumbled, or when tree branches scratched and clawed. Meredith trembled in fear at the depth of passion in the man. He was quick to anger, she realized. Would he be as quick to strike out at others? At her?

A few of their curses had him chuckling, low and deep in his throat. That sound caused strange feelings to curl deep inside her. Feelings that were most unsettling. He was a rough, unlettered man, born and bred for cruelty and killing, she reminded herself. Not the kind of man to cause a ripple of feelings in her.

She heard the change in his tone when turrets could be seen rising above the mist. "At last. We are home."

Home. She had a sudden desire to weep. Would she ever see her beloved home again? Or would she be condemned to die in this strange wilderness?

As they topped a rise Meredith stared at the sprawling structure of stone, standing between two towering peaks. Though not as heavily fortified as the Border castles, for they were constantly being attacked by the English, it was a solid fortress surrounded by wooded hills. What was more, it was luxurious, even opulent.

In her mind she had pictured these rough people living in hovels. Had her captor not said as much? But the roofs she saw among the trees were of solid, sturdy houses. A few even resembled the English manor houses.

The sound of voices could be heard in the forest. The voices of women and children coming to greet their men. The distant sound of hounds baying.

While she watched, the men saluted their leader and veered off the path toward their own homes. Women laughed and children shouted as they were lifted in brawny arms and hugged fiercely. Within minutes horses and riders had disappeared into the forest, leaving Meredith and Brice Campbell in a small enclosed courtyard that led to the castle's entrance.

Half a dozen hounds surrounded their horse, leaping and baying as their master called each name.

The door was thrown open. The first one through the doorway was a thin youth with fiery hair spilling about a wide forehead. A sprinkle of freckles danced across an impish, upturned nose. His arms and legs were as thin as a girl's, though the beginnings of muscles could be seen beneath the clinging sleeves of his saffron shirt. His sparkling blue eyes filled with joy at the sight of Brice.

Servants hurried out to catch the reins of the lord's horse as he dismounted.

The lad threw himself into Brice's arms. "You've been away so long I was beginning to fret."

"Over me, Jamie lad?" Brice tousled his hair and wrapped him in a great bear hug. "You know better. I'll always return to Kinloch House."

"Aye," the lad said with feeling. "And I'll always be here waiting."

"Until you're old enough to ride with me," Brice muttered with a grin. "Which will be soon from the looks of you." He held the lad a little away from him and studied him with a critical eye. "You've grown at least an inch since I left."

The lad laughed, then glanced shyly toward the vision in white who sat astride Brice's horse.

Seeing the direction of his glance, Brice reached up. Meredith was hauled roughly from the saddle and handed over to a bewildered serving wench who stared mutely at her master's captive.

"Take the woman to my chambers. I will deal with her later."

Meredith shivered at his tone. Her mind whirled as she was whisked inside and herded up great stone steps. She had a brisk impression of tapestries and banners lining the walls of the staircase before she was ushered into a chamber on the second floor.

"There's fresh water, my lady," the timid servant said. "And I'll fetch warm clothes if my lord approves." She backed from the room and closed the door.

This was obviously a man's private domain. The furniture was massive, like the man who lived here. A log burned in the fireplace and Meredith hurried to stand in front of it. She had been chilled clear through to the bone. The gauzy gown intended for her wedding had offered little protection from the cold. And though the warmth of her captor's body had offered some protection, she had been buffeted by the raw elements. Perhaps, she thought, she would prefer death by freezing to whatever torment Brice Campbell had in mind.

What did he have in mind for her?

Meredith turned, keeping her back to the fire while studying the sitting chamber. The walls were hung with tapestries and furs. The cold stone floors had been softened with fur throws, as were the chairs and settles.

She needed a weapon with which to defend herself. Sooner or later Brice Campbell would discover that he had killed the wrong man. She would be useless to him. And he would be forced to dispose of her. When that time came she would have to be prepared to fight to the death.

She moved about the room, searching for anything that might be used as a weapon. When she found nothing she entered the bedchamber. The flames of the fireplace cast the room in a soft glow.

A rough-hewn frame of logs supported a huge bed littered with pallets of down and fur. Meredith's gaze fastened on a shelf above the bed where a dozen swords and daggers lay strewn about.

She studied the weapons and selected a small dagger that would fit beneath the waistband of a gown. Clutching it to her, she ran a finger gingerly along the blade and was pleased to find it honed to perfection.

She glanced down at her waist. The filmy confection she was wearing could hardly conceal a weapon. She would have to hide the dagger until more suitable clothes were given her.

Kneeling beside the bed Meredith began searching among the linens for a place to hide her treasure. Her fingers encountered the softness of fur. She closed her eyes a moment, resting her cheek against the velvety smoothness. How drained she was. There had been so little time to rest in the past few days. First there had been her father's death and burial, and then the marriage plans. Marriage. She felt tears sting her lids. There had been no time to grieve for her father or for her husband of less than a minute. She pressed her cheek to the soft bed coverings and choked back a sob.

Though she was an excellent horsewoman, she had spent too many hours of the day and night in the saddle. Her muscles protested. How she yearned to rest her aching body. Oh for a few moments of respite from the fear that lay like a hard knot in the pit of her stomach. She sighed. A minute longer, and then she would get to her feet. She must be prepared when the barbarian came for her. She would rest only a short time. She could not afford to let down her guard. Against her will her lids flickered, then closed. With one hand holding the dagger, the other curled into a fist at her side, she slept.

Brice finished the last of the mutton and washed it down with a tankard of ale. His hunger abated, he leaned back and stretched out toward the warmth of the fire. The dogs at his feet stirred, snatching up the scraps he tossed them, then settled back down to drowse.

He was in a foul mood. Now that he had eaten his fill, he would have to give some thought to the woman.

If he was cold, the woman had to be much colder. The thin gown had afforded her no protection from the chill of the night. But she had brazenly rejected his offer of a warm cloak. What arrogance. He felt the beginning of a grudging admission of respect before brushing it aside. What foolishness.

She was a most unusual woman. Not once had she cried or complained. And not once, when they had made brief stops, had she climbed from his horse and demanded a moment of privacy.

A bride and a widow within minutes. And yet she had not shed a tear. Remarkable.

What was he to do with her? His hand atop the table clenched and unclenched. It had not been part of his plan to steal the woman. In fact, it bothered him more than he cared to admit. But the fool who had defied him and fired the arrow would have to bear the guilt. The terms had been clearly stated. One among the MacKenzie clan had no conscience.

Across the table Jamie MacDonald watched in silence. He had learned to hold his tongue when Brice was in one of his black moods. Jamie did not see Brice's bouts of temper as a flaw. Any man who carried the weight of responsibilities that Brice Campbell carried had every right to moments of doubt. If someone had suggested that Jamie was turning a blind eye to Brice's faults, he would have fought them to the death. He adored Brice Campbell. His devotion to the man was absolute.

Brice looked up as the door was thrown open. The dogs rushed to the door and sniffed, eager to greet the visitors who carried a familiar scent. Angus Gordon, Brice's most trusted friend, burst into the room. Behind him strode

Holden Mackay, whose clan had recently joined forces with
the Campbells in the feud with the MacKenzies.

One look at Angus's stormy features told Brice that
something was very wrong.

"You've killed the wrong man, Brice."

"What are you saying? You saw him fall at the altar, Angus. It was Gareth MacKenzie."

"Nay, Brice. 'Twas his younger brother, Desmond. Holden and I stayed behind to learn the name of the one who
had fired the arrow at you."

"And did you?"

At Brice's arched brow Angus nodded. "Gareth Mac-
Kenzie. He would be the only one fool enough to continue
the feud after you had announced it over." His tone lowered. "Holden tried but could not get to him. There were
too many MacKenzie men. And the kirk was crowded with
women and children."

For a moment Brice could only stare from one man to the
other. Suddenly scraping back his chair, he raced up the
stairs toward his chambers with Jamie, Angus, Holden and
the hounds on his heels.

"Woman." The door was slammed against the wall, the
sound reverberating along the hallways of the castle. He
gazed about the empty room. "Do not try to hide from
me."

In quick strides he crossed to the bedchamber and kicked
in the door. Jamie, Angus and Holden remained in the
doorway, watching, listening.

The dogs circled the figure by the bed.

In that one instant before her head came up, Brice saw her
kneeling beside the bed, her hair spilled forward like a veil.
He could read her confusion when her lids flickered and
lifted. Eyes as green as the shimmering Highland lochs

watched him as he strode toward her. By the time he reached her she was on her feet, prepared to meet her fate.

The dogs growled low in their throats. But not one of them made a move toward the woman. They would wait, forever if necessary, until their master gave them the signal to attack.

In her hand was a dagger. A very small, very sharp dagger. Though Meredith's heart pounded painfully in her chest, her hand remained steady.

It was a giant who faced her. A giant whose rough clothes and speech sent terror racing through her. He stood, feet apart, hands on hips. On his face was a scowl that gave him such a fierce look she wanted to flee. But though her heart was nearly bursting, she reminded herself that she was now the MacAlpin. The MacAlpin was no coward. Meredith lifted her chin a fraction and met his look with one of defiance.

He saw the look. Even in his anger he admired her for it. There were not many in this land who could face Brice Campbell without flinching, be they man or woman.

The dagger? Though he had no doubt that he could best this small female in a battle, it irritated him that she would dare to draw a weapon against him.

"Put it down."

Her eyes widened at the icy command.

"If I am forced to disarm you, my lady, I assure you I will not be gentle."

She stared at the muscles of his arms, then lifted her gaze to the challenge in his dark eyes. For a moment longer she held the knife. Then slowly, with no change in her expression, she let it drop from her fingers. It fell to the floor and lay there among the furs, glinting in the light of the fire.

"Your bridegroom," he said, watching her through narrowed eyes. "Was he not Gareth MacKenzie?"

She wanted to hurt him as he had hurt her. She wanted to twist the knife, while he writhed in pain. If not the dagger, then the words that could cut as surely as any blade.

A half smile touched her lips. "Nay, my lord. It was not."

His eyes narrowed fractionally. Damn the woman. She was enjoying his confusion. "The man I killed. Who was he?"

"Gareth's brother, Desmond."

She saw the way his lips pressed together. A little muscle began working at the side of his jaw.

"You lie, woman. Why would the younger brother be allowed to wed before the eldest?"

Especially to one as lovely as the woman standing before him. For the first time Brice allowed himself to see, really see, the woman he had captured. With that wild mane of hair falling in tangles to below her waist and that gown of gossamer snow revealing a lush young body ripe for the picking, she was stunning.

"Because Gareth knew that I would never consent to be his wife. He offered Desmond instead."

"Consent?" Brice Campbell threw back his head and laughed. "And why would he need the consent of a mere girl? Why did he not go to your father and offer for you like a man?"

"I need the consent of no man," she said in a haughty manner that had him lifting an eyebrow in surprise. "Now that you have killed my father, I am the MacAlpin, heir to my father's land and protector of his people."

"I killed your father?" Brice took a menacing step closer and saw the way she watched him with the wariness of a doe in the forest. "Who accuses me of such treachery?"

"Gareth MacKenzie."

He clamped his mouth shut on the curse that rose to his lips. "At least the lie was spoken by one who does not matter to me."

"He matters so little," she said with a look of fury, "that you invaded the sanctity of the kirk to try and kill him."

At her sarcasm Brice felt his temper rising. But just as quickly, her next words had him feeling contrite.

"And succeeded in killing an innocent lad in the bargain."

"I regret having killed Desmond MacKenzie," Brice said with sudden honesty.

For a moment Meredith found herself astounded by his admission. Could it be that the barbarian was almost human?

"But the next time I will succeed," he added in a tone of pure venom. "From this moment Gareth MacKenzie is a dead man."

"And what of me?"

He took a step closer until they were almost touching. The hounds, taking a cue from their master, inched closer, sniffing the hem of her gown.

To her credit, Meredith did not back away, but stood facing him. He reached out a hand, intending to catch her roughly by the shoulder. The instant his fingers encountered her skin he felt the heat. Heat that raced and pulsed until he felt as if he were on fire.

"I haven't yet decided just what I'll do with you." He stared down into her eyes and was astounded by the sexual pull.

"What is your name?" His voice was a mere whisper.

"Meredith." She was surprised at how difficult it was to speak. At his touch her throat had gone dry. All the blood seemed to have rushed to her brain, leaving her feeling weak and light-headed.

"Meredith MacAlpin."

"Meredith." An unusual name for an unusual woman. He had to remove his hand or he would be burned. He clenched his fists by his side and took a step back. "Daughter of Alastair MacAlpin?"

At her nod he said simply, "He was a good man. And a fair one."

His mind began working feverishly while he studied her. "Perhaps I'll use you as the bait in a trap."

He saw the way her lips pursed as she started to protest. The words died on her lips as he added, "If Gareth Mac-Kenzie sees your land slipping away, I'll wager that he'll do anything necessary to get you back."

"Are you suggesting that Desmond was ordered to marry me only to enlarge the MacKenzie holdings?"

He saw the sparks in those green eyes and nearly laughed aloud. So he had struck a nerve. Swallowing back the smile that threatened he murmured, "Was there any doubt?"

He watched the way her features darkened with fury. Aye, a nerve. God in heaven. What a temper. What a fascinating, fiery little creature.

"Oh, Gareth MacKenzie will come for me." She faced him, hands on hips, eyes blazing. "But not to enrich his estate. He will come for me because he is a gentleman. A man of honor. And not a—barbarian."

He did laugh then, a deep, joyous sound that sent little tremors along her spine.

"A barbarian, am I?" His smile faded. In its place was a look of pure venom. "Aye. That is what I must be if we are to believe that Gareth MacKenzie is a gentleman."

He stooped and retrieved the dagger before crossing the room to remove all the weapons from the shelf above the bed.

"Angus," he shouted. "Holden."

Instantly his friends were at his side.

Brice handed them the weapons. "See that these are kept away from the lady." He emphasized the word "lady."

Angus nodded toward Meredith. "Angus Gordon, my lady."

Meredith studied the man who stood beside his friend. Smaller by a head, sandy hair fell in a riot of curls over his freckled forehead. His blue eyes danced with the promise of laughter lurking just beneath their clear depths. In her state of anger Meredith refused to acknowledge him, except for a slight nod of her head.

"Holden Mackay," Brice said by way of curt introduction. "Of the clan Mackay to the east."

Meredith studied the burly man. At first glance he appeared to have no neck. His head seemed to rest upon his massive shoulders. His upper arms, like his chest and shoulders, were corded with muscles. As he lifted several weapons with the ease of a seasoned warrior, he turned and, for the first time, stared directly at her.

"My lady." He inclined his head slightly. "Your stay at Kinloch House should prove to be most interesting."

Meredith shivered at the suggestion in his words. But it was his eyes that frightened her. They were cold, lifeless. Like his soul? she wondered.

"I will join you below stairs," Brice called to his friends.

When the two men left, Jamie continued to stand in the doorway staring with fascination at the beautiful woman who was Brice's captive.

"Jamie. Be gone, lad."

The boy blushed clear to his toes before rushing from the room.

When they were alone Meredith lifted her head a fraction and faced her captor.

Again he felt the pull and had to force himself to step back, away from the heat of her.

He deliberately turned his back on her and walked to the adjoining sitting chamber.

"I will have food sent to you. My servants will see to your comfort." At the door he turned toward her with a look that struck terror in her heart. His eyes were dark, dangerous. "If you try to leave this room you will find yourself most uncomfortable."

"Do you think I fear death at your hand?"

He gave her a chilling smile. "Perhaps it is not death I have in mind, Meredith MacAlpin. Perhaps it is something far worse for a lady such as you. At the hands of a—barbarian like myself."

His words sent a shiver along her spine. She had been prepared to die. But the thought of being used by him like some tavern slut sent her into a state of near hysteria.

He called to the hounds and they ran eagerly from the room.

When the door closed, Meredith began to pace the length of the room and back. She must find another weapon with which to defend herself.

With a feeling of desperation she searched every inch of the room. She was not a woman who accepted defeat gracefully. But defeated she would be without a weapon. As she turned dejectedly toward the bed, she spotted a rough cloak dropped carelessly in the corner of the room. Beneath it she found a dagger, small and sharp. With trembling fingers she concealed it beneath her gown.

This time her captor had not even bothered to disarm her—had merely ordered her to drop her weapon and she had. Now he would think her too puny, too insignificant, to dare to defy him. Hopefully he would not bother checking her for a weapon again.

She strode toward the fireplace and stood, deep in thought. The next time Brice Campbell came for her she knew what she must do.

Chapter Three

When the door to the sitting chamber opened, Meredith's hand automatically moved to the dagger at her waist as she swung around to face her captor. In her eyes was the look of a warrior.

"I brought you food, my lady."

Upon seeing the serving girl Meredith let out a long hiss of breath.

The girl was nearly as tall as a man, with blond hair neatly plaited and twisted about her head. As she set the tray on a table near the fireplace, Meredith noted that her hands were large and work worn.

"What is your name?"

"Cara."

"Have you served Brice Campbell long, Cara?"

With ease the girl pulled a massive chair in front of the table and waited for Meredith to seat herself. "I was born here in Kinloch House while my lord Campbell and my father were in France. When my father died in France, my lord arranged for my mother and me to stay on here."

"And you do not object to being forced into service?"

"My lady, it is a fine life for us. If my lord Campbell had turned us out, where would we have gone?"

"Have you no family?"

"My mother has two brothers, but both had already taken wives. We would have become a burden to them, and in time they would have resented us. Knowing that, my lord Campbell provided for us."

Meredith noted the warmth in the girl's tone whenever she mentioned Brice Campbell's name. "How can one so cruel elicit such devotion?"

"Cruel?" Cara gave a sweet laugh. "My lord Campbell is a good and fair man. I have never known him to be cruel." She lowered her voice. "But he is cursed with a quick temper. Mother has often said that Father told her he would ne'er be the one to cross swords with him in battle."

Meredith recalled his curses in the darkness, low and savage, and felt herself shiver. Aye, the man had a temper.

"But he is quick to forgive and forget as well. A kinder, fairer man there is not in all of Scotland. His kindness even extends at times to his enemies."

"I do not understand."

Cara gave her a level look. "Jamie MacDonald's father was a Lowlander."

"I had thought the lad to be Campbell's son."

"Son?" Cara smiled at the thought. "Ian MacDonald and his wee son were all that was left of a clan that had been burned and looted in the dark of night. Blaming Brice Campbell, Ian MacDonald journeyed to the Highlands to seek his vengeance."

"What happened to Ian?" Meredith asked softly.

"He was killed in battle. When Brice learned that there was no one left in the Lowlands to raise the lad, he took him in. And Jamie MacDonald is like a son to Brice."

Cara swallowed suddenly, dismayed at the looseness of her tongue. "I pray I have not betrayed a confidence by telling you this, my lady. But let no man call Brice Campbell an unjust man." She avoided Meredith's eyes, fearing that she had overstepped her bounds. "I will leave you to your meal. When you have finished I will return with warm clothes." She stared pointedly at Meredith's gown. "Though there is nothing wrong with the clothes you wear. You look as lovely as a bride."

The food, which only minutes ago had seemed so inviting, now tasted like ashes in Meredith's mouth. She pushed the plate aside. "I was a bride. For a moment."

Seeing the bleak look on Meredith's face, Cara cried, "Oh, my lady. What happened?"

Meredith's voice held a dreamy, far-away note. "He was hardly more than a lad. Doing what his family ordered. As was I." Her tone hardened. "He was killed at the altar." Meredith scraped back her chair and crossed the room to stand in front of the roaring fire. She was suddenly cold. So cold. The scene played once again in her mind and she gripped her hands together so tightly they were white from the effort. "Killed by an arrow from Brice Campbell's longbow. The same Brice Campbell you claim is an honorable man."

"I am sorry, my lady."

Meredith was so deep in thought she didn't even hear the door close as the serving girl took her leave.

In the great hall Brice paced back and forth before the fireplace while Angus and Holden emptied their tankards. Though Jamie MacDonald's eyes were heavy, he resisted the urge to go to bed. The need to be close to Brice, to hear all that had transpired in the Lowlands, was more compelling than the need for sleep.

The hounds lay in a circle before the fireplace, their eyes firmly fixed on their master.

"How could I have made such a blunder?"

"The MacKenzie brothers are nearly identical. From so great a distance it was a natural mistake." Angus added softly, "Do not fret, old friend. We will kill Gareth next time."

"Next time." Brice whirled on his friend, his eyes blazing. "Do you think I can ask my men to risk their lives going down to the Borders again, just to honor my good name?"

"Why not?" Angus shrugged. "You know they would carry your standard anywhere."

"They have wives and children to consider. I will not place them in danger for the sake of my reputation."

"Then you and I will go." Angus grinned. "You know I like nothing better than a good joust. Especially with the likes of Gareth MacKenzie."

"And I will ride with you," Jamie said, jumping to his feet. "I have no need to stay here."

Brice's temper cooled. "Aye. We're three of a kind." His frown turned into a smile. He could never resist Jamie's enthusiasm.

"Then we'll go back down and make good our promise?"

"You have a duty to stay here and grow to manhood," Brice murmured gently to the boy. Circling the room, Brice clapped his hand on Angus's shoulder. "I'll ponder your offer and give you an answer on the morrow."

"What of the girl?" Holden asked.

"Aye, the girl." Brice tried not to think about the way he'd felt when they had touched. The mere thought of it brought a rush of heat. He shrugged. "I'll think on that as well." He crossed the room, then paused on the stairs.

The hounds circled his feet, eager to accompany him to his room.

"Pray she's asleep," Brice muttered. "I'm near exhausted. All I want is a chance to rest this tired body."

"Aye." Angus followed him up the stairs and turned toward his rooms on the far end of the hall. "It's been too many hours since last we slept. I will see you on the morrow."

"You are both fools," Holden hissed. "Do you not know what to do with a warm, soft woman's body on a night such as this?"

Brice turned on him with a look of fury. "Do not talk so about a Scotswoman. Especially in front of the lad."

"I've heard such talk in the stables."

"But not in this house."

"Think of her as the spoils of war," Holden said with a sly smile. "And enjoy this gift you've been given."

"We'll talk no more of it." Brice's tone was low and commanding. "Until I decide what to do with the woman, she is to be treated with civility."

"Aye." Holden laughed. "I will be most civil with Lady Meredith MacAlpin."

Brice recognized the sarcasm in Holden's tone but was too weary to argue further. With a lift of his hand he dismissed his friends and made his way to his chambers.

Meredith heard the door close and was instantly alert. She listened to the slight shuffling sound as Brice crossed the room. She heard the occasional scratch of dogs' paws as they walked to the fireplace and settled down for the night.

The dogs. She had not planned for the dogs to be in the room.

Brice tossed another log on the fire and the flames danced and leaped as they licked at the dry bark. The room was suddenly bright from the glow of the fire.

At the foot of the bed Brice removed his tunic and shirt and she heard them whisper through the air as he tossed them on a nearby chair. The pallet sagged as he sat and tugged off his brogues.

When he pulled down the linens her heart began a wild hammering. Was the man actually going to sleep in the same bed with her? She had thought, nay, hoped, that he would be gentleman enough to sleep on the settle across the room.

The dagger in her hand was damp and slippery.

She was wearing only a sheer night shift, which Cara had brought earlier. Her gossamer gown and kid slippers had been taken away at Cara's insistence. On the morrow they would be clean and ready for their mistress. But their mistress, Meredith thought with a smile, would be miles from here. She would borrow a cloak and boots from Brice Campbell's wardrobe.

Patience, she counseled herself. Despite these unexpected changes in her plans, the dogs, the man in bed beside her, she must bide her time. She must wait, pretending to be asleep, until Brice Campbell relaxed his guard. If he had any warning, all would be lost.

From the warmth of his breath on her cheek she knew that he was facing her. She dared not chance a look at him. If his eyes were focused on her, he might detect the slight flickering of her lids. She would have to wait until the fire burned low and his breathing became even.

Her lids were heavy. Her body begged for the blessed release of sleep. But though the urge to sleep was nearly overpowering, she resisted. Her only chance to escape would be to plunge the dagger into Brice Campbell's heart and disappear into the dense Highland forests.

He shifted slightly and his thigh came into contact with hers. She lay perfectly still, willing herself not to move.

How strange to be lying, not in her marriage bed, but in the bed of a brute who had taken her captive. How warm his flesh where it pressed hers. The thought left her shaken. She must not allow herself to think of him as a man. He was a cruel savage, who would rue the day he had tangled with a MacAlpin.

He sighed and moved a foot. Before she could recover her wits he brought his foot down, dragging the fur coverings from both of them.

From beneath veiled lashes she chanced a quick look around. The dagger was clearly visible if he would but open his eyes. She held herself rigid, afraid to breathe, afraid even to swallow. By the light of the fire the dagger's blade glinted ominously. There was no place to hide it.

He moaned and dropped an arm about her waist. Her gaze flew to his face. His eyes were tightly closed. Gathering courage, she allowed her gaze to scan him.

God in heaven. The man was practically naked. She was so stunned she started to push away before she realized what she was doing. At the movement his fingers closed around her waist, dragging her closer.

The hand holding the dagger was slick with sweat. She clutched it between herself and him, praying that she would not drop it in her nervousness.

Sparks shot from the fireplace, sending a tiny explosion of light into the room. Reflexively he moved, bringing himself even closer to her. His face rested just beside hers, his lips brushing a tangle of hair at her temple.

The nearness of the man was driving her to distraction. All her carefully laid plans were unraveling. With his lips pressed to her temple she was unable to think, to even move. Saliva pooled in her mouth and she forced herself to swallow. The sound seemed overloud in the quiet of the room.

He murmured something in his sleep and tightened his grip on her, drawing her firmly against him. Never in her life had she been this close to a man. Even one with all his clothes on.

With each breath his hair-roughened chest brushed against her breasts, creating a tingling sensation deep inside her. She was achingly aware of his hips touching hers, of the thigh that rested against hers. The hand at her waist was warm, so warm that she felt as if her flesh were on fire. The heat spread, radiating a warmth that threatened to engulf her.

Despite the thundering of her heartbeat she forced herself to listen carefully to the sound of his breathing.

Soft. Even.

It was time. Before she forgot who she was and why she was here. Before she forgot that he was a monster who had killed Desmond MacKenzie and carried her off like a prize to be claimed. Before she allowed herself to be frightened by the presence of his dogs. It was time to buy her freedom even at the price of his life.

Her fingers closed around the hilt of the dagger. Wet, slippery fingers. For one moment she allowed the knife to slip from her fingers while she wiped them on the bed linen beneath her. Then, picking up the dagger, she clutched it firmly and raised herself to her knees.

She lifted her arm and brought the dagger down with all her might. At the last second she closed her eyes. She could not bear to watch the blade pierce his heart.

Brice was dreaming. A beautiful woman dressed all in white was running toward him, her arms outstretched, her long dark hair streaming behind her on the breeze. He caught her and lifted her, pressing his lips to hers. Slowly, languidly, she slid down his body until her feet touched the ground. He could feel the press of her breasts, her hips, her thighs. His hands spanned her waist as he drew her closer. Suddenly she was pulling away from him. Her smile twisted into an evil leer. Her hand snaked out. Instead of caressing him, she slapped him. Hard.

Brice awoke, twisting away from the dark, angry vision.

Meredith felt the mattress shift as Brice rolled aside. The dagger caught the edge of his shoulder, barely biting into flesh. Blood spurted and ran down his arm. She pulled the dagger free and lifted it again, intending to take better aim. But before she could once again plunge the blade her hand was caught and pinned in a grip of such strength she cried out.

He swore, loudly, viciously, as he crushed her small hand in his. "You will drop the dirk or I swear I'll break every bone in your lovely body."

"Nay. I'll not submit to you." She was still on her knees, straddling his prone body, struggling for control of the dagger.

"Submit?" The word was a snarl as he rolled over, pinning her beneath him. "You'll do more than submit, woman. You'll die unless you give up the weapon. Now."

He pressed a thumb to her wrist until the bones threatened to snap. With a shriek of pain she let her fingers go slack until the knife dropped from them.

He picked up the knife and tucked it beneath the bed linens, then stared down at the figure pinned to the mattress beneath him.

"I thought it was a dream." His voice was low, dangerous. "Had I not awakened in time, you would have killed me."

"Aye. You deserve to die for what you did." She felt the sting of tears and tried to blink them back.

Her hand was so numb she had no feeling in it. Had he broken it? She tried to move her fingers and felt searing, burning pain.

"What I did was avenge my honor." His hands continued to hold her roughly. "Gareth MacKenzie has made false accusations against me, attributing crimes to me that he knows I could not have committed."

"What has that to do with me?"

"Nothing." His tone was abrupt, cutting off her protest. "My fight is not with you. You just happened to be a minor obstacle in the path of my justice."

"Justice. What you have done is far from just."

"Aye." He looked down at her and felt his anger continue to stir him, though it was already beginning to diminish. "I had not intended to involve you in this, lass. It just happened."

"Then you are honor bound to release me." She felt a moment of hope before his next words dashed it.

"The MacKenzies do not respect honor. They respect only strength. I have already told you. You will be the bait that lures Gareth MacKenzie to my lair."

Her heart plummeted. Was there no reasoning with this madman?

From the floor he lifted a shirt and tore a strip of fabric. With an economy of movement he wrapped the cloth about his wound and turned to her.

"Tie this. 'Twill stem the flow of blood."

She fumbled with the cloth and managed to secure the dressing. It was incongruous that moments ago she had been prepared to kill him. Now she was bandaging his wound.

A million hot needles pierced her hand as the feeling returned. He noted the way she tentatively wiggled her fingers.

"It's broken." Her voice was flat. "You've broken it."

He stared down at her hand in silence.

Her tears started, and though she made a valiant struggle, they flowed freely.

She knew it was not only the hand that caused her to cry, but the knowledge that she had lost her chance to escape.

Moved by her tears he caught her hand in his and expertly ran his fingers over hers. His tone was gruff. "Not broken. But probably badly bruised. If you lift a weapon against me again I will be even harder on you."

Without realizing it he continued holding her hand. So small. So soft. How could one small hand hold his life in it? The anger inside him merged with other, newer emotions. Instantly his touch gentled.

"Such lovely bait. How can Gareth MacKenzie resist?"

She saw the look that came into his eyes and felt a new terror grip her. She was too vulnerable. He was too dangerous.

"As you said, Gareth has no feeling for me. He will not be ensnared in your trap."

His voice was suddenly harsh. "I think you place too little value on yourself, woman. There are not many men who could turn away from your obvious charms."

Her heart leaped to her throat. Aye, he was far too dangerous.

He lowered his face until their lips were inches apart. She felt the heat of his breath as it mingled with hers.

Damn Holden Mackay, he thought. He had planted a seed in Brice's mind this night. And now, with the woman so near, the thoughts expressed by Holden were taking hold of Brice's will.

"I fear I shall have to sample the bait."

"Nay." She tried to pull away but was held fast.

His lips brushed hers.

She felt the first rush of heat and turned her head, avoiding the lure of his lips.

With a muttered oath he placed a hand on either side of her head, holding it firmly as he brought his mouth over hers.

In that first instant he felt a jolt, like a blow to the midsection. Her lips trembled and he knew that she felt it, too.

He was so startled by his reaction he lifted his head a moment, staring deeply into her eyes. Wide, shimmering pools of green stared back at him. He could read surprise there. And innocence.

Innocence. God in heaven. A virgin?

But she had been betrothed. Could it be that she and Desmond MacKenzie had never known each other?

He studied her face, mesmerized by her beauty. Beneath the beauty, beneath the innocence, he could read something more. There was fire there. He was nearly consumed by the heat.

Slowly, seductively, he touched his lips to hers and thrilled to the feelings that poured between them. With a sigh he took the kiss deeper, savoring all the sweetness, all the innocence he could taste.

Meredith had been kissed before. There had been lads waiting to steal a kiss along a darkened lane. There had been wedding banquets, where the young people were allowed to taste the brew. Such things often led to the first stirrings of youthful desire. She had once been kissed by Gareth MacKenzie. It had frightened and repulsed her. She had sensed something dark and unsavory in Gareth's manner. From that moment on she had avoided him. She had kissed his brother, Desmond. But they had both been children and the kiss had been no more than a touching of lips to lips.

But this. This was something so new, so breathtakingly sensual, she could hardly contain her heart. It was hammering so painfully in her chest she was certain he could hear the sound.

The hands that cupped her face were rough and callused, and strong enough to break her in two. Yet their touch was so unexpectedly gentle, she felt herself melting into him.

Brice felt the gradual change in her as he lingered over her lips. Though she was still tense and frightened, she was responding, like a woman awakening from a deep sleep.

If he held her here long enough, she would be his.

The thought startled him. And disturbed him. If he was right, she had never been with a man. He had not expected this. Had not expected one so innocent. Had not expected to want her. It complicated matters. He knew he had to end it.

Still he lingered for a moment longer, unwilling to break the contact. Never had he felt such a desire to lie with a woman and take all she had to give.

The need to take became a need to give. Unless he ended this now, he could very well find the situation out of control and not at all to his liking. It had never been his way to take a virgin.

He lifted his head and drew back.

Meredith lay very still, watching him. Her breathing was ragged, her heartbeat erratic.

"A very nice sample," he whispered.

"May you be damned to hell."

He smiled, but the feeling curling in the pit of his stomach was still there, still prodding him to take what he had no right to.

He thrust her away from him. "Go to sleep." His voice was rougher than he'd intended.

He saw the look that came into her eyes. Relief. Gratitude. She had thought she'd have to fight him.

"I'll not sleep in the same bed with you."

He gave a careless shrug of his shoulders. "Then sleep on the floor. But beware the dogs."

He pulled the furs over himself and rolled away from her. His pulsebeat was as wild as if he'd just led a charge of brigands through the Highlands. His hands, he noted, were certainly not steady enough to hold a broadsword.

Meredith rolled away, curling herself into a tight little ball at the edge of the mattress. What choice had she been given? The floor or the bed—with him in it. But then what had she expected from a lout like Brice Campbell?

She would never be able to sleep in the same bed with this brute. If she dared to fall asleep, he might take advantage of her weakness.

As her eyes grew heavy she was forced to admit that it was not she who had ended the kiss but Brice Campbell. If he had wanted to take advantage of her, she would have been powerless to stop him. Powerless. The feeling enraged her. She had been powerless to refuse the marriage offer between herself and Desmond, despite the fact that she had not loved him. And now she was once again powerless to escape this barbarian who held her prisoner in his Highlands.

She would be powerless no more.

She thought about wrapping herself in a fur and sleeping with the dogs in front of the fireplace. But she was so weary. So drained.

Before she finally fell asleep, she spent a very troubling night wrestling with the dark thoughts that plagued her. And all of them centered on the man who slept as peacefully as a bairn beside her.

Chapter Four

Meredith clung to the safety of sleep. Outside the windows a breeze whispered through the trees. A chorus of birds filled the morning with song. Water splashed. A nearby waterfall, Meredith thought, rolling to one side. Her hand encountered a warm spot among the bed linens. Instantly she opened one eye. The place beside her was empty. But the warmth of Brice's body still remained. She fought a sudden chill. She had spent the night in his bed.

The splashing grew louder. A waterfall inside the room? She looked up to see Brice washing his face and arms in a basin of water. Her gaze fastened on his muscular shoulders and she felt her throat go dry.

He was terrifying. He was magnificent. Never had she seen a man to match him. His shoulders were wide, corded with muscles. His waist and hips were narrow beneath the bit of cloth tied about his lower torso. She watched as he lifted his head and shook it, sending a spray of water into the air before pressing a linen square to his face. He turned. She studied the mat of dark hair that covered his chest and disappeared below the cloth tied at his waist.

He caught her watching him. God in heaven, she was lovely. Her dark auburn tresses spilled across the pillow and framed the most beautiful face he'd ever seen. Though she had modestly pulled the bed linens to her chin, he could still recall the lush young body beneath the sheer night shift.

"I trust you slept well."

"Nay." She avoided his eyes. "I am not accustomed to sharing my bed with a man."

She saw the frown on his lips before he turned away and began pulling on his tunic. He did not bother to add that her presence in his bed had cost him more than a little sleep as well. He'd been forced to wage a terrible battle with himself over her.

The hounds had been sitting, watching Meredith from across the room. Now they began timidly approaching the bed. One by one they pressed their noses to her. And though she told herself they were big ugly brutes, she found herself scratching behind their ears, rubbing their thick coats. Two stayed beside the bed, enjoying her tender ministrations. The others turned away, having satisfied their curiosity about this strange female.

"Cara has brought your clothes." Brice indicated the neatly folded pile of garments. "I will leave you to your privacy. We will break our fast as soon as you join us below stairs."

Meredith watched as he pulled on his brogues and tossed a length of plaid over his arm. His strange manner of dress, leaving his limbs bare, was appealing to her. The sight of his muscular legs was oddly arousing.

"Will I dress for traveling?" she called to him.

He paused in the doorway. The dogs milled about his feet. His tone was sharp. "Where would you be traveling?"

"Home." She tossed aside the fur throw and sat up. He caught a glimpse of thigh before she slid the night shift down modestly. "I had hoped that you would return me to my people."

"And why would I do that?"

"Last night you said that I had no part in your plan for revenge."

"Aye. But I also told you that now that you are here, you will become the bait."

He saw the frown that darkened her features. She clamped her mouth shut on whatever angry words she was about to hurl.

When the door closed behind him, Meredith sprang from the bed. If he would not take her out of this wilderness, she would find a way to go by herself.

Meredith crept down the stairs. In her arms she carried a coarse woolen cloak and a fur throw. Both would be needed for the arduous journey home. She might be forced to wander through these mountain forests for days before finding her way out. She had decided to borrow a few warm things from Brice Campbell's own closet.

At the foot of the stairs she paused to listen. Judging by the voices, the refectory was at the far end of a dim hallway. Casting a furtive glance around, she hurried in the opposite direction and pushed open a door. Inside was a cozy room where a fire had already been prepared in the fireplace. There was a large desk and several oversize chairs, as well as a settle draped with fur in front of the fireplace. Atop the desk were books and ledgers.

Meredith stared around the room with a sense of wonder. This library was even more magnificent than her father's. Did this mean that Brice Campbell could read? She had thought all the Highlanders, and this man in particular, were vulgar and uneducated.

Locating a tall armoire she thrust her bounty inside and quietly latched the door. Then she made her way back down the hallway and followed the sound of voices to the refectory.

She paused outside the door and listened.

". . . to the Borders alone." It was Brice's voice, low, calculating.

"But why can I not go along?"

Meredith peered inside. Angus and Holden sat across the table from Brice. Angus was arguing with his friend. She could not see his face, but she could hear the note of protest in his voice. "The MacKenzies are not the only ones who will kill you on sight. Do not forget, old friend, that you have incurred the wrath of the MacAlpin clans as well. You have their woman."

"Their leader," Brice corrected.

"Leader?" It was another man, tall, red bearded, who had ridden with Brice on the morning raid.

Meredith saw Brice's head nod. "With Alastair MacAlpin dead, she is now the MacAlpin."

There was a murmur among the dozen men at the table. Jamie, seated on Brice's left, looked impressed. "Why, she's no bigger than I am. How can a helpless female be leader of her clan?"

"Helpless?" Brice gave a mirthless laugh, recalling her attack of the previous night. "Never let the looks of a woman deceive you, Jamie lad. The lady is far from helpless."

Though Brice's words were more amused than irritated, Meredith was more impressed by what she'd heard before that. She stood back, pondering all that had been said. Brice Campbell did not sound like a man who had knowingly murdered her father. Nor did it sound as though Angus or the others had anything to do with that terrible act.

Obviously Gareth MacKenzie had been wrong. But why had he seemed so certain that Brice Campbell was guilty?

When she returned home she would confront Gareth. But for now, there was only one thought. She must elude her captors and make her way back home.

Brice and the others looked up as she entered. The hounds circled about her ankles, then settled down once more by the fire.

Beneath the bulky shawl, she was wearing the filmy white confection. Her wedding gown. Brice felt a swift pang of remorse. How she must hate him for altering forever the course of her life.

He stood and held a chair as Meredith seated herself beside him.

"You may serve, Cara," he called.

The young serving wench came forward with a tray of steaming meats, followed by other servants bearing trays of warm bread and biscuits and platters of sweet puddings.

Meredith's stomach was in knots. The very thought of what she was about to undertake had her hands trembling, her insides turning over. But she must eat all she could in order to sustain her energy for what lay ahead.

Brice watched as she loaded her plate with meats and breads. Each time he looked away, she slipped some of the food onto her lap and hid it among the folds of her gown.

Jamie, busy feeding the hounds who lurked beneath the table, thought it amusing that the lady's hands were also working beneath the table. Odd that she had befriended the hounds so quickly.

"So ye be the MacAlpin now, lass?" A burly man in coarse woolen garments addressed her.

"Aye."

"Alastair MacAlpin withstood many an attack from the English," he said, tearing off a strip of meat with his hands. "He was a clever warrior."

"You knew my father?"

"We met from time to time. He sat on the king's Council, as did Brice's father. The Campbell clan and the MacAlpin clan were part of the king's own guard."

She knew that. Knew also that there had been little trust between the Highlanders and the Borderers. She'd been raised to believe that the Highlanders were a breed apart from other Scots.

"Then you know that my father was a man of peace."

"The English who raided his lands would not agree with you, lass. The man was the devil himself when his land or people were threatened."

"Aye," Brice added. "He wielded a sword with the best of them. But the lass means that Alastair MacAlpin argued for peace among the clans. He said it was our only weapon against the mighty English."

"Some would call his cry for peace a cowardly act."

Meredith's hand balled into a fist. "What would you know about the world beyond your fortified mountains? Do you know what it is to live on the Border? To be raided constantly by hordes of English hoping to steal your flocks, your cattle, even your women?"

"More meat, my lady?" Cara stood beside her with a tray. In her eyes Meredith could read a warning.

Meredith bit down on the words that she had been about to hurl. What good would it do to goad these savages?

Without a word she filled her plate. Beside her, Brice bit back a smile. The lady was not above speaking her mind.

He marveled also at the amount of food the lady was capable of eating. Just moments ago her plate had been piled high with bread and meat. Where did such a tiny little lass put all that?

"You were blessed with a healthy appetite, my lady."

"Mayhaps all the Borderers are taught to eat quickly, before the English can steal it," Angus said.

She heard the thread of laughter in his tone and bristled.

"If I must remain a prisoner in your castle, my lord Campbell, then at least I shall indulge my palate."

"By all means. Would you like some pudding?"

She shook her head a little too quickly. The thought of sticky pudding running down her gown nearly caused her to choke. "I thank you but I have had sufficient."

Out of the corner of her eye she saw Jamie watching her. She rolled the excess material of her gown around the food and prayed that she could escape the room without being caught.

When they were finished Brice pushed back his chair. "Angus, you will be responsible for the woman until I return."

Meredith was careful to grasp the folds of her gown, hugging the food to her bosom. The ends of the shawl were the perfect cover. "I implore you one last time," she said softly. "Take me with you."

"You will remain here." His eyes were cold, his manner implacable.

As he turned away she muttered, "You will regret that decision."

He turned back and caught her by the arm. In that instant he felt the jolt and cursed himself for his foolishness. To touch this woman was to invite feelings that had no place in his life. Abruptly he dropped his hand to his side.

"I already regret having brought you here. But here you will stay until I decide to return you to your people."

Meredith wondered if the trembling deep inside her was caused by his touch or by the fear of having her plot discovered.

They all looked up at the sound of horses. While Brice and Meredith stared out the window, his men took up their weapons and prepared to defend the castle.

Peering through the opening, Meredith saw a company of riders led by a dainty, auburn-tressed young woman. On her wrist perched a falcon. Behind the woman there were at least a dozen men and women in elegant dress.

Meredith glanced at Brice in time to see his grim look melt into a warm smile. What a truly handsome man he was when he was not glaring at her. She was startled by the wave of alien emotion that washed over her. Jealousy? What nonsense. How could she possibly be jealous of the effect this stranger had on Brice Campbell?

He seemed not to notice Meredith. With a laugh he motioned for his men to put away their weapons. And then, as the woman was being helped from her mount, he was rushing out the door with Jamie and the dogs at his heels. His men followed and came to attention, forming two columns on either side of Brice and the woman.

Meredith lingered only a moment longer. This was the perfect opportunity to make good her escape. While the others were occupied with their visitors, they would never notice that she had slipped away from the castle. Perhaps, if the Fates were smiling upon her, she would be miles from here before she was missed.

She hurried along the dim hallway and pushed open the door to the library. Opening the armoire she pulled out the heavy woolen cloak and filled the pockets with the bread and meat she had secreted among the folds of her gown. She slipped her arms into the sleeves of the cloak. Because it had been made to fit Brice, it engulfed her, the sleeves completely covering her hands, the hem dragging upon the floor. She pulled up the hood, covering her head and leaving her face in shadow.

She stooped and lifted the fur throw from its place of concealment, folding it over her arm. No matter what weather she encountered on her escape, this would afford more than enough protection.

She closed the armoire and crossed to the door of the library. At the sound of voices she froze in her tracks. God in heaven. The voices were coming this way. With a cry of dismay she raced across the room and pulled open the armoire. Just as the door to the room opened, she leaped into the cupboard and pulled the door shut. With the door to the armoire closed, she was in total blackness.

"I cannot believe you are here." At the sound of Brice's voice, Meredith gritted her teeth.

"Nor can I." The young woman's voice was low, with a trace of an accent.

Meredith heard the dogs sniffing at the door to the armoire.

"Why did you not send riders ahead to announce your arrival? I would have prepared a more fitting welcome."

"I wanted to surprise you. Besides, just being here at Kinloch House is welcome enough."

"How did you manage to slip away from your brother?"

"James has other things on his mind these days." The sound of feminine laughter drifted across the room. "He is enamored of Agnes Keith. I hope it will soften him somewhat."

In the armoire Meredith crouched in a most uncomfortable position. She could neither sit nor stand, but was forced to stoop. To add to her discomfort the woolen cloak was so heavy it weighted her down. The warmth from the cloak and the fur draped over her arm, combined with the heat of the fireplace, left her soaked with perspiration. And still the dogs sniffed. When would they settle down before the fire? Why had they taken this occasion to pay her any interest?

"Ah, yes. Agnes, his new bride. How do they fare?"

"At least he has someone other than me to bully."

"Has it been terrible?" Brice's tone was tinged with concern as he crossed the room and cuffed the hounds' heads. "Off with you now."

With a whimper the dogs moved away a few paces before renewing their sniffing at the armoire.

"Oh, Brice. The tales I could tell. The last days in France were worse than the torments of hell."

"Poor Mary." Meredith could hear the sound of footsteps and sensed that Brice had crossed the room to the woman's side.

Peering through a crack in the door, Meredith watched as Brice drew the young woman into his arms.

"I know how much you miss Francis."

"My darling François. Aye, I miss him terribly. But it is more than that. It is this place. It is so forbidding. All the gaiety, the laughter, seem to have died since I returned." Her voice lowered. "And all because of that horrid little man who preaches fire and brimstone."

"Ah. Knox. He has caught the ear of the people."

"He watches and waits, Brice."

"For what, madame?"

"For me to slip so that he can publicly humiliate me."

There was silence in the room and Meredith watched as Brice and the young woman strolled to a window overlooking a vast expanse of forest.

The dogs did not follow their master. Instead, they continued sniffing at the armoire.

The heat in the tiny space was becoming unbearable. Soon, Meredith thought, she would suffocate.

"Be very careful not to offend him, Mary. He could cause you great harm."

"I am only now learning that." The young woman gave a deep sigh. "I long for the dancing, the singing, of France. I long to give elegant parties, to laugh, to—flirt. Oh, Brice.

I am eighteen years old and no longer have a husband, nor any sort of life. It is terrible. Terrible."

Meredith detected a note of unspoken laughter in Brice's tone. "You are too beautiful, Mary, too full of life and laughter, to be condemned to a life alone. What man in his right mind would not lose his heart to you?"

"Did you?" It was the voice of a coquette, warm, inviting.

"You know I did. We all did while we were with you in France."

"Oh, you. I know better. Brice Campbell, you were the only Scotsman who never let himself be swept away by the charm of France."

"Only because I yearned for the Highlands. I feared it would be too easy to be seduced by the life you offered us."

"Is that why you left so abruptly?"

"Aye. I had to return to my home. Or be lost."

"Poor Brice. Has it all been worth it?"

There was silence. For long minutes the only sound Meredith could hear was the hiss of the fire. She staggered and leaned heavily against the door to the armoire. If she did not slip out of this heavy cloak soon she would faint from the heat. While she listened to the growing silence she wriggled out of the cloak. When she had managed to free one arm she sighed and began the struggle to free the other.

She was so engrossed in her struggle to free herself from the cloak she did not hear the sound of footsteps.

"So."

The door to the armoire was yanked open, causing Meredith to fall forward into Brice's arms. She would have slumped to the floor if he had not held her firmly.

Instantly the dogs circled around, yelping and baying.

"Why are you spying on us?" Brice's tone was low, menacing.

Meredith's cheeks reddened. She was mortified as she faced the haughty young woman who stared at her as if she could not believe her eyes. How she must look. Like some sort of ragged beggar. The cloak hung from one arm, dragging behind her on the floor. The fur throw was caught about her feet, threatening to trip her. Jagged scraps of bread and meat spilled from the pockets of the cloak. The hounds leaped up, snatching at the scraps and dragging them from her pockets.

At the sight Brice's eyes narrowed. "Are you ready to explain what this is all about?"

She swallowed. She was caught. There would be no use trying to lie. "I—intended to run off while you were occupied with your guest."

"Run off?" The young woman took a step closer, studying Meredith with open curiosity. "And why would you do that?"

"Because I'm being held here against my will," Meredith cried.

"Brice." The young woman turned wide eyes toward her host. "Is this lass telling the truth?"

Meredith's heart soared. Surely this young woman would insist that Brice return her to her clan at once.

Brice continued to hold Meredith by the arm. His fingers tightened their grip. He could feel his temper rising.

"She is. This is Meredith MacAlpin."

"Oh, how exciting. I heard about the—incident at the cathedral. You must tell me everything." The young woman's eyes danced with mischief. "This is so..." She spoke in rapid French for several minutes, while Brice's eyes darkened with anger. Then, reverting to English, the young woman continued, "Such a dashing, romantic adventure. My heart fairly bursts with the thought of it. You are a devil, Brice Campbell. A rogue and a devil. And you, Meredith

MacAlpin. What a thrilling story you will one day tell your grandchildren.''

"You are daft." Meredith kicked the fur throw from her feet and shrugged out of the confining cloak. Around her feet the dogs slathered after the last of the food scraps. "I am being held captive by a barbarian and you suggest that I should faint for joy."

At her insulting words the young woman's laughter faded. She tilted her head at a regal angle and regarded Meredith with a look of contempt.

"You do not have permission to speak to me in that tone. Kneel at once and beg my pardon."

Meredith's mouth dropped open. For a moment she could scarcely believe her ears. She turned toward Brice and found him grinning. That only served to further enrage her.

"Of all the vain, arrogant, pigheaded . . ."

Brice's fingers fastened upon her arm. In a tone tinged with laughter he said, "Hold your tongue, woman. Have you not yet realized who our visitor is?"

Meredith gazed upon the haughty young woman who continued to watch her through narrowed eyes.

"Kneel, Meredith," he murmured. "And pay homage to your queen.".

"Queen?" Meredith's throat went dry. For long moments she studied the woman. Then, with a gasp, she fell to her knees. "Oh, Majesty. Forgive me."

She had heard the stories, of course. All of Scotland had heard that the young queen, having recently buried her husband, Francis, the Dauphin of France, had been returned to her birthplace to assume the throne.

She was kneeling before Mary, Queen of Scots.

Chapter Five

Vain? Arrogant? Pigheaded?'' The queen enunciated each word with great care.

Meredith, kneeling before her, flinched as though lashed by a whip.

"She goes too far. This time, Brice," the queen said haughtily, "you have found a woman with a temper to match your own."

"Aye." He seemed not at all concerned that the queen continued to glare at the lass who knelt abjectly at her feet.

"I could have you publicly flogged for your disrespect of the queen's person."

Meredith lowered her head, afraid to meet the queen's eyes.

"Would you like the flogging to take place here?" Brice inquired, struggling to hold back his laughter. He knew that the queen was far too tenderhearted to ever follow through on her threat. "Or will you have her dragged back to Edinburgh?"

"You mock your queen?" Mary arched an eyebrow and glowered at Brice.

"Nay. In fact, I will send Angus to fetch a whip from the stables."

As Brice turned away the queen caught his arm. "Wait. You are too eager. I have thought of a better punishment for this disrespectful subject."

Meredith braced herself for what was to come. Whatever punishment was meted out by the queen, she had certainly earned it. How could she have been so foolish as to express herself in such forceful language?

"Rise, Meredith MacAlpin, and face your queen as you learn the consequences of your actions."

Meredith stood on trembling legs. She glanced at Brice's face but could read nothing in his hooded gaze.

"I will give you a choice," Queen Mary said. "A public flogging or..." She bit back the smile that twitched at the corners of her lips. "An opportunity to entertain your queen. You must relate to me and my ladies-in-waiting every detail of your—encounter with this rogue, Brice Campbell. From the first moment you saw him."

The queen burst into laughter at the look of astonishment on Meredith's face. Even Brice could not contain his laughter.

"That is all that you require, Majesty? A simple narrative?"

"Not simple," the queen corrected. "Every little detail must be included. I want to know everything." She turned to Brice. "And you, scoundrel, must leave us alone for at least an hour. This is woman's talk, you understand. And when she has finished, your servants can provide us with a banquet before we return to Falkland."

The queen clapped her hands, summoning the women of her hunting party. "Oh, Brice, this will be better entertainment than any poet or musician. I am greatly in need of such excitement. My life has been so drab since returning from the gaiety of France."

Brice lifted the queen's hand to his lips before departing the room. "Your loyal subjects are most happy to oblige." He shot Meredith a warning look. "Beware what you say in the presence of your queen. The next time you might not fare as well."

Within minutes Meredith found herself surrounded by five women named Mary. The young monarch introduced her four closest friends, Mary Beaton, Mary Fleming, Mary Seton and Mary Livingstone. The four Maries had been with the queen since early childhood. And like all best friends, they shared everything, even their most intimate secrets.

While servants poured tea and passed around biscuits, the women arranged themselves in chairs and settles in front of the fireplace. When the servants left the room, the queen commanded Meredith to begin her story.

While the others listened in awe, Meredith detailed her father's tragic murder and her agreement to marry Desmond MacKenzie in order to assure protection for her people.

"Those of us who live on the Border know the danger of invasion by the English."

"My beloved cousin, Elizabeth of England," Mary said through clenched teeth, "assures us that she is doing all she can to protect our land and people. And while she sends us messages of assurance, her soldiers continue to plunder."

Meredith was surprised at the queen's outburst. Was the young monarch always so outspoken? Was she not aware that even in the presence of her friends her words would not be kept secret? A queen, more than any other, must guard her thoughts carefully.

"Go on with your story," the queen commanded.

"Did you love Desmond MacKenzie?" Mary Fleming interrupted.

"What nonsense, Flem," the queen interjected. "What woman has ever been allowed to marry a man for love?"

Stunned by the queen's comment, Meredith openly studied the young monarch. It was common knowledge that Mary Stuart had been betrothed to Prince Edward of England when both had been mere children. But his death had released her from that bondage. The rumors had been that she was fairly happy with the young, fragile dauphin, whom she had married at the age of fifteen. But his mother, Catherine de' Medici, had been more than happy to be rid of the headstrong Queen of Scotland upon his untimely death.

"Well? Did you love him?"

Meredith studied the toe of her kid slipper. "We were friends when we were children."

"Were you eager to wed him?" Mary Seton asked.

"Or bed him?" Mary Fleming added.

Meredith's face flooded with color.

It was the queen who came to her rescue. "This lass has not been exposed to such bold discourse. Hold your tongues and allow her to tell the story."

"I—was reluctant to wed Desmond. I do not think I would have ever loved him the way a woman wants to love a man. But I knew that the union would assure my people the protection of the MacKenzie armies. I would do anything for my people."

"Spoken like a true Scot." The queen smiled warmly at Meredith. Despite her earlier insult, the queen admired the girl's spirit.

"So you were willing to wed him though you did not love him. Was he as handsome as Brice Campbell?"

Meredith felt her cheeks growing warmer by the minute. "He was fair of face and hair. Not much more than a lad."

"Brice Campbell," the queen said with a smile of appreciation, "is no lad. He is all man." Seeing Meredith's embarrassed flush she said with an impatient sigh, "Pray go on with your tale."

When Meredith described the murder of her husband at the altar, and the deception by his brother, Gareth MacKenzie, the women gasped.

"Did Gareth not realize that he was placing your life in danger by defying Brice Campbell's orders?"

"I had not thought about it," Meredith said. "It all happened so quickly. When Gareth fired the arrow I saw this giant glide through the air and take hold of me. And then I was in his arms and soaring over the heads of the people in the cathedral."

"How exciting."

"How terrifying."

"How romantic."

"Did you cry?"

"Nay." Meredith lifted her chin, nearly overwhelmed by these outspoken women. "I would not give Brice Campbell the pleasure of seeing me cry."

"Oh, how wonderful." Queen Mary clapped her hands and urged the others to silence. "That would infuriate a man like Brice. Now you must tell us everything that happened to you since your momentous meeting with Brice Campbell."

"Aye. Momentous." Meredith described her abduction, the tedious journey to the Highlands, and her attempt to kill Brice in his bed. During the entire narrative the queen's eyes glittered with a feverish light, as though she were living each incident in her mind.

"Brice Campbell is the strongest man I have ever met," the queen said with a trace of awe. "It is known throughout Scotland that there are few men who can best him in a fight or a duel. I have heard many a man declare that he would wish to have Brice on his side in a battle. And yet you dared to attack him.''

"In his own bed," Mary Fleming said with a knowing wink.

"I was desperate to return to my own people, Majesty. In my place, would you not have done the same?''

The queen nodded her head. "How did you get into his room while he slept?''

Meredith looked away, too ashamed to meet the queen's eyes. "I was being held prisoner in his room.''

The queen turned toward her friend, Mary Fleming, who was watching in silence. "What say you, Flem?''

"Pray, continue with the tale," Mary Fleming said without much enthusiasm. She seemed distracted. While Meredith proceeded to struggle through the story of her abduction, Fleming studied the queen and then allowed her gaze to scan the young woman seated beside her.

Suddenly she blurted, "What a remarkable similarity.''

"What are you babbling about, Flem?'' The queen arched one brow in a regal manner.

"You and Meredith MacAlpin bear a strong resemblance. You could be sisters.''

Meredith felt herself flushing as the others began to study her with great interest.

The queen stood and walked a few paces, then turned and watched the others. "Do you think so?''

"Why, of course," Beaton said. "Look at the hair.''

The three women caught at strands of Meredith's hair, lifting it and examining it in the sunlight.

"It is the same color as Your Majesty's. If we were to plait Meredith's, or brush Your Majesty's loose, they would be the same," Seton said.

Queen Mary was obviously intrigued by this unexpected turn of events.

"And both are small of stature, delicate in appearance."
Fleming caught Meredith by the hand and led her to the
center of the room while the others circled about her.

While the others laughed, the queen stood apart. On her
face was a look of intense concentration. Suddenly she took
a step closer. "The gown you are wearing. Is it your wedding gown?"

Meredith nodded. There was an inflection in the queen's
tone, of guarded excitement, that puzzled her.

"Have you no others?"

"I had no time to choose a wardrobe, Majesty. You will
recall that I was abducted at the altar."

"So Brice and the others have seen you only in this?"

Meredith waited, knowing that the queen was leading to
something.

"Fleming and Beaton. Help me out of my clothes."

The women stared at the queen without moving.

"And Seton and Livingstone, you will help Meredith off
with her gown. Oh, what a fine joke we shall play," the
queen said, twirling about like a little girl.

"I do not understand."

"It is the sort of game we could have enjoyed in France,"
Mary said, her face animated. "We will change clothes and
see who discovers our little deception first."

When Meredith began to shake her head the queen said,
"How many people really look at others? If they expect you
to be in the clothes you have been wearing since your arrival, they will expect that the woman at the table wearing a
white gown is you. And since I arrived in this hunting outfit, they will believe that the woman wearing it is the queen."

When Meredith continued to shake her head the queen
motioned to the others. "Hurry. Brice promised us an hour.
It will soon be time to sup with the others."

In a daze Meredith stood helplessly as the women, caught up in the queen's plan, removed her gown and kid slippers and replaced them with the queen's jeweled burgundy velvet hunting outfit and high kid boots. While Mary Seton laced the boots, Mary Livingstone brushed Meredith's hair and dressed it in the identical fashion to the queen's.

Meanwhile the queen was dressed in Meredith's white gown and kid slippers. Her plaited hair was brushed loose, falling in crimped waves to her waist.

When both women were ready, they walked to a looking glass, where they stood side by side and examined their appearance.

"Something is wrong," Mary Fleming said softly.

"It is the eyes. Anyone seeing Meredith's green eyes would know that she was not the queen."

"A veil," the queen muttered.

"Of course." Fleming removed her veiled hunting toque and placed it upon Meredith's head.

The dark weblike netting veiled her eyes and most of her upper face.

"Perfect." The queen studied the girl beside her, then stared at her own reflection. "Do you not feel regal in my garb, Meredith?"

It took the young woman a moment to respond. "Aye. It is a strange feeling to know that my queen is wearing my clothes and that I am wearing hers."

At a knock on the door they turned. Cara entered and curtsied before Meredith. "My lord Campbell announces that a banquet has been prepared for Your Majesty."

Meredith was so stunned by the servant's reaction that she gave a little gasp and stepped back in surprise. The women around her giggled. Beside her the queen, dressed in the wilted wedding gown, was nearly doubled over with spasms of laughter. The poor girl, confused by the unexpected response to her announcement, bowed her way from the room, keeping her gaze lowered.

"You see," cried the queen. "She never even looked up at you. She saw the gown, the auburn tresses, and believed that she was in the presence of the queen. Come," she called to Meredith and the others. "We will enjoy Brice's feast and see who discovers our little joke first. Seton," she said suddenly. "I am betting a gold sovereign that our deception will not be discovered until after the first course of our banquet."

"Aye, Majesty," Mary Seton said softly. "I will take your bet."

"Majesty," Mary Fleming said discreetly. "If you are to be believable, you must stand back and allow Meredith to lead the way. And you must assume the mannerisms of a hostage and set aside your usual strong will."

"Dear Flem. How clever of you." The queen stifled a laugh and stepped aside, allowing Meredith to take the lead.

Brice frowned, deep in thought, as he changed into clothes more appropriate for entertaining the queen. He had planned on returning to the Borders this day to search for Gareth MacKenzie. Once he rid the land of that villain, he would be free to return Meredith to her people. The sooner that was accomplished the better. She was proving to be a stronger distraction than he had anticipated.

It was odd how his plans were constantly being changed by the whims of others.

At a summons from a servant he strode from the room.

The women were already assembled in the great hall along with Brice's men and the men from the queen's hunting party.

When Brice entered, Mary Fleming nudged Meredith. "Your Majesty will want to lead us to the banquet tables.

Perhaps our host will be gracious enough to accompany you.''

Brice offered his arm to his monarch and felt the small hand on his sleeve. As they led the merry group to the table he murmured, ''Did you find Meredith's tale entertaining?''

''Very,'' the voice beside him whispered.

''I hope you and the others did not shock her overmuch.''

''And why would you say that?''

He placed a hand over hers and squeezed. ''Do not play the queenly role with your old friend. I know you and the other Maries better than anyone else could possibly know you. You say and do the most shocking things just to see the reaction of others.''

When the woman beside him remained silent he studied her bowed head and was puzzled. From their earliest days together he had never known the queen to be at a loss for words, especially when being taken to task for something.

He brought his lips close to her ear and whispered, ''Just what have you and the others done this time?''

''Done?'' With her head lowered she murmured, ''I fear I do not understand.''

The queen was behaving in a most strange manner. Brice knew her well enough to know that it meant she was up to one of her tricks.

''Come,'' he urged, pausing while the others caught up. ''Tell me, for I shall surely discover your game soon enough.''

''There is no game. I am merely overcome with hunger.''

Brice, giving up for the moment, gave her a smile. ''Then you shall enjoy a feast fit for royalty.''

At the head of the table he held her chair, then seated himself at her right hand. As always the four Maries flocked around their monarch, interspersed with the men from their hunting party. At the far end of the table Brice noted that Meredith was seated between Angus Gordon and Jamie MacDonald, and though she kept her face averted, there was a smile on her lips. Odd. Until now, she had done nothing but scowl at him.

Crystal goblets were filled and Brice lifted his, exclaiming, "To Mary, Queen of Scots."

"To Mary," repeated the entire company before lifting the goblets to their lips.

At the head of the table, the object of their toast nodded her head slightly and drank.

In the silence that followed, the young woman at the far end of the table spoke. "When you leave, will you take me with you—Majesty?"

Everyone gasped at the boldness of the hostage's words. Angus placed a hand on her arm as if to warn her, but she shook it off as though no one had ever before dared to touch her in such a way.

Beside him, Brice saw the queen's head nod slightly. He felt a rush of seething anger at Meredith's crude attempt to escape from Kinloch House with the queen's blessing. When the others left he would deal with her harshly. For now, he would keep a tight rein on his temper and deal with her more diplomatically.

"It is not proper to address the queen unless she first invites it."

"May I speak, Majesty?" came the bold reply from the far end of the table.

Again Angus tried to stifle her outburst. Ignoring him, she opened her mouth to speak.

"Nay. We will eat." Brice held up a hand to silence her.

At his signal, the servants began circulating among the guests, offering from trays of steaming deer, rabbit, goose, pheasant and partridge. There were breads still warm from the oven, as well as steamed puddings.

From the far end of the table, the woman in the white gown called, "Such fine food, my lord."

Brice's eyes narrowed. Was it Meredith's intention to dominate the conversation? Perhaps she hoped to continue to call attention to herself in order to invite the queen's protection.

"There are those who say the Highlanders live like royalty while many in the Lowlands starve." All eyes turned toward the woman in the white gown who sat beside Angus. With a wide, innocent smile she added, "Is that not true, Majesty?"

Brice heard a slight choking sound from the woman beside him. "Aye" came the voice. Then, with just a trace of French accent, she added, "'Tis said that many covet the holdings of the Highland lords. What say you—Meredith?"

Brice turned to study the woman in the burgundy velvet gown. Though the gown and hair were that of the queen, the voice, though similar, was not hers. He and Mary had been friends for too long. He had heard her when angry, happy, ill and well. He would know her voice anywhere.

He strained to study the face beneath the veil. Why would the queen wear a hat and veil to a banquet? A hint of a smile began at the corner of his lips. To hide behind? His smile grew.

"Do you remember that time when you and I and the dauphin went riding in Paris?" he asked.

Beside him the woman went very still.

"Surely you have not forgotten, Majesty. We had a race. I believe the bet was one hundred gold sovereigns."

Still the woman beside him remained silent.

"Unfortunately for you, I won by several meters," Brice said with a trace of triumph.

From the end of the table came the thunderous response. "How dare you, Brice Campbell! I won that race. And the bet was five hundred gold sovereigns. By the time you caught up with me I had turned my mount over to a groom and had retired to my rooms. You threatened to have your horse drawn and quartered for stumbling and losing the race."

Around the table there was stunned silence.

Brice threw back his head and roared with laughter. "And how does my captive, Meredith MacAlpin, know of such things?"

At the foot of the table the queen stood, shocking those guests who had not yet caught on to the joke.

"You knew all along, did you?"

"Nay, Majesty." Brice wiped tears of laughter from his eyes. "Not until I heard the poor imitation of your French accent beside me."

"Ah. Then it was Meredith who gave it away."

"It was the boldness of the one who pretended to be my captive. You have a very—regal presence, Madame. A trait that does not allow you to blend in with a crowd. How much did you have riding on this little prank?"

"A mere gold sovereign." The queen gave him a wide smile. "It is worth losing this bet to Flem just to put you in your place, Brice Campbell." She looked around at the others. "Let no one at this table think that any Highland lord can best his queen in a race. Shall I challenge you again, Brice?"

"Perhaps another time, Majesty."

While the others chimed in the laughter at the queen's prank, Brice turned toward Meredith. In a voice the others could not hear he whispered, "Well done. For a few moments you managed to fool me, little wildcat."

Beside him Meredith merely smiled. Why in the world should Brice's words please her? He was, after all, still the same barbarian who had captured her and held her against her will in the Highlands.

Or was he?

Meredith thought about the loyalty of his people, so unexpected in one of his reputation. And the library of books and ledgers. Did that not indicate an educated man? And what of his friendship with royalty?

So many questions. And yet, long after the queen left, she would be forced to remain here and perhaps learn the answers.

She glanced at the far end of the table where the queen was accepting the congratulations of those who admired her latest trick. Had not the queen herself brought up the question of what would be done with her? Perhaps she could yet persuade the queen to take her with her. At least then she would be free of Brice Campbell. After all, was that not what she truly wanted?

At the far end of the table, Jamie MacDonald remained rooted to his chair. He was sitting beside the queen. And he had just been privileged to witness one of her renowned pranks. Could life be any more wonderful than this?

Chapter Six

When the feasting was over, the queen insisted upon summoning her musicians who had traveled with her. When they took up their instruments, Brice brought Jamie before the queen.

"The lad plays several instruments, Madame, including the lute. He would be honored to join the royal musicians."

"They would be honored to have him."

Jamie felt his cheeks redden as he picked up the lute and joined the musicians. At a nod from Brice he began to play. Within minutes he forgot his nervousness as the music flowed through his fingers.

"I have not danced since I left France," Mary said with a pretty little pout, "seeing that dancing has been forbidden here in Scotland, as has anything else that brings pleasure. But here in the Highlands," she said, brightening suddenly, "that horrid John Knox cannot hear even a whisper of scandal about our adventures."

"Or misadventures, knowing you," Brice added with a smile.

"Hush. Now that I am once again gowned as your queen," Mary said with a glance at the burgundy hunting outfit that had been restored to her, "I command you to show a little respect. Further, I command you to learn the latest dances from Paris."

"I am your obedient servant, Madame." Brice bowed over her hand and escorted her to the center of the room.

From her position between Angus and Holden, Meredith was forced to watch as the queen and her friends taught Brice and the others the latest dances.

It was almost scandalous to see the way the women directed the men to hold them close while the music played. Their feet moved in perfect rhythm, their bodies swaying gently. One shocking new dance even ended with a kiss.

Meredith watched in stunned silence as the queen lifted her face to Brice. Their lips brushed. The men and women around them clapped their hands and called out encouragement.

Young Jamie MacDonald watched in stunned silence. Brice was actually kissing the queen.

"Ah," Mary said, smiling. "You have not lost your touch, Brice. You are still able to make my heart leap to my throat with a single touch."

"And you, Madame," he said with a smile, "are still the most outrageous flirt, as well as the finest dancer in all of France or Scotland."

"You flatter me."

"Nay, Mary," he said, offering his arm and leading her across the room. "Your love of the dance is obvious. You move like a leaf in the wind."

"The heart of a poet beats in the breast of this warrior," the queen said to the others with a laugh.

"I believe it is my dance, Majesty."

The queen turned into the arms of one of the men from her hunting party and together they twirled away. Over her partner's shoulder Mary called, "Dance with your hostage, Brice. I think it only fair that you teach her the dances of Paris.''

Brice's smile remained in place until he turned away. At that moment Meredith saw the little frown of frustration that was gone as quickly as it had appeared. He held out his hand and Meredith was forced to accept it.

"I do not dance, my lord."

"Your queen has commanded it."

He saw her bite her lip as she moved into his embrace.

As his arms encircled her the feeling was swift, immediate. It was not at all a pleasant sensation.

Against her temple he growled, "You might try smiling. Learning the dance is not quite as painful as a public flogging."

"Are you so certain? I did not see you smiling a moment ago." She tried to ignore the feeling that curled deep inside.

"I was thinking that I should first search your person to determine if you carried a knife."

She gave him an exaggerated, beguiling smile. "If I did, my lord, it would not be in my hand. It would be in your back."

She felt his hand tighten at her waist as he led her through the intricate movements of the dance. Their bodies moved together, stiffly at first. But as the music of the harp and lute washed over them, they began to relax in each other's arms.

There was warmth along her flesh where his hand rested. Meredith could feel each of his fingers at her back, and was alarmed at the prickly sensation his touch aroused. His breath was warm against her temple. In the crush of dancers he drew her closer, until she could feel his lips pressed to a tangle of her hair. The hand holding hers was strong and firm as he led her with ease. She felt a trembling inside that had nothing to do with the fact that she was disobeying the law of the kirk by dancing. Nay, it was not the dance that was her undoing; it was the man holding her.

As Brice turned her, he was acutely aware of her breasts crushed against his chest. Her thigh brushed his and he felt the heat. Her hand, so small and soft in his, showed the bruises from his show of force the previous night. He felt a trace of remorse at the way he'd been forced to treat her.

"I had hoped to return to the Borders this day and finish this business between myself and Gareth MacKenzie. Then you could be restored to your people."

"Instead you dance to the queen's musicians."

"It cannot be helped."

"Aye. So many things, it seems, cannot be helped." Her eyes grew stormy. "You could not help killing Desmond. You could not help taking me prisoner."

There was heat now of a different kind as Brice held her in his arms. He was not proud of having mistakenly killed an innocent. Nor was he happy about having taken her hostage. She had hit a nerve. He wanted to shake her. He wanted to throttle her.

Meredith fought back the feelings that simmered inside her. She had hoped that by insulting him, by reminding herself who this man was, she could sweep aside this insidious reaction to his mere touch. But nothing, it seemed, could save her from her weakness.

"The dance is ending," the queen called. "We must all kiss."

Meredith pulled away but she was no match for Brice's strength.

Brice bent, determined to casually touch his lips to hers. This was, after all, not really a kiss. It was nothing more than the latest silly fashion from Paris.

It was the merest touch of lips to lips. It lasted only the briefest moment in time. And yet, in that single second, she felt the fire and reacted as if she'd been burned. The moment his lips brushed hers, she flinched.

Brice felt it as well. He forced himself to absorb the shock with absolutely no expression on his face. The hands at her waist remained still as he commanded them not to draw her closer. But he could not control his pulsebeat. It throbbed at his temples, causing his blood to heat until it was a raging fire.

"Thank you for the dance, my lady." He lifted his head. "Angus." His voice was a low, angry growl.

Instantly his friend was on his feet and moving toward them. Meredith happened to glance over Brice's shoulder toward the place where Holden Mackay was sitting. On his face was a look so dark, so filled with fury, she nearly trembled.

"Dance with the lady," Brice said, handing her over to the surprised Angus.

Without another word Brice turned away and left the room.

Behind him, Meredith lifted her chin, determined not to watch his retreating back. But against her will her gaze locked on him, following his every move. In silence she endured the dance with Angus Gordon.

Jamie, too, watched as his hero retreated. There was nothing the man did that Jamie did not wish to imitate.

Across the room, the queen saw the way Brice stormed away. She saw also the way Meredith's gaze fastened on him, following him until he was out of sight.

And while the queen watched with avid interest, a slow smile of understanding touched her lips.

By late afternoon the queen and her company prepared to depart. Before leaving, she sent a servant to fetch Meredith.

The queen received her guest in the cozy library and Meredith was reminded of her earlier embarrassment when she had fallen out of the armoire into Brice's arms.

Her cheeks took on a becoming shade of pink. "You have decided to take me with you, Majesty?"

The queen shook her head. "I would not impose my will upon an old friend. Whatever Brice Campbell has in mind, I trust his judgment."

She saw Meredith's face fall at the news. "But at the table..."

"At the table, I was having fun at Brice's expense." To ease Meredith's pain she added softly, "But know this. Though his quick temper and skill with a broadsword are legend, Brice is a fine and honorable man. Although he bears a grudge against the MacKenzies, he will see that no harm comes to you."

No harm? What of the feelings he aroused in her? Feelings she had never even known existed within her? She trembled just thinking about the way she had nearly melted into his arms when they danced. And that kiss. It was no more than the brush of a butterfly's wings. And yet it had caused her heart to pound so loudly in her chest she had feared the others must surely have heard. God in heaven, what was to become of her?

Meredith felt a sudden wave of despair. Was she to be left to languish in this prison forever?

"I wish to go home, Majesty."

"Aye. Home." Mary Stuart heard the plea with a woman's heart. Did she not still think of France as her home? And did she not yearn to return to the opulence, the gaiety, of the French Court? The grim tone of Scotland since the popularity of John Knox was depressing to a woman like Mary. "I have no doubt that you will soon be returned to your home, Meredith. But until Brice makes that decision, I am loath to intervene. Your future lies in his hands."

Mary stood, effectively dismissing Meredith. And although the young woman yearned to throw herself into the queen's arms and beg for her intercession in this matter, her pride would not allow it. She stood, head held high, spine stiff, as the queen summoned Brice to escort her from the castle.

With her hand upon Brice's arm, the queen swept along the hall and into the courtyard. Behind her trailed the men and women of her hunting party. And behind them Meredith walked between Angus and Jamie.

As Brice helped the queen into the saddle, she stared over the heads of the crowd until her gaze came to rest upon the young prisoner. "I think, Brice, that you have captured more than you bargained for. In that one, you may have a wildcat by the tail."

She saw the thoughtfulness lurking in Brice's eyes behind the smile, though he said nothing.

Queen Mary gave a knowing look. "Farewell, my friend. I hope to see you soon in Edinburgh."

"The name of Campbell is not well received these days in the Lowlands."

The queen's eyes sparkled. "You are also the Earl of Kinloch. That makes you the queen's protector and a member of her Council."

"That title was my father's," Brice said softly. "It died with him. I am simply Brice Campbell."

Her tone was soft. "You are—simply one of my dearest friends." Her voice grew firm. "Despite what others say, a Campbell is always welcome in the home of the queen." Mary urged her dancing steed into a trot.

With a clatter of hooves the queen's hunting party followed their monarch across the courtyard and along the forest path. When they were no longer visible, Brice turned to find Meredith watching their departure with a look of naked hunger in her eyes. He felt her pain, sharp and swift, for he knew what it was to miss his home.

"Come," he said in a tone softer than he'd intended. "They could be the last visitors we shall entertain for a long time."

"Do you not find it lonely here in the Highlands?"

Brice offered his arm and she placed her hand upon it. Instantly he felt the rush of heat and marveled that this woman could be the cause of such discomfort.

"I have never felt lonely here."

He led her to the library and instructed a servant to bring two goblets of wine. Pulling the settle close to the fire he indicated that she should sit, while he chose to stand beside the fireplace. His arm rested along the mantel.

"Have you never known loneliness?" Meredith asked.

"Aye." He accepted a goblet of wine and sipped. "I accompanied the queen to France. Those were the loneliest days of my life."

"Why did you go?"

"My father feared for the safety of the young queen. He wanted her to be surrounded by friends who would remain loyal. Also, he argued that I could get a better education in France than I could here in Scotland." Brice gave a bitter laugh. "I did receive a fine education at the French Court. I learned that not all animals stalk the woods. Some dress in fine clothes and pass themselves off as aristocrats. And wait for a chance to attack unknowing prey."

Meredith heard the venom in his tone and wondered about it. What had happened to him in France to make him so bitter?

For long minutes he stared broodingly into the flames, before pulling himself from his dark thoughts. He set down the goblet on a low table and summoned a servant.

"Accompany the lady to my chambers," he said. "And fetch Angus and Holden to stand guard over her until I return."

Meredith turned, about to protest his latest order. But one glance at the tight set of his mouth convinced her to hold her tongue. Brice Campbell was in no mood to answer to her. Or to anyone.

The aroma of wood smoke mingled with the lingering scent of roasted meat. Two men lounged outside the door of Brice's chambers.

"'Twas truly a banquet fit for the queen," Holden Mackay said thoughtfully.

"Aye."

"Plovers and partridges by the dozen," Holden taunted, watching his friend's mouth water. "Not to mention rabbits, geese, venison. But the plump partridges were my favorite."

"I wonder if Mistress Snow has any partridge left," Angus said, stretching out his long legs.

"You cannot be thinking of food after all we ate this day." Holden grinned. It was common knowledge that Angus Gordon, thin as a rail, was always hungry. The mere mention of food made him salivate. Besides, the young widow Snow, who worked in the kitchens along with Cara's mother, was as appetizing a little morsel as the food she prepared. Angus spent an inordinate amount of time in her presence.

"I could eat a bite or two. But Brice wants us here until he returns."

"Brice will probably be gone until dawn. You saw the look on his face. When those black moods come upon him, he rides the woods for hours."

"Aye." Angus stood and began pacing. "But I intend to be here when he returns. I have faced his anger before when his orders were disobeyed."

Holden leaned back on the bench, stretching his hands above his head. "Mistress Snow makes a fine pudding. And her scones are the envy of every woman in the Highlands."

"Stop talking about food." Angus turned and paced the other way.

"If you wish, I will stay here and keep watch." Holden glanced at the closed doors. "There has been no sound from within for an hour. I'll wager the girl has fallen asleep."

"Aye." Angus stifled a yawn. "'Tis late enough. If I do not eat something soon, I'll not be able to stay awake."

"Go then." Holden was on his feet and turning his friend in the direction of the stairs. "Coax some food from Mistress Snow. And when you've had your fill—" he gave an evil leer "—of both partridge and Mistress Snow, come back here and we'll keep watch together."

"You do not mind?" Angus paused at the head of the stairs.

Holden shook his head and waved him on. "Nay. Go, old friend."

With a laugh Angus was gone.

When the sound of footsteps died, Holden peered about, then walked to the door of Brice's chambers. With his ear to the door he listened intently for several minutes. Then, taking a last glance around, he pressed a shoulder to the door and entered without a sound.

Meredith had decided to take matters into her own hands. Since Brice had seen to it that guards were posted outside the door of the chambers where she was being held, she would simply have to find another way out of her prison.

She knelt on the floor tying strips of linen together. Because there were still servants moving about the courtyard below from time to time, she was unable to drop the rope of linens from the window of her upper room to test its length. But she had determined that when these last three strips were attached, she would have enough to at least get her close to the ground. Under cover of darkness, with the servants snugly in their beds, she would slip from the window to the courtyard. If the rope was too short she was prepared to drop the rest of the way and pray that she broke no bones in her fall.

In preparation for her escape she had removed her soiled wedding gown and, having rummaged through Brice's wardrobe, had donned tight breeches and a shirt of lawn. On the floor beside her lay a tunic and warm cloak, which she intended to pull on just before she made good her escape.

As she knotted the linen strips her hair swirled forward in a wild tangle of curls. There was no time to plait it. With one hand she brushed the tangles aside and continued working.

The only sound in the room was the occasional hiss and snap of the burning logs on the grate. It was not until a shadow fell across her that she looked up in surprise.

"So. What is this?" Holden reached down and snatched the linen from her hands. Studying the knotted rope he arched a brow and looked down at her with sudden respect.

Meredith sprang to her feet with the agility of a cat. Another chance for escape was slipping through her fingers.

"Give it to me," she cried, her voice low and husky. As she made a grab for it his fingers closed around her wrist, holding her still.

"Brice's anger will be a fearsome thing when he sees this."

He studied the way her hair streamed down her shoulders and across her bodice. His gaze fastened on Brice's saffron shirt fastened snugly against her high, firm breasts. Even if he had not been sufficiently aroused, the strange sight of a woman in tight breeches was more than he could endure.

"By all that is holy you are the most beguiling woman I have ever seen."

At the look of hunger in his eyes she was gripped by a sudden, paralyzing fear. She tried to step back but he kept his hand firmly around her wrist.

"Perhaps," he said in a voice meant to seduce, "Brice need never know what you had planned."

"You would keep this from him?"

In one quick movement he looped the linen rope about her neck and drew her roughly toward him, until their faces were nearly touching. "I could be persuaded."

Meredith's heart lurched. There was no mistaking Holden's meaning.

While he held the rope with one hand, his other hand moved to the fasteners of her shirt. When she resisted, he caught at the collar and pulled. With a ripping sound the fabric gave way and tore open, exposing a delicate lace chemise beneath.

"Please. I've..." She swallowed down the hard lump of fear. She must not scream. That would bring the entire staff of servants down upon her. And there was still a chance that she could break free and escape. "I've never been with a man."

She saw the light that came into his eyes as he regarded her. "All the better." He twisted the rope until he heard her sudden intake of breath. With mock seriousness he whispered, "Forgive me, my lady. Am I choking you?"

Her hands clawed at the rope but he only twisted it more until her eyes swam with tears.

"Please." She struggled for a breath. "I cannot breathe."

"Would you like me to loosen it, my lady?"

She nodded her head and clutched at his hands but he only laughed and gave the rope a final vicious twist. "Do not fight me, Meredith MacAlpin. Soon you will lose consciousness. And when you awaken, you will find out what it is that men have enjoyed from the beginning of time."

"Nay." She felt the floor tilt and the room begin to spin and still he would not relent. Though she kicked and fought and clawed at his hands he never loosened his hold on the rope.

She heard a strange buzzing in her ears, and tiny black specks seemed to float through the air. Though she fought the feeling, she was slipping, slipping. Her hands went limp and she felt her knees buckle.

As she slid to the floor he knelt over her and loosened the rope, then reached both hands to her torn shirt.

In some dark corner of her mind she heard the ripping sound as the shirt was torn from her.

Chapter Seven

Though she was barely conscious, Meredith continued to fight her attacker. She felt a sense of outrage as strong hands tore at her breeches. With no weapon, she used her fingernails to scratch and gouge at the offending hands. And when Holden ignored her feeble attempts, she sank her teeth into his hand, drawing a spurt of blood.

He was stunned by her determination. Though he had seen traces of her fire and spirit, he had convinced himself that this female would be cowed by his superior strength.

"Stupid wench."

He slapped her so hard her head was snapped to one side. Pain danced through a haze of bright stars before she fell back defeated.

As Holden's hands reached for her, a voice from the doorway caused him to pause in midair.

"Step away from the woman."

Holden turned to see Brice facing him. By the flickering flames of the fire, Holden could see the glint of a knife in Brice's hand.

Meredith's attacker felt a trickle of sweat mingle with the blood that oozed from his wounds. He recognized the look of fury that darkened Brice's features. There were many men he would fight for a beauty such as this one. But never would he wish to fight Brice Campbell. Especially in a temper like this.

Thinking quickly he said, "The wench called out to me. And when I entered your chamber she acted the part of a temptress. Look how she is dressed."

He scrambled quickly to his feet, stepping a little away from Meredith. Brice saw, for the first time, the tight breeches, the gaping shirt.

Meredith opened her eyes and felt her head swim as she tried to sit up. At a glance she took in Brice, dagger in hand, facing Holden. She felt a momentary rush of relief. Safe. Now she would be safe from her vicious attacker. It was Holden's words that sent her hopes plummeting.

"The wench thought if she could seduce me I would be persuaded not to tell you that she was trying to escape. But I remembered your orders, Brice. Though she put up a fierce struggle, I was able to keep her from slipping out the window."

Meredith thought about protesting. But why would Brice Campbell accept her word against that of one of his own men? With a feeling of desperation she lay back, prepared for even more punishment from the man who should have been her protector.

Brice took a step closer. "Aye. I see the tunic and warm cloak folded atop a fur throw in preparation for travel. Woman, there is no denying that you intended once more to attempt an escape."

His gaze locked on the knotted rope of linen that trailed the floor. "You are a clever lass. You even prepared your escape from a dangerous height."

Suddenly his gaze followed the trail of linen rope from the window, to where it was still coiled loosely about her throat. Dark purple welts were already forming on her flesh. From the way her shirt fell open he knew that it had not been merely unfastened by a woman about to seduce. It was rent nearly in two. And the torn breeches were further indictment.

His gaze lifted to Meredith's face. He saw the dull pain that glazed her eyes. And something else. Terror. Sheer terror.

His fury bubbled dangerously close to the surface. He felt the warmth of the dirk in his hand and fought a surging desire to bury it in Holden's massive chest. What chance did a fragile, unarmed woman have against an animal like Holden Mackay?

In the blink of an eye the anger and guilt transferred from Holden to Brice himself. Who had left the lass in this brute's hands? Who had foolishly thought that a man, far from the comfort of his own clan, could be trusted with the care of a prisoner as beautiful as Meredith MacAlpin?

Had it not been for his own complicity in this, Brice would have killed Holden Mackay for this ugly deed.

In a tightly controlled voice he rasped, "Mackay, you will leave us. You have violated someone under my protection. Return to your people. You are no longer welcome in Kinloch House."

Holden experienced a wild surge of relief. He had feared, from the savage look in Brice's eyes, that he would have to battle him to the death. But just as quickly the relief disappeared, to be replaced by a growing sense of wrath.

"Aye." Holden's eyes glinted with sudden anger. "Turn on your old friends from the north for the sake of a wench who has bewitched you. But the day will come when you will regret this. On that day, when you need the might of the Mackay armies, we will remember this night and take up arms with your enemy."

"So be it."

Holden thought about killing the man who all but ignored him while he studied the woman. Brice's head would be quite a prize to take to his people. The name Brice Campbell still brought fear to the hearts of men in the Highlands. But Holden was aware of the barely controlled fury in the man, and knew that with Brice in such a rage he had no chance to win. Without another word he turned and fled.

Brice fell to his knees and touched a finger to the bruises about Meredith's throat. "The lout choked you."

At the intimacy of his touch she flinched and tried to back away from him. "Do not touch me."

"I must examine your wounds." When he tried to subdue her she mistook his intentions and began wrestling for control of the knife still held firmly in his other hand.

He saw the raw emotions in her eyes and cursed himself for his clumsiness. Tossing aside the dirk he lifted both palms to her to prove that he meant her no harm.

"I am unarmed, my lady. I wish only to make amends for what has been done."

At his submissive gesture Meredith felt the prickle of tears against her lids and blinked furiously. She must not let him see her weakness.

"Do not touch me. I can—take care of myself."

The more she tried to be brave, the more helpless Brice felt.

With a savage oath he yanked the rope free and tossed it aside. Then he lifted her in his arms and strode across the room. Kicking open the door to the bedchamber, he crossed the fur-strewn floor and laid her gently upon his bed.

The room was dim except for the flickering flames of the fire. His voice was as still and hushed as the night that seemed to have wrapped them in its soft, dark cloak.

"Forgive me, Meredith. It never occurred to me that one of my own men would be the cause of such pain."

When she did not respond he whispered, "I regret that I must cause you further discomfort." As he spoke he reached his hands to the waistband of her breeches. "There is blood upon your clothing. I must find the source."

"Nay. Nay." Though she tried to fight him, he managed to remove the torn clothing.

Beneath the breeches and shirt her ivory chemise bore more traces of blood. But when he untied the ribbons that laced the chemise across her breasts, she cried out so sadly he was forced to stop.

He sat on the edge of the bed and leaned close, placing his hands on either side of her head. "Holden has hurt you, Meredith. You are bleeding. Let me help you."

At his gentle concern she felt some of the terror dissipate. Perhaps it was not his intention to harm her. Perhaps he was merely trying to help.

"I am not bleeding," she whispered.

Her breath was warm against his cheek. So warm he had to resist the urge to turn his mouth to hers.

"There is blood on your garments."

"Holden's blood," she whispered.

"Holden's?" He drew closer, staring intently into her eyes. "But you were unarmed."

"Aye. But I had my hands. And my teeth."

"You bit him?" He felt some of his fury begin to melt. In its place a hint of laughter bubbled.

"Aye. I bit him."

"Then I suppose I need not remove your chemise in search of more blood."

"Nay."

"A pity. I was prepared to do my duty no matter how unpleasant."

How could it be that only moments ago she had suffered the terror of the damned, and now, with Brice as protector, she was able to smile and even respond to his silly joke?

"If you should think about removing my chemise, my lord, think about this. If you try, you will need the queen's own physician to repair the damage these teeth will inflict upon your hands."

"These are noble warrior's hands, my lady. They must be ever prepared to protect the weak and suffering."

"They will be exceedingly damaged warrior's hands if they are found where they are not wanted."

He gave her a long, lingering look. "What an amazing woman you are." He saw the hint of color that touched her cheeks. "You are truly unharmed, Meredith?"

The tenderness in his tone was nearly her undoing. He felt her tremble.

"Aye, my lord." Her voice trailed off as she fought a shudder that passed through her body. "I have survived. I am fine."

His voice was suddenly gruff. He recognized the shock and fatigue that was beginning to overcome her. "You are indeed a fine woman. But you are far from recovered. You will sleep now."

He pulled the bed linens over her and added a fur on top of them, smoothing it until she was warm and snug.

Meredith caught his hand. "You will stay with me? You will not send someone else to guard me?"

"If you wish."

"Aye." She clung to his hand. "I wish."

He stared down at the small hand upon his. At this moment he would move heaven and earth if she but asked it.

"I will be right beside you."

"All night?"

"And late into the morning if you desire."

He pulled a chair beside the bed and dropped a fur across his knees. While the fire burned to embers he watched her as she slept.

Thin morning sunlight filtered through the windows, sweeping away the night shadows. Beneath the covers Meredith lay very still, replaying in her mind the events of the previous night.

She recalled clearly the attack by Holden and the tender way Brice had carried her to his bed. Less clear in her mind were the dreams that plagued her as she slept. Several times she had cried out. And each time Brice had been there beside her, soothing, holding. The last time she had sobbed as though her heart would break and it had been Brice who held her in his arms, rocking her as tenderly as if she were a wee bairn.

Brice. She opened her eyes and stared at the chaise drawn up beside the bed. It was empty. She felt a swift stab of disappointment. He had broken his word and left her.

A movement beside her in the bed startled her. Turning she found herself face-to-face with Brice.

Without a word he touched a hand to her cheek. The sweetness of the gesture brought a lump to her throat.

She studied the stubble of beard that darkened his chin, and had to clench her hands into fists to keep from reaching out to him. The nearness of the man did strange things to her. Her throat was dry. Her heartbeat was wildly erratic. And she was suddenly far too warm.

As she sat up and swung her feet to the floor he closed a hand around her wrist.

"You should stay abed, my lady."

"Nay. I have a need to be up and about."

He watched as she crossed the room toward the basin and pitcher. Pouring a little water she began to wash her face and arms.

He sat up. From this vantage point he could admire her Creator's handiwork. How truly lovely she was. The sheer chemise clearly emphasized every line and curve of her body. As she bent to splash water on her face, he studied the dark cleft between her breasts and felt a rush of heat. His gaze traced the waist so narrow he was certain his big hands could easily span it, then moved lower to her flare of hips. Her legs were long and shapely, her bare feet as dainty as a child's.

She dried her face and began to run his brush through the tangles of her hair. Tossing her head, she brought the hair forward over one breast and continued brushing until it was sleek and shining. Then she tossed it back and allowed it to cascade down her back like a shimmering veil.

She crossed the room to a stool and picked up the crumpled white gown. He watched her with a smile of appreciation. It was then that he spied the bruises on her throat.

He was across the room in quick strides. Without a word he caught her chin in his hand and lifted her face.

Meredith was about to protest his rough actions until she saw the pained look in his eyes. "What is it, my lord?"

"I should never have allowed him to walk away." Brice's nostrils flared as he gently examined each bruise. "I should have killed Holden Mackay for what he did to you."

"I will heal." Embarrassed at his scrutiny she brought a hand to her throat.

"If I but had it in my power," he said, bending his lips to the bruises on her throat, "I would willingly take each of your hurts upon myself."

She stood very still, absorbing the waves that shuddered through her at his touch. Never before had a man dared to press his lips to her throat. And yet the touch was so tender, so loving, she was helpless to step away.

He glanced down at the soiled gown in her hands. "Do not put that on," he said in a low tone of command.

"But it is all I have." As she made a move to pull away he yanked the gown from her hands and tossed it in a heap on the floor.

"I will send Cara up with something more appropriate."

He turned away and pulled on a tunic before leaving the room. It would never occur to him to admit, even to himself, that the gown offended him because it reminded him of the marriage she had almost been allowed to consummate, and the husband who would have bedded her.

Cara helped Meredith into the gown provided by the young widow, Mistress Snow. Though not a perfect fit, it was far more comfortable than the white gown that she had discarded.

The fabric was the color of heather, with deeper purple ribbons banding the bodice and hem. The sleeves were full, then gathered at elbow and wrist with shirring. The color was a lovely counterpoint to Meredith's green eyes and brought a bloom to her cheeks. Best of all, the high ruffled collar hid the bruises that marred her throat.

"Oh, you look lovely, my lady," Cara said as she finished dressing Meredith's hair with matching ribbons.

"Thank you. And thank Mistress Snow for me."

"I will, my lady." Cara crossed the room and held the door. "If you are ready, the others are waiting to break their fast."

Meredith followed her from the room and made her way to the great room, where the rumble of masculine voices alerted her that the others were already assembled.

She took a seat between Brice and Jamie and accepted food from the servants in silence.

Beside her, Brice cleared his throat. Odd. When they were alone, he had no trouble conversing with her. Now that they were with the others he felt the old awkwardness returning.

"You look lovely," he murmured in a voice meant for her alone.

"Thank you, my lord. I would like to go to the scullery later to thank Mistress Snow."

"I will take you myself."

They continued to eat while the conversation swirled around them. There was talk of the queen's visit, which led to a discourse on the scandalous marriage feast the queen had given her brother, James and his wife. The guests had openly danced, knowing they violated the laws of the kirk. The discussion then turned to the latest invasion of the Borders by English troops.

Beside Meredith, Jamie fidgeted. He had heard the whispers and rumors this morrow. Brice had banished Holden Mackay from the castle. Some said the lady had seduced poor Holden, while others whispered that Holden had forced himself on her. No matter what the truth of the rumors, Jamie was unnerved by them. He had witnessed glimpses of Holden's cruel vengeance. He would not wish to endure the man's wrath.

He glanced uneasily at the beautiful creature beside him. Though he was only ten and two, he was already as tall as she. And stronger, he suspected, risking a quick glance at the delicate hand resting beside her plate.

She was very quiet this morrow. But since her arrival he had heard her say very little. Her voice was unusual: deeper in timbre than most females, and as whispery soft as a lullaby. It was the voice he imagined his mother would have had, if he could but recall his mother who had died when he was a bairn.

Meredith sensed the scrutiny of the lad beside her and turned to give him a shy smile. He returned the smile before coloring and turning away quickly.

It mattered not to Jamie what the others whispered about the lady. He knew in his heart that she would never attempt to seduce a man like Holden. To Jamie, Meredith Mac-Alpin embodied all that was good and fine and noble.

No one mentioned the absence of Holden Mackay, and Meredith fretted that word of her attack had already been whispered about the castle. She frowned and quickly dismissed such thoughts. She would not dwell on somber things.

After their meal, she followed Brice from the great hall and through the maze of dimly lit passageways to the scullery.

The air was thick with the aroma of fresh bread baking in the ovens. A small deer was slowly roasting on a spit, in preparation for the evening meal. Servants were busy fetching buckets of water, while more servants scurried about, scrubbing, cleaning, cutting and preparing.

"Mistress Snow," Brice called.

A small, thin woman looked up from a floured table where she was kneading dough. Seeing the lord of the manor she quickly wiped her hands on a linen square and hurried forward.

Her dress of pale pink was covered by a soiled apron. She touched the end of the apron to her brow as she walked. Dark hair was pulled back from a pretty oval face. Little tendrils of hair clung damply to her forehead and cheeks. Blue eyes danced with laughter as she studied the way her best gown looked on the beautiful woman beside Brice Campbell.

"Lady Meredith MacAlpin came to thank you for the use of your gown."

"It looks far more beautiful on you, my lady, than it ever did on me," she said with a slight bow.

Brice took a moment to study Meredith while she faced the young servant. Indeed she did look beautiful in the heather gown. But it was the exchange between Meredith and his servant that he found most fascinating.

Meredith caught Mistress Snow's hands in hers, ignoring the dusting of flour that clung to her skin. "It was very kind of you to entrust me with the use of your gown. I shall find a way to repay your kindness."

"I desire nothing of you, my lady. It is enough to know that you are pleased with my simple gown."

"I am more than pleased. I am most grateful. Thank you, Mistress Snow."

As they turned away, Brice was aware that the entire staff of servants had watched and listened to this exchange. It was a rare thing to see a highborn woman who would take the time to thank a servant for a kindness.

When they left the scullery they were aware of someone who appeared to be waiting for them. Brice's hand went to the dirk at his waist. Meredith's hand leaped to her throat in a gesture of distress.

Angus Gordon stepped from the shadows and put a hand to Meredith's arm to stop her.

"My lady," Angus said, his face turning a bright scarlet. "Forgive my boldness for approaching you in this manner. But I must beg your forgiveness for leaving my post last night. I am shamed by my lapse of duties."

Now it was Meredith's turn to blush. The young man seemed truly contrite.

"It was not your fault, Angus," she said, avoiding his eyes.

"Aye, but it was." Angus took a step closer, forcing her to look up at him. "Brice had ordered me to guard you. I ignored his orders, and allowed harm to come to you. If Brice had not returned, I shudder to think what would have happened to you at the hands of that coward, Holden Mackay."

"It is forgotten," she said in a tone that left no question of her feeling. "I would ask only that you never mention the name Holden Mackay again."

Angus bowed slightly over her hand. "As you say, my lady. The man no longer exists."

She shivered as Angus accompanied them along the hall. If only Angus's words were true. But the fact was that somewhere in the forest surrounding Kinloch House, Holden Mackay dwelled. And in his heart he could very well be nursing anger and a desire for revenge.

If she ever managed to escape this fortress, there would be another danger added to the elements. A man who would show her no mercy.

Chapter Eight

In the courtyard a dozen horses were being readied for a journey. But though the men awaiting Brice were familiar to Meredith, they were no longer dressed like Highlanders. Instead of being bare legged, they wore trews, the long hose of the Lowland clans. Many wore breeches, as did Brice, and shirts of gray and dun instead of saffron. The colorful belted plaids they usually wore had been exchanged for simple wool cloaks. All the men wore daggers fastened to their belts. Most carried swords and had longbows slung over their shoulders. But though they were dressed in the garb of the Lowlanders, nothing could hide the fierce pride or the rawboned strength of these Highland warriors.

"You are leaving with your men?"

"Aye."

Brice saw the fear that leaped into Meredith's eyes. "Would Holden Mackay dare to return while you are away?"

His eyes narrowed. "This fortress is nearly impenetrable. But to assure the safety of those inside, I leave a dozen men capable of withstanding any attack."

At his words of reassurance she took in a long, steadying breath. "Where do you go?"

"We ride to the Borders."

"Then you must take me home."

He saw the eagerness in her eyes and wished he did not have to be the one to dash her hopes. "Nay, my lady. We ride on a mission of revenge."

Her heart sank once more. "Gareth MacKenzie."

"Aye." He draped the cloak across his shoulders at a rakish angle and pulled himself into the saddle. "When the MacKenzie is dead I will return you to your people."

"And if you die instead?"

"Would that please you, my lady?"

When she remained silent he gave her a rare, heart-stopping smile. "If I oblige you by being killed, I would suppose the MacKenzie would come for you. That is," he said with a sweep of his plumed hat, "if he still desires to align your two clans."

"He will come for me," she called.

But Brice did not hear her words above the clatter of hooves. Or if he did, he chose not to answer.

"Jamie," he called to the lad who watched their preparations from the doorway. "I leave the lady Meredith in your care until I return."

The boy's cheeks flamed until they matched the color of his hair. "Aye, Brice. I'll see to her."

With shouts of eagerness the men whipped their horses into a run. Within minutes they had disappeared into the surrounding forest.

Meredith sat by the window watching the path of a shooting star. How strange life was. So often, when she got what she had wished for, it turned out to be not at all what she wanted.

She had wished for Brice to leave her alone long enough so that she could slip into the forest and make her way back home. But now that Brice had finally left her, she was unable to leave. Someone now lurked in the forest beyond Kinloch House who wished her even greater harm than could befall her at the hands of Brice.

And so she sat, alone and lonely.

Lonely? She did not miss Brice Campbell, she told herself firmly. How could she miss the quick temper, the cold, dark looks? Why would she care about the absence of the low, taunting voice, the occasional burst of teasing laughter?

At a knock on the door she looked up. Jamie MacDonald stood poised in the doorway. At his feet were several of Brice's hounds.

"Come in, Jamie," she called.

He took a step in and glanced about uneasily. He had never had occasion to enter a lady's room before. The hounds, following his lead, proceeded cautiously.

"I—wanted to see if you needed anything, my lady." His Adam's apple bobbed up and down with each halting word.

Meredith smiled. "How kind of you, Jamie. I was just sitting here feeling lonely. I would treasure your company for a little while." She indicated a chair pulled before the fire. "Sit awhile."

He crossed the room and perched on the edge like a bird ready for flight. The hounds circled the room before settling at his feet.

"What do you do while Brice and the others are away?" she asked.

"I help in the stables, and sometimes go with the men who keep watch along the trails."

"What do they keep watch for?"

"Surprise visitors," he said with a trace of a smile.

Meredith was reminded of another's smile. "Do you miss Brice Campbell when he is away?"

"Aye. Kinloch House is never quiet when Brice is in residence. But when he goes away, it is as if everyone lies sleeping, waiting for Brice to awaken them."

What an oddly accurate description, she thought.

"And the hounds? Do they switch loyalties when their master is away?"

Jamie reached a hand to the head of one of the dogs. Instantly the dog sat up and rested his chin on the boy's knee, staring sorrowfully into his eyes.

"Nay. The hounds follow me and allow me to pet them. But they leave no doubt as to their loyalty. They love only Brice Campbell. As do I," he added fiercely.

Meredith was moved by his simple statement.

"Cara told me how you came to live here. Do you miss your home in the Lowlands?"

Jamie shook his head slowly. "I no longer remember it, my lady. I was but a babe when my father and I came here."

"Do you not feel disloyal to your clan when you swear allegiance to a Highlander?"

Jamie stood and crossed to the window where he stared in silence for several minutes. When at last he spoke, his voice was as soft as a night breeze.

"I know that it could have been Brice's arrow that slew my father. And I know here," he said, touching a finger to his temple, "that I should avenge my father's death. But here," he said, touching a hand to his heart, "I know only that Brice gave me shelter when I had none. He gave me food and clothing, and has taught me to read, to chart the stars, to ride and handle a weapon like a warrior. When he scolds me, I know it is because he expects me to grow to be a man of honor. And when he praises me, my heart swells with pride. Though I am a MacDonald from the Lowlands, Brice Campbell is my father now. I would do nothing to dishonor him."

With a lump in her throat Meredith crossed the room and touched a hand to Jamie's shoulder. "I have a little sister," she said softly, "named Megan. She is near your age. And much like you."

"A sister?" Jamie tried to picture a younger, smaller version of the woman beside him.

"Aye. Two sisters, in fact. Brenna, with dark hair and eyes to match the heather. She is a gentle girl who would never harm a living creature. And Megan," Meredith said with a laugh that bubbled forth just thinking about the child. "She is fair as the sun and as wild and free as the breezes that blow off the river."

Meredith stared at the darkness beyond the window, knowing that Jamie's loneliness was as acute as her own.

"Sit and tell me about your life here," she said.

He smiled and followed her back to the chair. He couldn't think of any place he would rather be at this moment than right here, in the company of the most beautiful woman he had ever seen.

They talked and laughed for nearly an hour before looking up at a knock on the door.

Cara entered, carrying a tray of tea and biscuits.

"Mistress Snow thought you might be hungry." The serving girl placed the tray on a low table in front of the fire.

"When the men ride to the Borders," Meredith asked softly, "how long do they usually travel?"

"Oh, my lady, it could be days. There's no telling how long they'll stay away this time."

Days. Meredith's heart fell. She glanced at Jamie and saw that he, too, was dismayed. As she poured two cups of tea she had a thought. "Is there cloth here at Kinloch House? Enough for a gown?"

"Aye, my lady. There is fine cloth in the storehouse."

Meredith smiled suddenly. "Tomorrow, Cara, after we break our fast, I would like Jamie to show me the storehouse."

"But why, my lady?"

Her smile grew. "I owe Mistress Snow a gown. There is no better time to start than now."

"And when you tire of sewing," Jamie said with a wide smile, "I shall be happy to show you the stables. Brice said I can handle the horses as well as any of his men."

"I would like that."

Together Meredith and Jamie passed another pleasant hour before they bid good-night. And when at last Meredith drifted off to sleep, she felt more relaxed than she had at any time since her shocking abduction.

The line of mourners stretched around the manor house and up the lane for as far as the eye could see.

An old man, slightly stooped, with a walking stick in his hand, joined the crowd and moved slowly toward the house. A rough, shapeless cloak fell from his shoulders to his ankles. When someone in front of him asked his name, the old man cupped a hand to his ear and strained to understand the question.

"He's likely from the MacKenzie clan," one of the women called from behind him. "With Gareth MacKenzie spending so much time on MacAlpin land these days, the MacKenzie clansmen are everywhere. So many strangers," she complained. "There was a time when we knew everyone who passed us on the lane."

"What do you expect?" cried a thin youth. "With old Duncan MacAlpin and two wee lasses the only ones left to lead the clan, the MacKenzies have a free rein in MacAlpin affairs."

"Aye," another responded. "First Alastair, and then Meredith. Both were born leaders. But the younger lasses have not the heart for it. And Duncan is a beaten man."

The crowd moved along and the old man struggled to keep up. Those around him, intent upon their gossip, ignored him.

"Some say old Duncan and Mary will never be the same now." A plump woman with a baby at her hip spoke to the crowd.

"Aye. The murder of an only grandson is too hard to bear," said a ruddy-cheeked man.

"Especially since Duncan's son, William and his wife, Margaret, can have no more bairns." It was a young, pretty woman speaking. Her coloring was similar to Meredith's, since they were distant cousins. "Young William was the light of their lives."

"Aye. Especially Duncan's. He doted on the lad. He and Mary had depended upon young William to help with the chores." An old woman lowered her voice slightly as she addressed those around her. "Gareth MacKenzie himself witnessed the murder of poor William. When he tried to stop them from beating the lad, he took a dirk in the arm from one of them."

"Something must be done to stop the killing."

The crowd murmured its approval.

"Aye," said the ruddy-cheeked man. "And from what I've heard, something will be done."

"What have you heard, man?"

"Gareth MacKenzie is planning to lead an army against the man who would murder even children in his lust for power."

"The filthy, murdering coward," someone in the crowd spat.

"Aye. Brice Campbell must be stopped before he manages to kill the entire MacAlpin clan."

At that the shabby old man stopped in his tracks. Then, keeping his head bowed, he plodded slowly along with the others. When they reached the manor house he studied the faces of the crowd, nodding occasionally when his gaze met that of someone familiar, partially hidden beneath similarly shabby attire.

As they passed the simple wooden casket, the old man paused to study the lad who was being mourned. Young William, grandson of Duncan and Mary MacAlpin, dead at the tender age of ten and five. On either side of the casket stood the parents and grandparents, as well as the three pretty granddaughters who were openly sobbing.

Beside them were two young lasses who stood together, heads high, hands linked. The old man paused to study them carefully. Though their coloring was distinctly different, he knew them to be sisters. The younger sisters of Meredith MacAlpin.

The older of the two, with coal-black hair and eyes more violet than blue, stared above the crowd, drawing into herself to keep from feeling the pain. The other, with hair the color of the sun, eagerly scanned the faces in the crowd as though expecting at any moment to see the one she sought.

Meredith, the old man thought, noting the intensity of the gaze. The younger one had not yet accepted what the older one knew to be fact: that Meredith was not free to return to them in their time of need.

The old man's eyes narrowed as he noted Gareth Mac-Kenzie standing just behind the two lasses. Around him were a dozen or more of his most trusted men, all of them bearing arms.

As always, Gareth set himself up in a position of importance and made certain that the crowd of mourners heard every lurid detail of the lad's murder.

"'Twas Brice Campbell," he said loudly. "And at least two dozen of his cowardly men. I saw and heard everything. They asked the lad's name, then began beating him with their fists."

"Dear God, stop." Duncan dropped an arm about his wife's shoulders as she started to cry.

"When was this?" the shabbily dressed old man asked in a voice that quavered with age.

"On the day before last," Gareth said. "I leaped from my horse and tried to go to the lad's aid, but one of the cowards plunged his dirk into my arm while another held me down and took my knife."

"'Twas Gareth's weapon they used on my William," Duncan said through trembling lips. "It was found, caked with dried blood, beside his body."

Gareth continued his story, eager to feed the crowd's appetite for gossip. "When the lad was no more than a bloody heap, they let me go."

"Odd they did not kill you as well," the shabby old man said haltingly. "Why would you suppose they let you live?"

Gareth shot a cold stare in the direction of the speaker, then shrugged off his comment as being unworthy of a response. The shabby old stranger was probably just another of the MacAlpin clan. Gareth's voice rose. "I call on all men of goodwill, be they MacKenzie or MacAlpin clan. It is time to show the Highland Barbarian, Brice Campbell, that he can no longer murder our young and helpless and then hide in the forests yonder. He captured your leader, Meredith MacAlpin, and holds her captive in his Highland fortress. Who knows what unspeakable things are being done to her this very day."

Out of the corner of his eye the old man saw the two lasses tighten their grips on each other's hands. Neither made a sound. Neither showed any sign of emotion, except for a tightening of their mouths.

In the corner of the room a woman began sobbing.

Still other women gasped before turning into their men's arms and crying silently.

Gareth waited, judging the mood of the crowd. With a voice of triumph he shouted, "And Brice Campbell has murdered another MacAlpin. What say you?" Gareth looked around as a hush fell upon the crowd. "Who will join me in putting an end to his reign of terror?"

For a moment there was only silence. Every man here was aware of the reputation of the man they called the Highland Barbarian. There were none eager to risk their lives at the end of his sword. Still, the sight of the young lad in the casket and his grieving family left them too outraged to dwell on the risk.

"With enough force we can storm Campbell's fortress and save the woman who was to wed my brother. With Meredith MacAlpin at my side, I vow to unite the Border clans and stand against any attack."

The room was rocked with shouts and calls as the men hurried forward to shake Gareth's hand and offer their arms.

"In the days to come," Gareth shouted above the din, "I will raise up an army of men. And we will ride to the Highlands and rid ourselves of this scum."

"Aye. Here's to the death of Brice Campbell." Fists were raised in a salute as the men, their blood hot for revenge, surged forward.

"And just to tempt you further," Gareth MacKenzie shouted, "I will offer a price of one hundred pounds sterling to any man who brings me the body of Brice Campbell."

While the rooms of the manor house rocked with the fury of the crowd, the shabby old man nodded to several others before making his way slowly from the house. In the lane he continued hobbling until he came to a stand of trees. He glanced around, and seeing no one behind him, stepped into the shelter offered by the trees. Several horsemen greeted him. He pulled off the shabby cloak, and with an agility that belied his stooped appearance, pulled himself into the saddle.

"Well, Brice," one of the men said softly. "What news have you?"

He nodded to the others who had accompanied him to the house. Once they reached the safety of the trees they also shed their shabby cloaks and pulled themselves onto their waiting horses.

Brice's tone was as grim as their faces. "By all accounts I have lived up to the name these Borderers have given me." His eyes narrowed fractionally. "I have just discovered that on the very day I was dancing with the queen, I was also here in the Lowlands murdering young William MacAlpin."

"That is an amazing feat even for a Highland warrior," one of the men said with a laugh.

"Aye." Brice's eyes narrowed as he added, "And Gareth MacKenzie has put a price on my head. One hundred pounds sterling for any man who brings me to him. Alive or dead."

"MacKenzie," Angus spat. "Come, Brice. Let us kill him now."

"Nay, friend." Brice turned his mount and motioned for the others to follow. "Already he surrounds himself with too many men. Think of your women and children waiting for you in the Highlands. Within days there will be dozens of men riding through the forests hoping to cut down anything that moves."

"What will we do now?"

Brice slowed his horse until Angus caught up with him. As they rode side by side Brice murmured, "We will do what our ancestors have done for centuries, old friend. We will take up arms and fight anyone foolish enough to dare to enter our Highland forests."

"And what of our families?"

"They remain at our sides," Brice said. "We will bring them inside the protective walls of Kinloch House. And there they will stay until the siege is over."

"And the lass, Meredith MacAlpin?"

A little muscle worked in the side of Brice's jaw as he urged his mount ahead. Aye, he thought. What to do about Meredith? If he were to return her to her people, she would prove the lie that Gareth MacKenzie had spread. That could, once and for all time, clear his good name. But it would be impossible for him to remain with her forever. And left at the mercy of Gareth MacKenzie she would soon be conveniently murdered, as the others had been.

But, Brice reasoned, if he kept her with him, she would be forced into a life of hardship and deprivation while the invaders were repulsed. Yet for now, he could think of no other solution.

Over his shoulder he called, "The woman stays with me at Kinloch House."

"Oh, my lady. This is far too grand for me to wear." Mistress Snow studied her reflection in the looking glass. "I look like the lady of the manor."

"And well you should." Meredith stood beside her, proud of her accomplishment.

It was Brenna, the sister who was younger by a year, who sewed the finest seams. And it had always been Brenna who could add a bit of ribbon or lace and make the plainest gown look splendid.

Meredith had taken great pains with this task. And it had served its purpose well. The long hours alone in Brice's chambers had passed far easier than she had expected. And when she wasn't sewing she was visiting with the servants. She had learned the names of all of them, as well as their family histories.

Like a shadow, young Jamie had been constantly at her side, watching, listening. And though he felt strangely disloyal to his idol, Brice, he found himself becoming enchanted with the beautiful young woman who was being held prisoner in their home.

"I think," Mistress Snow said, interrupting Jamie's musings, "that I should take back the simple gown I loaned you, and give you this one."

"And I think," Meredith said with a smile, "that Angus Gordon will not be able to stay away from the scullery when he sees you in this."

"Oh, my lady." The young widow blushed furiously before burying her face in her hands.

Jamie stifled a giggle. He had repeated a litany of gossip during the days that he and Meredith had spent together. Apparently the lady had paid more attention than he'd thought.

They all looked up when they heard the clatter of horses' hooves entering the courtyard.

"The men have returned." Mistress Snow raced to the door, then seemed to remember her position. Holding the door for Meredith and Jamie, she followed them down the stairs.

Men and horses milled about in mass confusion. Many of the men stood in a circle, listening intently as Brice spoke in low tones. Others trudged to the storehouse and began carrying an assortment of supplies toward the main door of the castle. As Meredith watched, the circle of men broke up. Most of the men mounted and rode away, while others joined the group carrying supplies.

Brice spoke quietly to Angus and another man, then looked up to see Meredith standing in the doorway with her hand on Jamie's shoulder. For long moments their gazes met and held.

It was strange to see this woman, his captive, standing protectively beside the boy he loved more than his own life. Strange and—pleasant.

Meredith felt the hypnotic pull of his gaze and couldn't stop the tremors that coursed along her spine. How odd that the man she wished to escape from was also the man who could cause such wild stirrings deep within her.

Brice said something more to Angus, then strode impatiently toward her.

She studied his grim features and waited for him to speak. Instead, he stopped before her without a word, then called out orders to the men in the courtyard.

It was vexing to be ignored in this fashion. In a snappish tone she asked, "Have you extracted your revenge?"

He shook his head and turned to speak to one of his men.

"Then what news do you bring? Am I to be returned to my home?"

He turned toward her but kept his gaze on the procession of men and arms. "Jamie," he said in a patient tone, "go and help the men carry supplies to the main house."

"Aye." Jamie gave Brice a long, questioning look before turning away.

"As for you, my lady," Brice said, still watching the progress of the men, "I fear it will be a long time before you see home and family again."

Meredith swallowed down the knot of fear that leaped to her throat. "What are you saying?"

"We will soon be under siege, my lady. These forests will be teeming with men bent upon my destruction."

She felt a flare of hope. "Gareth MacKenzie? He comes for me?"

"Nay, my lady." Brice turned and met her gaze squarely. "He comes for me."

"Surely Gareth MacKenzie would not be fool enough to bring his men into the Highland forests where they would be outnumbered."

"He and his men do not come alone. They bring the MacAlpin clan with them."

She brought her hands to her hips in a fit of outrage. "My people do not fight in the Highlands. They understand the folly of it."

"They fight when they are persuaded that the life of their leader is threatened."

"You have threatened my life?"

"Nay. But your people believe I have. And," he added tersely, "they agreed to fight when the grandson of Duncan MacAlpin was murdered by the Highland Barbarian."

"What are you saying?" Her hands balled into fists as she turned on him. "You killed William?"

He caught her fists in his big hands as easily as if they were no more than wispy flowers blowing in the wind. "Nay, my lady. The lad was killed on the very day I was dancing with the queen."

"I do not understand."

"The ones who killed young William wanted the murder to be blamed on me."

"Why? Who would benefit from such a thing?"

"Aye. Who indeed?" He studied her in silence for long minutes. "Did I mention that Gareth MacKenzie has offered one hundred pounds sterling for the Highland Barbarian?"

Several men pushed past them, their arms laden with the supplies of war.

When she continued staring at Brice in openmouthed surprise, he said softly, "It could mean that Gareth MacKenzie is so incensed by the death of one of the MacAlpins that he would lead his own men into certain danger." His lips curved into a smile, but his eyes, she noted, were dark and unfathomable. "Or it could mean that Gareth MacKenzie hopes to silence the Highland Barbarian before the truth can be revealed."

"It could also mean that Gareth is determined to avenge the senseless murder of his brother."

Without a word in his defense Brice swung away and strode toward the storehouse.

While she watched the frantic preparations for war, Meredith felt a growing sense of dread. This feud was growing into something far more dangerous than vengeance. Someone was going to a great deal of trouble to ruin Brice Campbell's reputation. Someone who would stop at nothing, even the murder of the young and helpless.

Young William. She felt as if a knife had pierced her heart. She had watched the tenderness between Duncan and Mary and their young grandson. His death would be a heavy burden.

And what of her people? They were being dragged into a war not of their making. If they were persuaded to leave their homes and follow Gareth MacKenzie, they left their own families open to attack by the English across their border. They lacked strong leadership. And all because she'd had the misfortune of being captured by the Highland Barbarian.

Chapter Nine

I can handle a broadsword, Brice."

Meredith looked up at the sound of Jamie's pleading voice.

"Nay. I'll not allow it." Brice grasped the weapon, yanking it fiercely from the lad's hands. "'Tis not fit for close combat. It takes two hands to wield, leaving no protection of a shield. Besides, I expect you to play the pipes when I give the command."

"Bagpipes." The lad's face mirrored his disgust. "That is a task for children and old men."

"Is it now?" Brice crossed the room and ran a hand lovingly over the bagpipes resting on the mantel above the fireplace. "When I was no younger than you my father ordered me to play these when we were attacked by the powerful Murray clan. When I saw him about to be attacked from behind by Cedric Murray, I dropped the pipes and reached for my sword. But my father ordered me to continue playing. He said it was what gave him the strength to go on."

It was plain to Meredith that Jamie felt a thrill of pride at being compared with Brice.

"But how could you play while all around you men were dying?"

"I did what my father commanded," Brice said simply. "I knew that it meant more to him to hear the sound of the pipes than to hear the sound of his son's clumsy attempts at a man's work." His voice lowered with feeling. "He knew there would be time enough for that."

"But what if I am attacked?"

"Here." Brice handed the youth a small, deadly dirk. "When fighting a man within these walls, this is your best weapon."

"What about this?" Meredith asked.

Two heads turned toward her. Both faces held puzzled frowns. She was standing in the doorway holding one of Brice's swords in a menacing fashion.

Brice walked toward her until he was the blade's length from her. "It is never wise to take up a weapon unless you know how to use it."

"You think I do not know how to defend myself?"

"Stick to women's work," he said softly.

"Women's work." There was a note of contempt in her voice.

"Aye. Mistress Snow tells all who will listen about your skill with a needle."

"I made her a gown because she had loaned me hers. But that does not make me less skilled in the ways of battle. I can handle a sword as well as you, Brice Campbell."

"Can you now?" Without warning he reached out and yanked the weapon from her hand. He sent it crashing to the floor before taking a step closer and facing her. "So much for your skill with a sword." With a smile he half turned toward Jamie and winked. "How will you defend yourself now, my lady?"

"With this." With a look of triumph she reached into the waistband of her skirt and removed a small, sharp dagger.

"So. You dare to conceal weapons. When you are within these walls, under my protection, you have no need of such things."

She gave him a chilling smile. "It would seem that you forgot to tell Holden Mackay."

Brice flushed. Caught off guard, he advanced toward her.

She lifted the knife in a threatening gesture. "I think you should be warned. I learned such skills at my father's knee. Though I have no wish to harm you, I will not back away from a fight."

At the incongruous sight of the small, delicate figure facing down a giant of a man like Brice, Jamie burst into gales of laughter.

"What will you do now, Brice? Do you risk hurting Meredith just to prove you are the stronger, or do you let a Lowland lass bully you with a dirk?"

Brice studied his opponent. She was perfectly composed. There was no hint of fear in her eyes. The hand holding the dagger was steady. About her lips there was the merest hint of a smile.

"So, my lady, do you think, like Jamie, that you have me at a disadvantage?"

Her smile blossomed. "Aye, my lord. I do. I think it is time to persuade you to release me to my people before they reach the Highlands and engage you in battle."

He moved so quickly she had time only to blink. With one hand he caught her wrist and swung her around. Both his arms came around her, crossing her arms beneath her bosom and pinning her to the length of him. The knife slipped from her hand and clattered to the floor.

His breath was hot against her temple as he pressed his lips to a tangle of hair and muttered, "Now, my lady, I believe the advantage is mine. We will speak no more of releasing you to Gareth MacKenzie."

Her breath came out in a hiss of air, and although she struggled, she was held fast.

"It is not Gareth who will claim me. It is my own people."

His voice was low with anger. "Who are now in league with the MacKenzies."

"If I am free, my people will follow me."

"A woman of strength and leadership, of course. As you have often pointed out to me."

Across the room Jamie laughed and clapped his hands. "Now what say you, Meredith? Do you admit defeat?"

She stopped fighting. The tremors that rocked her had nothing to do with combat. They had everything to do with the man who held her imprisoned in his arms.

"Aye, Jamie." She lowered her gaze, afraid the lad would see the fire that burned inside her at the nearness of her captor. "Defeat perhaps. But only for the moment."

Against her temple Brice murmured, "I will settle for even a fleeting moment of victory over you, my lady." He allowed his lips to linger while he inhaled the soft scent of her. His thumbs brushed the underside of her breasts and he was startled by the rush of desire caused by even that slight contact.

He was aware of the tension in her and felt a thrill. Could it be that he was the cause of such feelings? Or was the lady merely tense at the thought of the battle yet to come?

With a smile he dropped his hands and stepped away. When she turned to him he gave a slight bow. "I look forward to our next round of combat, my lady."

Meredith watched as he crossed the room and continued with Jamie as if they'd never been interrupted. How could he be so calm when her heart was near bursting?

She waited a moment longer until her heartbeat returned to normal. Then she stalked from the room, unaware that

Brice watched her every movement. But Jamie noted that Brice seemed distracted as he took up the weapons for another lesson in the art of defense. And long after she was gone, Brice stared at the closed door, deep in thought.

"Riders approach."

It was what Meredith had been fearing for days. The word was passed from men perched atop high, rocky crags to others who concealed themselves in trees or behind boulders. Runners carried the warning to the guards posted at the door of Kinloch House.

Bands of Highlanders had roamed the forests for days, encountering only scattered clusters of armed Lowlanders. The bulk of Gareth MacKenzie's army stayed close together, knowing there was safety in numbers. Their number made it impossible for the Highland warriors to attack. Instead, in groups of three and four, the men loyal to Brice Campbell watched and waited, and made their way back to Kinloch House, where their families awaited their safe return.

Inside the castle all was in readiness. Entire families had been ensconced in every room and made as comfortable as possible. No one knew how long they would be forced to endure such close quarters. Even the sheep and livestock were brought inside the compound, to protect them from being slaughtered by the enemy. It was Brice's intention that the enemy, denied all food save what they had brought with them, would soon be forced to withdraw and return to the Lowlands.

The women shared the duties of cooking and caring for the children, while the men honed their weapons to a fine edge and went out in clusters of twos and threes, attacking small bands of Lowlanders and then returning to the protection of the castle before dark.

Chores were assigned to everyone except the youngest.
Provisions had been stored in the dank dungeons below the
castle, in case the women and children were forced to spend
a prolonged time within its safe confines.

Meredith had hoped that Brice would relent and allow her
a chamber of her own. She yearned for a few moments of
privacy, away from this man who seemed to dominate her
every moment, both waking and sleeping. But now that the
others had taken over the rooms of the castle, there was no
hope for such a luxury. She was forced to share Brice's sitting chamber and bedchamber. At her insistence, she was
allowed to sleep in a settle pulled before the fireplace rather
than share Brice's bed. But it did nothing to ease the tension between them. She was still achingly aware of the man
whose soft breathing punctuated the darkness between
them.

Their close quarters did allow her to see how carefully
Brice prepared for the anticipated attack. His weapons
gleamed atop the mantel. The broadsword, a two-handed
weapon with terrible killing power, had been honed until it
was capable of severing a man's head with a single blow. A
second weapon with a shorter blade and a basket-shaped hilt
of gold encrusted with jewels, also displayed a razor-sharp
edge. A longbow and quiver of arrows stood at the ready.
And though Brice possessed more than half a dozen dirks,
each one had been sharpened to perfection.

At the call to arms, Brice glanced across the room to
where Meredith stood. "You will go below now with the
women. I have assigned two of my warriors to guard the
door. They will protect all of you with their lives."

She felt the rush of anticipation that had always flowed
when her father's castle had come under siege. As the eldest daughter she had been assigned the task of seeing to the
safety of her sisters. She had been trained to fight. And al-

though there was a knot of fear in the pit of her stomach, she would never back away from the fight.

"For the last time I beg of you, Brice. Set me free. Send me forth to meet my people. They will turn away from this battle, if only they see that I am free."

"We will speak no more of this thing. My decision is made."

She decided to try a new course of persuasion. "If you will not set me free, then let me at least stay here." Her glance strayed to the weapons atop the mantel, then back to where Brice stood facing her. "I could assist those who are wounded."

A hint of a smile touched his lips. "Indeed? Help them die faster, perhaps?"

"I cannot stay in the dungeons, Brice. As leader of the MacAlpins I claim the right to be present at the battle."

"Do you think I could concentrate on the battle at hand, knowing you are vulnerable to attack?"

"The men who ride with Gareth would never harm me. They are my own people."

"Are you so certain of that?" Brice studied the way the sunlight streamed through the windows, turning the ends of her hair to flame. He longed to touch it, to feel the silken strands sift through his fingers. Abruptly he pushed away such thoughts. "What if the men of the MacKenzie clan do not recognize you, and in their lust for blood slay the very one they have come to free?"

Such a thing had never entered Meredith's mind. Though she felt a moment of uncertainty, she persisted. "I am the reason for this attack. If you show my people that I am unharmed, and allow me to return to the Lowlands with them, your life can go on as before."

"Aye." His tone hardened. "And as before, more innocents will be murdered, and their death blamed on the

Highland Barbarian. Who is to say that even you will be safe on the journey back to your people?''

She stiffened. ''Are you suggesting that there are those who wish my death?''

He saw the pain in her eyes and regretted his sharp words. If only they had time. Time to discuss the suspicions he had begun to harbor about those around her. Time to share his thoughts about Gareth MacKenzie and his dead brother. But there was not even time to prepare her for what was to come.

He crossed the room and caught her roughly by the shoulder. ''We will speak no more of this.''

''But . . .''

His gaze focused on her lips. With no warning he lowered his mouth to hers and kissed her with a savageness that left her stunned and reeling.

He took the kiss deeper, filling himself with the taste of her. God in heaven. What was wrong with him? Never before had he allowed anyone or anything to distract him from the task at hand. Never before had he been forced to wage such a difficult battle with himself. This female, who should mean nothing to him, was intruding too often upon his thoughts. He was worried about her safety. And that worry could mean the difference between living and dying. In a battle to the death, even the simplest distraction could cost him his life.

He lifted his head and stared down into eyes that glittered with a strange light. The woman was bewitching him.

He experienced a wave of self-loathing. In a voice low with fury he whispered, ''Go now and join the women and children below the castle.''

He shouted for one of his men. Angus Gordon opened the door and stood awaiting his orders.

''Take the lady below. And see that she does not leave.''

Meredith backed away from Brice's touch and gave him a look of pure venom. "Aye. I shall go below while you and the others settle this thing."

She moved past him and hurried to the door. With her hand on the door pull she called, "But though you fancy yourself a mighty warrior, be warned. Do not turn your back on your attackers, my lord. Or you may find a MacAlpin dirk buried between your shoulders."

He watched as she flounced away beside Angus. As he bent to his weapons, the taste of her was still on his lips.

Chapter Ten

Dust plumed in great clouds as the horsemen crowded through the entranceway and milled about in confusion. Above the din of horses' hooves in the courtyard there was a great roar of men's voices shouting encouragement to one another as they prepared the attack on Kinloch House. The door to the castle was rammed. And although the massive door had been braced by thick timbers, it eventually sagged and gave way beneath the assault. Swarms of men poured through the doorway of the castle, their voices a chorus of cursing and screeching.

At the sudden mournful wail of bagpipes they seemed to fall back for a moment before regaining their momentum.

Brice saw the looks in the eyes of his men. They had expected no more than a dozen or more Lowlanders. But there were ten times that number. And many of them, though dressed like Lowlanders, had the look of the Highlands about them.

A warning bell rang in his mind but there was no time to fathom it. Something did not ring true about the men attacking them. There was something very wrong here.

In that one brief moment of confusion the Highlanders returned the attack with a vengeance. The air was filled with the sound of sword clanging against shield, of fierce battle cries, of the moaning and shrieking of the first to fall in battle.

In the light of candles set in sconces along the walls, the bearded faces appeared wild and frightening. And because Brice Campbell, the most feared of all men in the Highlands, had a price of one hundred pounds sterling upon his head, he found himself at the point of dozens of swords.

He had been raised with the sword. From his earliest days he had known that there would be men eager to challenge him. But though he willingly accepted the challenge, he took no joy in killing. It was something that had been thrust upon him as leader and warrior. It was his death or theirs. And in his hands rested the fate of his people.

There was no time for fear. He parried each thrust with equal skill, matching move for move. But though he was a skilled warrior, the endless fighting was wearing him down.

As the hour stretched into two, and then into a third, he glanced around at his comrades and felt a heaviness around his heart. This day many good men had fallen. And many more would never again rise up.

Below the castle, in the flickering light of the dungeons, the women rocked their babies and sought to comfort the crying, frightened children. Their eyes mirrored every emotion, from absolute terror to quiet resignation. The battles were as much a part of their lives as eating and sleeping. They had been the daughters of warriors. Now they were the patient wives of warriors. And every woman there knew, like a knife thrust to the heart, that they were also the mothers of future warriors.

Meredith stood with her ear pressed to the heavy door. When she heard the sound of the guards outside the door being engaged in battle, she clenched her hands at her sides and strained to make out the voices muttering savage oaths and barely coherent phrases. A scream pierced the air and

she heard the thud as a body dropped to the floor just outside the door. The fighting went on for what seemed an
eternity. She heard a second body fall. Then she detected the
sound of footsteps receding.

For long minutes she continued listening with her ear
pressed firmly to the massive door. There was only silence
outside the room. But from the upper floors she could hear
the distant sounds of battle.

How much longer should she remain here with the
women? This room offered shelter, a safe haven from the
battle. But those were her men fighting, dying. And they
were here to rescue her. Regardless of Brice's words, Meredith knew in her heart that she had no choice. She must
show herself to her men and order them to cease this battle
at once and return with her to the Lowlands.

She lifted sweating palms to the latch that secured the
heavy door from inside. Behind her the women lifted
pleading eyes that spoke of their disapproval.

"Please, my lady," Cara whispered. "There is only death
beyond this room."

"I must go. I have the power, the authority, to stop this
slaughter."

"Nay, my lady," Mistress Snow said, coming to place a
restraining hand upon her arm. "My lord Campbell ordered
us to stay here where we are safe. He is the only one who has
the authority to end this battle. I beg you, please do not
disobey him."

Meredith lifted her head a fraction. No one, not even
these well-intentioned servants, would dissuade her.

With her shoulder to the door she pushed it open an inch
and peered about. Two men lay in pools of slowly congeal-
ing blood. She recognized the two as men who rode with
Brice and her heart went out to their widows still waiting
bravely just beyond the door. At least for a little while

longer she would spare them the gruesome sight of their loved ones.

Motioning for Mistress Snow to latch the door behind her, Meredith slipped out and hurried to kneel beside each of the fallen warriors in turn. Both were dead. Judging by the bloody swords beside them, both had fought furiously before giving up their lives.

She lifted her head and listened to the sounds of battle being waged above her. Lifting her skirts she ran to the stairs and began to climb.

The great hall was littered with the bodies of the dead and dying. Blood spattered the walls and tables. The hulking forms of men writhed and twisted as they moaned or choked back sobs. Pain and death were everywhere.

Meredith walked among the fallen men, kneeling to whisper a word of comfort, to offer a tankard of water. Not one of them, she realized was a MacAlpin. All except Brice's men were strangers to her. Brice. She studied each face, and though she was not aware of it, her heart sought only one. When a search of the entire room did not reveal him, she let out a long sigh of breath. Brice had survived the first wave of attack.

Meredith heard the sound of the pipes from the direction of the courtyard. When she reached the door she looked out at a scene of such carnage it took her breath away.

The storehouse had been burned. Black acrid smoke filled the air. Animals, free of their pens, milled about while swordsmen battled all around them. Chickens, ducks, geese, were trampled in the melee. Goats bleated and ran about, seeking to escape.

Young Jamie, standing alone in a corner of the courtyard, struggled to play the bagpipes while all around him were fallen comrades. Meredith saw tears streaming down the lad's dirt-streaked face, but he continued to play, though she was certain he no longer knew nor cared what the song was. He played because Brice had ordered it. And he would go to hell and back for his beloved Brice.

Seeing a flash of saffron sleeve, Meredith cried out Brice's name and watched in horror as a tall man fell to the ground. His hands pried in vain at the blade of a sword buried in his chest. But when the man's head lolled to one side, she realized he was not Brice.

Her gaze scanned the swordsmen who milled about the courtyard. There were twenty men for every one of Brice's. Where had they all come from?

Hearing a cry from above her, Meredith looked up. A man was pushed from a balcony and hurtled past her, landing with a terrible shudder on the hard-packed earth of the courtyard. A bushy red beard covered his chin. He proudly wore the garb of a Highlander. His vacant eyes stared heavenward.

Meredith looked up toward the balcony. Peering down from his position of victory toward the fallen man was Gareth MacKenzie. On his face was a smile of supreme confidence.

Meredith was certain that Gareth had not yet spotted her. He was still staring intently at the man he had defeated.

Scanning the faces of the crowd, Meredith felt her heart lurch. Brice. Did he lie even now in a pool of his own blood?

She ducked back inside the castle and raced up the stairs toward Brice's chambers.

Outside the door she came to an abrupt halt. Brice, his sleeve hanging in shreds, his shoulder bleeding profusely, faced three opponents. His left arm dangled uselessly at his side. In his right hand was the gleaming broadsword. By the light of the fire the jewel-encrusted gold handle winked with brilliant color.

While she watched, all three men attacked.

Meredith longed for a sword. Though the men fighting Brice were MacKenzie clansmen, and therefore considered her protectors, she chafed at the uneven odds. With a weapon she could at least make the battle a bit more even.

As she watched the dueling swords she heard the sound of running feet. Dropping to her knees, she hid herself in a little alcove. It was a terrible thing to be forced to listen helplessly to the sounds of battle and be unable to join in. Nor could she any longer witness the outcome.

"So." The voice of Gareth MacKenzie rang through the hall. "At last we have backed the Highland Barbarian into a corner. Let us now show him how the Borderers fight scum like him."

Meredith got to her feet. She would show herself to these men to prove that she was truly alive and unharmed. And then she would demand that Gareth's men join her and follow her back to their home in the Lowlands. Though Gareth would insist upon taking Brice prisoner, she would at least see that he was kept alive.

As she began to step from her place of concealment, she heard Gareth's voice, low with fury.

"You men. Join these three and pin the Highlander against the wall. I want it to be my thrust that ends his life."

Meredith sprang from her place of concealment and stood in the doorway.

Five men held their sword points against Brice's chest while Gareth MacKenzie faced him. Brice's sword lay gleaming at his feet.

Seeing the flicker of movement in the doorway, Brice's eyes narrowed. God in heaven. Not now. Meredith must not be seen. If these animals caught sight of her, all would be lost. For there was no doubt in Brice's mind that Gareth MacKenzie was an evil man, bent upon destroying everyone who stood in the way of his lust for land and power.

"And when you have killed me, where will you lay the blame for your next murder? When innocent lads and old men are cut down in the night, whose name will you curse?"

"When I have taken over your land, and that of the MacAlpins, there will be no further need of deception," Gareth stated. "It will all be mine."

"And what of the woman?" Brice's lips curled in a hint of a smile. "What if Meredith MacAlpin refuses to be wed?"

"She will be given no chance to refuse. And I will see to it that this time she is not snatched from my clutches at the altar."

Meredith took a step forward, then froze at Gareth's next words to his men.

"Without her clan here to give witness, I will personally see to the woman. I want Meredith MacAlpin wed and then dead. We will take her body back to the MacAlpins for viewing."

"Why are the MacAlpins not here with you? It is, after all, their leader you fight for." Brice's voice was low with fury.

"They feared that their mistress would be harmed in battle. They favored bartering with you for her safe return."

"Then who are all these men who fight alongside you?"

Gareth gave an evil leer. "I have an unending supply of warriors. It seems the Highland Barbarian has incurred the wrath of many Scotsmen." With a low, mirthless laugh he added, "Now, if viewing the body of Meredith MacAlpin is not enough to secure the loyalty of the MacAlpin clan, the rest of my plan will be more than enough." He studied the bloodied foe who faced five of the MacKenzie's most skilled swordsmen. "I intend to place your sword through the heart of Meredith MacAlpin for all to see."

The men surrounding Brice burst into words of encouragement and taunting laughter.

"Every man on the Border will swear allegiance to me in our fight to rid the land of all Campbells."

"So you admit that it was you who killed the helpless and laid the blame on me."

"Aye."

"Then hand me my sword and fight one who is not helpless. I seek to clear my good name."

"Who would believe the word of a barbarian?" Gareth laughed and lifted his sword until the blade was pressing against Brice's flesh. "Especially a dead barbarian." To his men Gareth shouted, "I will strike the first blow."

Meredith saw the flash of blade as Gareth plunged his sword. Then, as the others attacked she leaped back into her place of concealment just as Gareth strode from the room. She pressed her hand to her lips to keep from crying out. And while Gareth seemed to take forever to descend the stairs, she was forced to listen to the sound of his men's crude laughter as they continued to thrust their blades into the already fallen Highlander.

When at last Gareth was out of sight, the battle was over. Five bloodied swordsmen strode from Brice's chambers and made their way to join their leader in the dungeons. One of them carried Brice's bloody sword, which he laughingly declared to his comrades would be used by Gareth to plunge into Meredith's heart.

On trembling legs Meredith crept from the alcove and made her way to Brice's sitting room. The fur throws that lined the walls and floor were stained crimson. Against a far corner of the room lay a crumpled form.

With tears streaming down her cheeks Meredith stood over Brice's body. Blood oozed from so many different wounds, she could not count them. And when she knelt and placed a hand to his throat, he did not move. In her over-whelming grief she could not detect a pulsebeat.

At the sound of footsteps on the stairs, Meredith looked up. From the rumble of voices, there were several men. Brice's men? Or Gareth's?

Her heart nearly stopped when she heard the deep, fa-miliar voice. Gareth. But why was he returning? What more could he do to the man who lay dead upon the floor?

Racing to Brice's bedchamber, she grabbed a dirk from the mantel. She watched as a shadow fell across the en-trance to Brice's sitting chamber. The sound of footsteps ended.

With the blood pounding in her temples, Meredith crawled beneath the bed. She heard the sound of booted feet scuffling about the other room.

"Campbell is dead."

"As I knew he would be. Did I not pierce him with my sword?" The sound of Gareth MacKenzie's voice sent tremors racing along her spine.

"What of the woman?"

"Search every room."

"We have already done so."

"There was no sign of her?"

"Nay, my lord. All of the women and children were be-low."

There was silence. Gareth swore. "The witch must have escaped into the forest during the battle. We must find her before she makes her way back to her people."

"Surely you do not think that one lone female can sur-vive the Highland forests?"

"We will see to it that she does not. Come. Let us fetch our dead and wounded and be done with this place."

"What will we tell the MacAlpin clan? They trusted you to return their leader to them."

Gareth paused, considering this new obstacle. "We will tell them that she has been spirited away by one of Campbell's men. I will order them to remain in the safety of their homes until my men and I can rescue her."

"But then you will not be able to blame her death on Brice Campbell."

"Even if Campbell's sword does not pierce her heart, I can still convince her people that it was his fault that their leader died. Was she not attempting to elude his grasp when she fled into the forest?"

One of the men nodded in agreement. "Will we burn the castle, my lord?"

Meredith's heart stopped. She forgot to breathe.

"Aye." Gareth's chilling words rang through the hall. "We have killed their leader. Now we will destroy his stronghold and scatter his clan. But work quickly. Let us waste no time in finding the woman."

Meredith heard the shuffle of feet and waited until she was certain they had gone. She lay under the bed and fought back the tears that threatened to choke her. She must do something. But what?

She pulled herself from her place of concealment and crawled to the other room where Brice lay. The tears that she had been fighting now spilled over, running in little rivers down her cheeks.

Brice. Her strong, angry, giant of a man was dead. She brought her hands to either side of his face and studied his proud, handsome features.

"How wrong I have been about you. You are not some cruel savage. You are a gentle giant, surprisingly fair with me, generous with your friends."

The tears began anew, and she struggled to hold them back. "You were even right about Gareth. And I have been so wrong. Gareth is evil incarnate."

Tears streamed down her cheeks and she made no move to check them. "What a fool I have been. If I had not been prevented by fateful circumstances from marrying Desmond MacKenzie," she said, pressing her forehead to Brice's, "I would already be dead, and my land and people would be in the clutches of the cruel Gareth.

"Oh, Brice. I see now that it was because of you that I have been given a chance to discover the awful truth about the MacKenzies."

The tears came harder now, and she struggled to subdue her emotions.

She felt a tingling at her fingertips and studied Brice's face, so handsome in repose. She thought she saw a flicker of pain cross his face. Impossible. Brice was dead. And then she felt the tingling again. A pulsebeat? She touched a finger to his lips and thought she felt a slight breath. With a last flicker of hope she pressed her fingers to his throat a second time. Aye. A pulsebeat. Feeble. Thready. But a pulsebeat all the same.

Alive. Brice was alive.

With a little cry she began to cut away the blood-soaked tunic. Tears sprang to her eyes and she quickly blinked them away. There was no time for tears now. There was work to be done. She would stem the flow of blood. She would warm him, with her own body if necessary. And she would keep him alive until he was strong enough to fight his wounds.

And then, together, they would fight Gareth MacKenzie, the brute who sought to subdue her people and steal her land.

Chapter Eleven

So great was Meredith's determination to save Brice's life, she forced herself to ignore the smell of smoke that crept up the staircase and invaded his chambers.

She added a log to the fire and placed a large kettle of water to heat. While it came to a boil she cut away Brice's garments and examined his wounds.

From the courtyard below she heard the sound of men being summoned, of horses being readied for travel. The sound of Gareth's voice calling out to his men set her teeth on edge. She forced herself to shut out all sound. For now there was only this room and this man. She would not leave his side, she vowed, until she was certain he would survive.

And what of the fire that threatened? One glance at the man on the floor told her that she could never drag him to safety. She would remain here and defy even the raging flames to save his life.

She stared down at his bloodied, battered body and felt a tremor of fear. If a giant of a man like Brice could be cut down, could anyone survive?

She thought briefly about the men below who had died in this bloody battle. And about the many more who still lay wounded. What of the women and children? Had Gareth and his men terrorized them, brutalized them? Or had they simply searched among them for the one they sought and then left them? She whispered a prayer for their safety, then bent to the task at hand.

There was no time to think about whether or not Brice would be caused further pain by her ministrations. For now, she would be forced to inflict some pain in order to properly care for him.

Tearing a strip of cloth, she dipped it into the rapidly heating water. With gentle strokes she sponged the blood that oozed from Brice's shoulder. Though the wound was deep, it did not appear to be life threatening, and she breathed a sigh of relief. When the shoulder was cleansed, she tied a clean cloth around it to stem the flow of blood, then moved to the next wound.

Blood flowed freely from a gaping hole in Brice's side. The tip of a sword had pierced cleanly through, then had been brutally withdrawn, tearing the flesh in jagged shreds.

Working quickly, Meredith washed the area, then pressed several thicknesses of clean cloth against the open wound and bound it tightly. It would be important to keep this wound clean. But for now, the most important thing was to stop the excessive bleeding.

She moved on to other, less serious wounds, where sword and dirk had pierced the flesh of Brice's hand, arm and both legs. He was a mass of bloody flesh. Yet none of these wounds appeared mortal. Why was he so near death? Why the pallor, the feeble heartbeat? Something had sapped his strength. One of his wounds was carrying him to death's door.

She heard a great cry from below and recognized the voices of Brice's men and servants as they battled the fire that threatened to destroy Kinloch House. Black acrid smoke filled the air as buckets of water caused the flames to sputter and smolder.

As Meredith sponged, her hand paused in midair. She noted the dark stain that slowly spread across the fur throw beneath Brice's body. For a moment she could only stare at it in dread. Then, struggling to roll him to one side, she discovered the small deadly knife still buried between his shoulders.

"God in heaven."

She thought of her final words to him before the battle had begun and felt a shiver pass through her. "Do not turn your back on your attackers, my lord. Or you may find a MacAlpin dirk between your shoulders."

Her gaze was riveted on the bloodstained hilt. It was little satisfaction to note that it was not a MacAlpin dirk that had gravely wounded him. It bore the mark of the MacKenzie clan.

The blade could not have pierced the heart or he would already have expired. But this wound was mortal.

There was no tenderness in her touch as she reached for the dirk. It must be removed, and the wound repaired quickly if she would save his life.

With both hands she pulled the knife cleanly from his back.

She looked up as the door to the sitting chamber was shoved roughly open. Smoke billowed inward and swirled like fog above a river. Wreathed in smoke, Angus Gordon, blood streaming from a wound to the head, stood framed in the doorway, leaning heavily upon the arm of Jamie MacDonald. Both of them were coated with soot from the raging fire they had been battling. Their hands were bloodied and raw from handling heavy buckets of water and beating out rapidly fanning flames. Their clothes were scorched. The pungent odor of burning wood clung to them.

Both of them stared at her, then at the bloody dirk in her hand.

Though he was obviously weak from loss of blood, Angus lifted his sword and faced her, his accusing eyes dark with fury, his lips a thin line of hatred.

"So. You would take your revenge even upon a dead man."

Before she could respond, he shouted, "Step away from Brice's body, my lady, or I will be forced to kill you where you stand."

"You do not . . ."

With tears streaming down his face, Jamie rushed at her, knocking her to the floor. Once on top of her his grimy fingers locked about her throat. His young face was a twisted mask of fury.

"Was it not enough that the MacKenzies killed him?" he sobbed. "Did you have to stick your dirk in his back to make certain that he is dead?"

"Jamie, listen to me."

With a cry of rage he closed his hands about her throat and squeezed. "I heard Brice say he had never meant to kidnap you. He vowed to see that no harm came to you. And this is how you repay him. How could you? How could you?"

Though the lad was young, he was bigger than Meredith. And surprisingly strong.

"Step away from her, Jamie." Angus staggered across the room and bent a hand to the lad's shoulder. "You've no stomach for killing. Least of all a woman. I'll see to it."

"You do not—understand." As Jamie was pulled from her, Meredith gingerly touched a hand to her bruised throat and took in long, choking breaths. "Brice is not dead. I was cleansing his wounds when I discovered the dirk."

"Oh, aye. And you thought you could bury it in his back rather than toss it away." With his sword lifted, Angus hovered over her, prepared to aim for her heart.

Jamie glanced at the still form of Brice, hesitated, then turned back to her. His look of fury had turned to one of question.

"Could it be that she speaks the truth?"

"She would say anything to save her life." Angus sneered.

"Perhaps. But see for yourself if you do not believe me."

As Angus brought his sword higher to strike, Jamie fell to his knees beside Brice. He ran a finger over the clean dressings at Brice's shoulder and side. Surely no one but Meredith could have applied them. And then he saw the river of blood that gushed from the wound in Brice's back.

"She speaks the truth," he whispered.

"What?" Lowering his sword Angus fell to his knees beside the still form of his friend. In a glance he took in the clean dressings, the kettle of water. "This cannot be. I heard Gareth MacKenzie tell his men that Brice Campbell was dead."

"Aye. He thought so. As did I." Meredith sighed. "But there is a pulse. Feeble, but a sign that life still flows within him."

Angus brought his fingers to Brice's throat and held them there for several seconds. Then he turned back to Meredith, who still knelt where he had left her. In her hand was the bloody knife she had pulled from Brice's back.

"Forgive me, my lady," Angus sputtered. "I thought..."

"It matters not," Meredith interrupted. "We must stem the flow of blood at once, or it will be as Gareth MacKenzie has said. Brice Campbell will be dead."

"Tell me what to do."

Angus offered a hand to her and helped her to her feet.

She shot him a look of gratitude. "Fetch some servants. I learned from my mother how to prepare potions for healing. But we must work quickly."

"Aye."

"You're not strong enough, Angus," Jamie said. "I'll go."

The lad seemed relieved to be able to be of some use. While Angus dropped to his knees beside Meredith and stared helplessly at his old friend, Jamie rushed from the room.

Within minutes he was back, followed by several smoke-darkened figures.

Though she had not allowed herself to dwell upon the fate of the others, Meredith was so relieved to see Cara and Mistress Snow alive, she felt the sting of tears in her eyes. She blinked them away.

"Were the women and children harmed?"

"Nay, my lady," Cara said softly. Soot smudged her face and hands. "Gareth MacKenzie flew into a rage when you were not found among us. He seemed intent upon finding you. He and his men were more than happy to be done with us so that they could scour the forests for a sign of you. But what of my lord Campbell?" The young serving girl glanced across the room and fell silent at the sight of Brice's still form.

"Jamie has explained what has happened here. Tell me what you desire," Mistress Snow said gravely. "And it will be yours."

Meredith noted the charred hem of the woman's gown and the raw, blistered flesh where she had battled the flames.

"Has the fire been contained?"

"Aye, my lady."

Meredith gave a sigh of relief, then spoke quickly, listing tubers, spices and fermented malt. After that she ordered Cara to fetch more clean linens.

"Should we not move him to his bed?" Angus asked.

"I fear it would only cause his wounds to bleed more freely. For now he will have to sleep here, before the fire. Bring me a pallet and several furs," she ordered Jamie.

When Mistress Snow had dispatched servants to find everything Meredith had requested, she returned. Though she struggled to keep her gaze averted from the man who knelt beside Meredith, she could not resist a quick glance at Angus's drawn features.

They had all been through hell this day. Yet they had survived. That alone was a bond that would not soon be broken.

"Is there anything else I can do, my lady?"

Meredith turned to glance at the housekeeper, then at Angus, kneeling beside her. His eyes, dull with pain, were set in an ashen face.

"Aye. You can take this man to his bed and see to his wounds."

Though the servant's face betrayed her pleasure, Angus seemed surprised. "My wounds are nothing, my lady. I cannot leave the side of my friend."

"You have been so concerned about Brice, you do not even know that you have been wounded." Meredith touched a hand to his shoulder in a gesture of kinship. "Brice will not mind that you have left him. He is in another world now. And it will be a long time before he decides whether to join his ancestors or return to us."

"Will you send for me the minute he awakens?"

If he ever awakens, Meredith thought sadly. Please, God, grant him the strength to fight this weakness. Then, brushing aside such emotional thoughts she nodded. "The very moment he is alert, you will be told."

With the help of Mistress Snow, Angus got slowly to his feet. He hesitated a moment, staring down at the woman who knelt beside Brice's still form, the woman who had been captive and was now healer.

"Forgive me, my lady, for doubting you."

"You had every right to think what you did, Angus." She gave him an encouraging smile. "I trust Brice Campbell is worthy of the love and devotion you have exhibited."

"Aye, my lady. He has more than earned my loyalty. And the loyalty of all who proclaim Brice Campbell their leader."

Meredith studied the man who would surely sacrifice his life for the one on the pallet.

"Rest now, Angus," Meredith said, as he leaned heavily on Mistress Snow's shoulder.

"If there is anything I can do, you must tell me."

She touched a hand to Brice's throat and felt the pulse that, though thin and halting, continued to beat.

"You can pray."

Meredith spread the poultice over the festering wound before covering it with fresh dressings. Then she pulled up the bed linens and sat back on her heels, studying the quiet figure on the pallet.

He was so still. So very still. As though his life was slipping away, breath by breath.

He had not moved since she had first found him. Nor had he moaned or cried out, despite the depth of pain he must be suffering.

The servants drifted into the room whenever they found time, as did all Brice's men who were able to walk. They would stay for a few minutes, studying his pale face, watching the woman who worked tirelessly beside him. On each face Meredith saw the love, the concern, for this man. It was evident in the way they studied him, with a kind of reverence, and the way they spoke, in hushed tones usually reserved for the clergy.

The light through the windows had long since faded into darkness. The only illumination in the room was the fire in the fireplace and a single candle beside a basin on a small table.

The sounds of activity in the castle had ceased. The dead had been removed to the burned-out shell of the storehouse until proper graves could be dug and the grieving families could see to their burial. The wounded had been ministered to and carried to beds and pallets.

Meredith continued mopping the sweat that beaded Brice's forehead. Her shoulders drooped in exhaustion. Her eyes blurred and she wiped a hand across them, blinking away the desire to shut them tightly.

Meredith looked up at the sound of the door being opened. Jamie crossed the room and knelt beside her. His gaze fastened hungrily upon the still form of Brice.

"You should be asleep," Meredith whispered.

"I cannot sleep."

She saw the fear lurking in his eyes. With great tenderness she brought her arm about his shoulder and drew him close. "When Brice awakens he will have you scurrying about fetching so many things you will have no time to rest. Then you will yearn for the luxury of sleep."

"Do you believe that, my lady?"

"I must," she whispered. "And so must you."

She felt the lad tremble. And then, in a burst of anguish, he cried, "I am so afraid, my lady. If I dare to fall asleep, I'm afraid Brice will slip away. And I will never have the chance to tell him how much I love him."

"Oh, Jamie." Meredith gathered him into her arms. Against his temple she whispered, "His fate is no longer in our hands. We have done all we can. But I promise you this. I will stay here beside him. And if he should need anything, anything at all, I will see that he has it."

The lad shook his head from side to side. "I am afraid to leave him."

"Then stay with him," she said softly. "Sleep here beside him."

"Here?" The boy seemed astounded by her offer. Never would he presume to sleep beside so great a man.

Meredith lifted the folded bed linens that Cara had left in case her mistress desired to rest. She would have no need of them since she would never be able to leave Brice's side this night.

Fixing a pallet beside Brice, she lifted a corner of the blanket and motioned for Jamie to climb inside.

"Brice will not mind?"

"I think he would be pleased," Meredith murmured, tucking the linens about him.

As she so often did with her younger sisters, she bent and brushed a kiss over the lad's cheek. "Sleep well, Jamie, along with Brice, in the hollow of God's hand."

The boy lay very still, absorbing the shock of her gentle kiss.

For as long as he lived he would never forget her kindness this night.

For long minutes he lay listening to the sound of Brice's shallow breathing. And though he struggled to stay awake and will life into the man who lay beside him, sleep at last overtook him.

Chapter Twelve

Brice awoke in the inferno he had always known would be his destiny. All around him drifted the acrid scent of fire and brimstone. And his own flesh felt seared beyond redemption.

So this was what it felt like to be doomed to an eternity of punishment. Pain throbbed until he writhed and twisted. And though he thought he moaned, no sound issued from his parched throat.

He knew why this punishment had been meted out to him. He had been so consigned to this penance for failing to save Meredith. In that brief moment when he had seen her in the doorway to his chambers, he had realized that if he did not succeed in fighting off MacKenzie's soldiers, all would be lost. Meredith, the innocent victim in all of this, would be forced into marriage with Gareth MacKenzie. Once married, he would claim her land and people. And once MacKenzie had what he wanted, Meredith would no longer serve a useful purpose. She would be conveniently disposed of.

That was what had distracted Brice and caused his downfall. It was the presence of Meredith there in the doorway that had made him lose his concentration. Never before had five or even ten opponents worried him. He was a warrior, born and bred for battle. His own mortality had never caused him a moment's worry. But that was before Meredith. Since meeting the fiery little beauty, everything had changed. The thought of what MacKenzie had in mind for her was more than he could bear. That moment's distraction had cost him the battle.

Now it had all come to pass. Brice felt an overwhelming sense of despair. He had lost. MacKenzie had won. Even now Meredith was no doubt standing at the altar of a small village kirk, surrounded by MacKenzie men, forced to speak vows that would seal her fate.

Brice was consigned to an eternity in hell.

The pain came again in waves, causing him to arch his body and roll to one side and then the other. There was no escaping it. The flames of hell licked across his skin and stabbed deep into his back. A fire raged inside him.

Something cool touched his face and he clutched at it, holding it to him when it would pull away. In his delirium he imagined that it was a small, delicate hand. Meredith's hand. But that was impossible. Meredith had been captured by Gareth MacKenzie. She was lost to him forever. Still he clung to the hand, needing to feel it, small and safe in his.

A voice sounded from so far away he could not make out the words. But from the soft, muted tones, from the low, husky whisper, he knew it was Meredith's voice. Calling him. Calling out to him from a lifetime away. He lifted a hand and tried to reach her, to answer her, to tell her that he was sorry he had failed her, that even now he would find a way to come for her. But his hand dropped weakly to the linens that covered him. He would rest awhile, to gather his strength so that he could plan his escape from this eternal damnation. One thought burned in his mind. He dare not rest until Meredith was safely away from MacKenzie and returned to Kinloch House. There she would be safe. There she would be loved.

Loved.

Aye. Though he would never have admitted it in life, he loved her. Loved her as he loved Jamie. Loved her more than he had thought it possible to love any woman. More than himself.

A dipper of cool water was forced between his lips. He swallowed and accepted another before turning his head away. A cool damp cloth was pressed to his forehead and he felt a moment's respite from the burning heat.

His lids flickered open and he found himself staring into green eyes the color of a Highland lake.

"Meredith."

His lips formed the word though no sound issued from his throat.

She smiled and he thought there would never again be anything as wonderful as her smile. As dazzling as the sun on a summer's afternoon. As warm and comforting as a fireplace on a cold winter's night.

A hundred questions danced through his brain, begging to be answered. How had she escaped MacKenzie's clutches? Was the attacking army still here at Kinloch House, holding her prisoner in this very room? His heart stopped. Or was she also dead? Had she been allowed this one visit before entering heaven?

Though his lips moved, the words were scrambled, making no sense. All he could manage was a weak croak.

"Rest now," she whispered, touching a hand to his cheek.

She was merely a vision, he realized. A lovely, ethereal vision.

His lids lowered. Though the fire raged on, he felt at peace. Anything could be endured, even hell, as long as he was granted an occasional glimpse of Meredith's beloved face.

"How does he fare?"

Angus tiptoed into the chamber and peered over Meredith's shoulder as she changed the dressing on Brice's back.

"He seems to slip in and out of this world," she whispered. "I fear he does not as yet comprehend where he is or who is with him."

"He is a strong man, my lady." Angus touched a hand to her shoulder and was reminded of how small, how frail, she was. Yet beneath her frailty he had witnessed enormous strength of will. Everyone in Kinloch House spoke in admiring tones of the way Lady Meredith MacAlpin tended their leader, refusing to leave his side even to take her meals. She slept curled up beside him, and ate whatever the servants brought her. And all of her waking moments were spent applying fresh poultices and changing his dressings, and seeing to his every need.

Jamie MacDonald had become her most loyal admirer. To the lad she was more than a great lady; she was a saint. He had told everyone who would listen how Meredith had encouraged him to sleep beside Brice for the first two nights, until he was convinced that his hero would not succumb if he left him. And although Jamie had now returned to his own chambers, Meredith encouraged him to drop by Brice's chambers as often as he wished in order to chart the progress Brice made.

"Brice will not easily give up his life, my lady. If he is fated to die he will not do so without putting up a fight."

She gave Angus a tentative smile. "How can you be so certain?"

"I know him, my lady. As well as I know myself. Brice is a warrior."

"Aye. And from the looks of both of you, there was great damage inflicted upon the other side. How do your wounds heal, Angus?" She glanced at the fresh dressings that bound his head, a sign of the loving care administered by Mistress Snow.

"The pain has nearly subsided. Now it only feels as if someone has buried an ax in my head."

Meredith laughed and Angus was pleased to know that he had managed to bring a smile to her lips.

What drove the lady? What caused her to stay by the side of a man who had taken her away from everything she loved? Was she suffering guilt because her own people had taken sides with the MacKenzies? Or was there some deeper emotion involved?

Angus glanced at the man who lay upon the pallet. So still. So pale. The two had been inseparable since childhood. Angus had never questioned the goodness of Brice Campbell. He had been privileged to witness Brice's kind deeds a thousand times. But this woman? What did she know of Brice and his way of life? How was it that she had, after only a glimpse into Brice's life, decided to trust him, to care for him?

"Do not fear for him. Brice will respond to your tender ministrations, my lady. That other life that tugs at him will give up its hold over him. He will come back to us."

Meredith gave Angus a grateful look.

At a knock on the door they both turned and watched as Mistress Snow entered, followed by a serving girl carrying a tray.

"This is the broth you ordered, my lady." Mistress Snow directed the servant where to set the tray, then turned to study Meredith, noting her pale features, accentuated by the dark circles that rimmed her eyes. "If you do not soon rest you will be joining my lord Campbell in a sickbed."

"I am fine." Meredith knelt and tasted the broth before nodding her approval to the servant. "Are the wounded below stairs beginning to heal?"

"Aye, my lady." The housekeeper chanced a glance at Angus before adding softly, "Though it has been a difficult task to keep some of them in bed long enough. Already some," she said, staring meaningfully at the man who faced her with a grin, "are determined to begin repairs on Kinloch House before their wounds have even begun to heal."

"I heard the sound of axes in the forest and trees being felled. I thought perhaps only necessary repairs were being made."

"Necessary." Mistress Snow gave a hollow laugh. "If Angus had his way, the castle would be as good as new before Brice had a chance to view the destruction left by the MacKenzies."

"It will cause him pain to know that his ancestral home has been burned by Lowlanders," Angus said softly. "I would spare my old friend any more suffering. And now I must go below and see to those repairs."

When he left the room, Meredith glanced at the housekeeper, who was staring at the closed door with a look of concern. "I know that you fear Angus is pushing himself and the others beyond their limits. But it is how a man deals with his feelings of hopelessness. With their leader cut down, and the enemy beyond their reach, they have a need to do something that is physically punishing."

"How did a sheltered woman like yourself learn such things?" The housekeeper watched as Meredith dipped the spoon into the bowl of broth.

"My father was a peace-loving man. But he was also a warrior." Meredith held the spoon to Brice's lips and watched as he swallowed the first trickle of broth. "Each time he was forced to recover from battle wounds inflicted by the English, he quickly undertook a difficult, draining task. My mother explained that it was a necessary part of healing.''

"Your mother was a wise woman." Mistress Snow gave a loud sigh. "As for me, I would prefer to take Angus to bed and find a gentler way of healing."

When she realized what she had revealed, the house-keeper blushed to the tips of her toes. "Oh, my lady. For-give me for my lapse."

Meredith's laughter rang through the room. "Oh, Mis-tress Snow. If you could but see your face."

"I—must see to the scullery," the woman said, hurrying to the door to escape her humiliation. "I will send Cara to see to your needs."

When the door closed behind her, Meredith shook her head and continued to laugh. Then, filling the spoon with more broth, she cradled Brice's head in her lap and forced a small amount of the liquid between his lips.

It was the sound of Meredith's laughter that seemed to penetrate the fog that shrouded Brice's mind. The sound trilled like the gentle warble of a bird. There was no mis-taking it. It was truly the beautiful Meredith, come once more to visit him in this place of misery.

He felt his head being lifted gently, as it was placed upon her lap. He inhaled the steaming broth as the spoon was placed to his lips. He tasted its delicate flavor as the liquid slid down his throat, warming, soothing. His parched throat was eased and he gratefully accepted a second spoonful.

From beneath slightly open lids he watched as she cra-dled his head in her lap and bent over him, intent upon her task. Her hair swirled forward, the silken strands brushing his hand. As she dipped the spoon once more in the bowl, she leaned forward slightly. He felt the imprint of her breasts and experienced a rush of heat that left him flushed and weak.

Now it was no longer the fragrance of the broth that filled his senses. It was the clean delicate fragrance of pine and wildflowers that seemed to surround her. He inhaled, filling himself with her scent, wishing he could fill himself with her.

She brought the spoon to his lips and he opened his mouth, accepting the broth. When he swallowed, the warm liquid snaked through his veins, giving him precious strength.

Again and again she fed him, grateful that he no longer fought her. It was the first time he had willingly accepted nourishment. When at last, unable to take more, he pushed her hand away, she glanced down and realized that he was watching her.

The spoon dropped from her hand, clattering to the floor. It lay there forgotten.

"Oh, Brice. At last you are awake."

"Am I?" On his face was a dreamy half smile. "I was afraid you were a ghostly specter, my lady."

"I am no ghost."

He glanced around, trying to focus his blurred vision. "Where are we?"

"In your sitting chamber at Kinloch House."

"Truly?"

"Aye. Truly." She laughed and laid his head back against a pillow of fur.

He wanted to tell her that he preferred to have his head in her lap. But it was proving difficult to keep his thoughts from scattering. And even more difficult to put them into words.

After a prolonged silence he murmured, "I dreamed I was in hell. And there were flames all about me."

"There was a fire. Gareth MacKenzie ordered his men to set torches to your home. But after the invading army left, your people were able to put out the flames."

"And you." Brice lifted a hand to her cheek. Even that small effort cost him. But it was worth it to satisfy himself that she was truly here and not just a vision. "I feared that MacKenzie had spirited you away and had forced you to wed him."

"Nay, my lord. I hid myself from view. Had I been braver I would have faced him with naught but my dirk. But like a coward I hid beneath your bed until he and his men were gone."

"You? A coward?" At her words he wanted to laugh, but his throat was too raw. He lay there letting strong new emotions wash over him.

"And I have been here with you since. Even though I feared I had lost you." She felt tears fill her eyes and spill over onto her cheeks, but she made no effort to wipe them. Instead she cupped his beloved face in her hands and studied him through the filmy haze. "Oh, Brice. I am so relieved that you have come back to the land of the living."

"Are you? Did you miss me?"

When she merely nodded he felt his heart soar to the heavens. "Maybe that is what saved me. Knowing that it was you I was coming back to." He caught her hands and held them in a death grip. "Do not leave me, little firebrand. Promise me that when I again awaken you will be here."

She would promise him anything at this moment. Anything. "I will not leave you, Brice."

His lids flickered, then closed. The hands holding hers slid down and dropped heavily against the linens. His breathing became soft and easy.

For endless minutes Meredith merely knelt beside him and watched as he slept.

Alive. Brice was alive. Truly alive. And for the first time since he had sustained his mortal wound in battle, she was convinced that he would not only survive but return to his former strength.

Suddenly she was exhausted beyond belief. The rush of energy she had experienced when he had first spoken was now slipping from her. All the long days and nights of nursing Brice through his ordeal were now beginning to take their toll. Her limbs were heavy. She felt light-headed. Her eyes yearned to close. She was drained. Drained of all strength. Drained of all thought.

With a sigh that welled up from deep within her Meredith curled up beside him and joined him in sleep.

Chapter Thirteen

Brice lay very still, fighting a wave of pain. His shoulder throbbed. His side ached. And something that resembled a flaming torch pierced his upper back.

He tried to roll over but there was a heaviness in his right arm and for one breathless moment he thought it might have been severed in the battle. His eyes snapped open and relief flooded through him as he gazed in wonder at the figure curled up alongside him.

Meredith lay facing him, her head pillowed on his arm, her hands resting lightly at his chest. Her hair spilled across the linens, a dark splash of color against stark white. Her breathing was slow, steady.

In these few moments before she awoke he took the time to study her. When had this fierce little woman taken over his life? How had she come to mean so much to him?

His men, on their frequent visits to his chambers, had relayed how she had ignored the threat of fire to stay with him, how she had stood up to Angus and Jamie when they had suspected her of aiding in his murder. Even the servants never seemed to tire of praising the way Meredith had protected him as fiercely as any she wolf during his recovery.

He had kidnapped her only as an act of defiance against the MacKenzies. It had been his intention to use her to flush out Gareth, and then to return her to her own people.

But now? Now he could not imagine being without her. Her presence filled these rooms, his home, his very life. And though he knew that her heart lay in the Lowlands, he yearned to change her mind.

If she returned his feelings, he reasoned, she would choose to stay here with him always.

If he truly cared for her, a little voice within him whispered, he would want only her happiness.

He did not love her. He could not. She was a lady, born and bred for the gentle life. And he was a Highlander, a barbarian.

But he did love her.

Love. Why was it never simple?

He had not meant to love her. And surely a woman like Meredith MacAlpin could never love the man who had stolen her freedom.

Meredith's lids flickered, then opened. For a moment she was strangely disoriented. The eyes staring back at her were dark, narrowed in thought.

Brice watched as the last clouds of sleep were blinked away and reality set in.

Brice. She had fallen asleep practically in his arms. And though she was fully clothed, he had little more than a strip of cloth for modesty. As she realized where she was, Meredith pushed herself away from him and sat up.

He studied the flush that colored her cheeks, and noted the guarded look that came into her eyes. Wonder of wonders. This same bold woman who had stripped him of his clothes and tended to his wounds with all the skill and care of the queen's physician, was now suddenly shy with him. Her reaction was oddly appealing.

Her hair fell in a tangle of curls and she dragged a hand through, pushing it away from her face.

"How do you feel this morning?" She tried not to stare at the dark mat of hair that covered his chest, or at the corded muscles of his arms and shoulders. For days he had been a mortal wound to be healed; today he was much more. Today he was a man.

"Like any man who just awoke with a beautiful woman in his arms."

"I did not mean to... I had not intended..."

"Meredith." He chuckled, low and deep in his throat, and reached out a hand to her chin, forcing her to meet his dark gaze. "It brings me comfort to know that, despite my grave wounds, my manhood is still intact."

Her face flamed. Scrambling to her feet she retorted, "I will see about some food. You have grown extremely weak in the days you have been recovering."

"I feel far from weak at this moment. And it is not food I crave."

She turned at the door. Arching a brow she shot him a haughty look. "I will speak to Mistress Snow about sending a Highland wench to see to your needs. There may be an old crone about the place who will not find you too offensive."

As she flounced from the room Brice lay back and gave in to a roar of laughter. The woman had fire. It was one of the many things he loved about her.

"Where are you off to?" Brice lay weakly against the cushions and watched as Meredith drew a warm cape over her gown.

"I ride with Angus to view the repairs being done to the homes nearby."

He nodded, oddly pleased that Meredith would take such an interest in the fate of his people. When she left in a flurry of cloak and bonnet he lay back and closed his eyes, annoyed at the weakness that kept him from taking charge as he had always done.

Angus had told him about Meredith's many kindnesses to the Highlanders who had been made homeless by Gareth MacKenzie's invaders. While the men repaired the burned-out cottages, the women and children had been made comfortable in Kinloch House. Meredith had given Mistress Snow permission to use whatever was left in the burned-out storehouse to see that everyone was given enough food and clothing. The refectory had become an open kitchen to all.

Brice lay back, listening to the sounds of activity. The forest rang with axes felling trees for new cottages. Below stairs was the bleat of a newborn babe. In the courtyard the women called to one another as they hung their clothes to dry. The halls resounded with the barking of the hounds as they romped with the children who seemed to fill every room. The sound of their joyous laughter was everywhere.

Because of Meredith's kind concern, his people shared his home, his food, his supplies, until they could once again see to their own needs.

Meredith had taken this cold ancient castle and had filled it with love and laughter. She thought it a simple feat. He found it amazing. Home. She had made his house a home.

Meredith's frequent forays into the forest were always a source of amazement to her. Every Highlander had a story about Brice Campbell. And every one of them was eager to share the story with Meredith.

"When I lost my husband in battle," Mistress Snow said, riding along beside Meredith, "the attackers began burning our cottages. I hid, along with my babe, in the forest.

And when the invaders had gone, I returned to the burned-out shell that had once been my home. That is where Brice Campbell found me. Sitting on a pile of rubble, rocking my babe in my arms."

"What did he do?" Meredith asked.

"He lifted me onto his horse and brought me to Kinloch House. Everyone there was so kind. And when I was strong enough to take charge of my life once more, I realized that I would rather stay at Kinloch and see to the running of the castle than return to live alone in my cottage in the forest."

"But what of the babe?" Meredith could not recall seeing a child.

Mistress Snow's eyes misted. "The babe had been dead for days before Brice came along and found us. In my grief I could not bring myself to bury her. She was all I had left of my husband, and I knew that when I consigned her to the earth, I would be completely alone."

"Oh, Mistress Snow." Meredith caught the woman's hand and pressed it between her own. "How you must have suffered."

"Aye. It was four years ago and the pain is with me still. But," the woman said softly, "I have learned that life must be lived. And each day the pain diminishes a bit more. Because of my lord Campbell's kindness and patience, I know now that I can survive anything."

It also explained to Meredith why, despite the fact that Angus was attracted to the housekeeper, and she obviously returned his affection, they made no move yet to wed. Mistress Snow needed time. And Angus, in his great love, understood her need.

Meredith stored Mistress Snow's story away in her heart. And when every family in the forest told of a similar experience at Brice's hand, she began to realize the depth of his goodness. She knew now why his people loved him so.

How strange, she thought, to discover so many mysteries about the man. She had believed the myth about the Highland Barbarian. If she had not been forced to learn of him for herself, she would never have discovered the wonderful, flesh-and-blood man beneath the myths.

His goodness was one more reason why she loved him so. Leaving him would be heart wrenching. Knowing that, she no longer made secret plans to escape. For now, her prison had become a haven.

"What is that damnable noise?"

Meredith looked up from the tunic she was mending.

Now that Brice's wounds were healing, he was beginning to show signs of resisting his confinement.

For days she had ordered Mistress Snow to prepare his favorite foods. She had encouraged Angus and the other men to visit Brice's chambers frequently, in order to pass the hours of inactivity. Jamie, too, spent long hours with his hero, reading from the precious books in Brice's library, telling and retelling the tales of heroics of Brice's men during the attack by the MacKenzies.

In time those same stories would be woven into the fabric of which legends were made.

But Angus and the others, having repaired the nearby cottages, were engaged in rebuilding the castle. They had little time to spend amusing their leader. And though Mistress Snow had the servants working overtime, Brice showed little interest in the special food they prepared for him.

"Your men are replacing the beams in the great room that were destroyed by fire."

"How can I be expected to rest with that pounding?"

"They are doing this for you." She bit through the thread and set aside his tunic. "They plan to have Kinloch House restored by the time the laird of the manor is up and about once more. They wanted to spare you the sight of all the destruction.''

With a sigh he squirmed about his pallet. ''I have remained idle long enough. The men need my direction.''

''The men are doing fine under Angus's leadership.''

She had no idea that her words only inflamed him further.

''Inform Mistress Snow that I wish to sleep in my own bed tonight, and not this miserable lump on the floor.''

Meredith stood, obviously stung by his sharp words. ''I will inform her immediately.''

As she passed him, Brice caught her hand. She looked down at him and saw his look of remorse.

''Forgive me, Meredith. I have never before been a man who complained about discomfort.'' He sighed and ran a thumb across her wrist. Instantly her pulse leaped. ''It is just that I have never before been forced to lie about while others cared for me. Though it may be the dream of many a man, it does not sit well with me.''

She smiled and dropped to her knees beside him. ''I know that, my lord. But I do not think you understand just how close to death you were. We feared each minute would be your last. Now that you have survived, we enjoy taking care of you. We all feared that you would not return to us from that other world that held you in its grip.''

''Had I not returned, would you have grieved, my lady?''

The words were spoken lightly, but Meredith was aware of the way he watched her while she responded to his question.

''Aye. I would have grieved, as would all the others who—care for you.''

Her reply gave a sudden lift to his spirits.

''Help me up, Meredith.''

''You wish to walk to the window?''

"Nay." He flashed her a smile and she felt her heart stop for a moment. "I wish to go below stairs and see what causes my men to disturb my rest."

"You have not attempted the stairs yet, my lord. The effort may sap your strength."

"It is high time I tried. Give me a hand."

As Meredith leaned toward him he wrapped his arm about her shoulder and got to his feet. Though she felt the jolt at his touch, she forced herself to behave as though nothing had happened.

"Stand very still for a moment," she cautioned. "It is only natural to feel light-headed when you first stand."

"And I thought it was because of the nearness of you."

She turned her head and was aware of his wicked smile.

"Be warned, my lord, that if you tease me beyond my limits, I shall be forced to take action."

"Will you put a potion in my broth?"

She laughed. "Nay, my lord. I will simply let you go. Without me to lean on, you are as helpless as a bairn."

"You would be so cruel to a man who has returned from death's door?"

She shot him a sideways glance and began to walk slowly toward the doorway, with Brice clinging to her. "You will only discover the answer to that if you overstep your bounds."

At the entrance to his chambers he bowed slightly, then caught her arm once more. "I will be the model of a Scots gentleman."

"That you most certainly shall. Or you will be forced to make a very ungentlemanly appearance at the foot of the stairs. In a heap."

With a laugh he made his way down the great stone steps. leaning heavily on her strength.

The stench of charred wood still clung to the lower rooms of the castle. Along the walls the rich tapestries, many of them woven a century earlier, hung in tatters. The fur-draped settles lay in a broken heap beside the fireplace, to be burned as needed. Blackened beams crisscrossed the ceiling, while soot-covered windows blocked all but a few jagged rays of sunlight.

A dozen men, stripped to the waist, strained beneath the weight of the trunk of a giant tree that was being lifted, by a series of ropes and pulleys, to the ceiling, where it would replace a beam destroyed by fire.

When the men spotted Brice they called and shouted their greetings. Those not engaged in the effort at hand crowded around him and clapped him on the shoulder or embraced him warmly.

Angus, in charge of a work crew, shouted a few orders before hurrying forward to greet his old friend.

"We had hoped to have all of this completed before you had a chance to see the damage."

Staring about him, Brice's tone was almost reverent. "From the looks of things it is a miracle that all was not lost. How did you manage to save Kinloch House, old friend?"

"Everyone helped," Angus said modestly. "The servants worked alongside our men until they could no longer stand. I saw men beating out the flames with their bare hands. And I saw women remove their skirts and use them against the fire. But in the end, we won."

"And now you labor to restore what was destroyed."

"It is good work. It has brought all of us together for a common goal. The anger we feel toward Gareth MacKenzie drives us, feeding our energy."

Brice cast an admiring look at his old friend, then turned to where Jamie and several men were planing a second timber.

"I thought it was time the lad learned other than battle skills," Angus said quietly.

With Meredith's assistance, Brice walked closer.

Jamie gave him a wide smile. "Bowen says I will soon be able to work alone, with only a bit of assistance from him."

"Then you must be doing a fine job. Bowen is the most skilled woodsman in our company."

Jamie beamed at the praise. Though he continued working, he often looked up to watch as Brice moved about the great hall. Leaning on Meredith's arm Brice walked slowly about, stopping often to talk with the men.

When Mistress Snow announced that their meal was ready in the refectory, the men set down their tools and pulled on their tunics before following their leader from the room.

It pleased Meredith to see Brice join his men at table. Servants passed around steaming bowls of soup and freshly baked bread. Joints of mutton and breasts of pheasant rounded out the meal, along with tankards of mead and ale. Although Brice ate sparingly, he seemed to gain strength just being a part of this jovial company.

When the others finished their meal, Brice stood and leaned heavily on Meredith's arm.

"Would you like to continue to watch the men, my lord, or would you prefer the solitude of your chambers?"

"It was good to join my men once more. They have renewed my vigor." He leaned closer and murmured, "But I believe the silence of my room will not seem nearly as confining as it did earlier."

As they climbed the stairs Meredith was surprised at the strength in him. In no time he would be well enough to sit a horse and wield a sword.

She experienced a stab of momentary regret. For these long days and nights she had been given a special gift. She had been forced to watch him lie helpless, had gloried in his healing, and come to learn a great deal about the Highland Barbarian. He was a true warrior, who would not give up even when all were against him. He was a man of high moral principles, despite the legend and lies that had sprung up about him. He was a man much loved by his people. And he was a man who had come to mean a great deal to her. When he was strong enough to return her to her people, she would miss him.

That thought shocked her.

She pushed open the door to his chambers and took his arm. ''I asked Mistress Snow to prepare your bed.''

They crossed the sitting chamber, then entered the dimly lit sleeping chamber. A fire had been set in the fireplace. Candles had been lit in the sconces set along the wall. The snowy linens had been turned down in preparation for his return.

She eased him down until he was sitting on the edge of the bed.

''I will be in your sitting chamber, my lord. If you desire anything, you need only call to me.''

''Do not leave me.''

When a look of pain touched his features, she knelt before him, her brow furrowed with concern.

''You are unwell. Where does it hurt, my lord?''

''Here.'' He touched a hand to a spot on his chest.

''But you were not wounded there.'' As she reached up he caught her hand and pressed it to his heart.

''Can you feel it?'' His voice was low, hushed.

''Feel what?''

''The way my heart thunders when you touch me.''

''My lord...''

As she tried to pull away he caught her hand and held it, palm flat against his chest. Though he held her as tenderly as a fragile flower, she could feel the carefully controlled power in his grip.

His words were softly seductive. "You said that if I desire anything, I need only call you."

"Aye, but . . ."

"I desire you, Meredith. You are the first thing I see when I awake, and the last I see before I close my eyes. Even in my dreams you are there, touching me, arousing me. All these long days and nights I have wanted you. And now that I am strong enough, I want to show you how I feel."

"You must not . . ."

"I cannot let you go, my lady."

"I believe I have something to say about that."

"Nay." His voice was gruff. "You do not."

He pulled her firmly against him. She brought her hands to his chest as if to hold him at bay. But it was already too late. His mouth covered hers.

This was no tender kiss, no gentle brushing of mouth to mouth. With an urgency that stunned them both, Brice poured out all the longing, all the needs, that had been building inside him for so long.

What was even more shocking, Meredith returned his kiss with a passion that left them both reeling.

Where had it come from, this need, this hunger? How long had it been growing inside them?

When they should have pulled apart they continued clinging to each other, his mouth avid, seeking, her mouth hungry for more.

"I want you, Meredith. God in heaven, how I want you."

At his words she went very still. For days now, while she had hovered about his still form, praying that he would find the strength to recover from his wounds, she had known. No other man would ever mean as much to her as Brice. No other man could touch her with a single word, a single look.

But wanting someone was not enough. If she gave herself to the Highland Barbarian, she would be sullied in the eyes of every other man in Scotland.

And yet, her heart whispered, even that would no longer matter. There was no other man in all of Scotland who could ever own her heart. There was only this man. Her love for him crowded out all other thought.

She continued to kneel, trapped between his knees, while he rained kisses on her upturned face. His lips skimmed the corner of her lips, her cheek, her temple.

The need for her was an ache far worse than anything he had experienced during his long recovery. The need for this woman clawed at his insides until he was nearly mad with the pain.

He had to have her. Or die trying.

Standing, he caught her hand and brought her to her feet. With his hands on either side of her face he studied her in the glow of the candles.

"I want you, Meredith. I love you, little firebrand." His love was the one thing she could not fight.

With a little moan she offered her lips to him.

"And I love you, Brice." She moaned.

Her words, murmured inside his mouth, filled him with such emotion he could only stand and hold her while he gloried in her surrender.

And then his arms were around her, holding her so close that two heartbeats thundered as one.

Chapter Fourteen

Needs shuddered through Brice, driving him farther and farther toward the edge of madness. But the woman in his arms needed time, needed patience and care. As much care as she had shown toward him in the past days and weeks while he'd healed. He would see to her needs and bank his own.

The lips on hers were gentle now, the kiss coaxing, seductive. He longed to plunge his hands through the tangles of her hair and take her here, now, on the fur before the hearth. Instead, he forced himself to go slowly.

He sensed her fear, her hesitation. But he was certain enough for both of them.

"Don't be afraid, love," he murmured against her cheek. "Think of it as a journey. A slow, easy journey we will travel together."

His lips skimmed her face, pausing to trace the gentle curve of her brow. How beautiful she was; how perfectly formed. He ran light kisses over her closed lids, then followed her cheek to the corner of her lips. With his tongue he traced the outline of her lips until she moaned and her lips parted for him.

With his tongue he explored the intimate recesses of her mouth, savoring all the sweet, wild flavors that were hers alone. And all the while his hands moved along her back, drawing her closer, then closer still, until she was pressed firmly against him.

She was aware of his arousal; aware, too, of the thundering of his heart. Its unsteady rhythm matched her own.

How long had she dreamed of being held like this, of being taken on a wild flight to the heavens and beyond? As his lips held her enthralled she flew high, then higher still, until she felt herself break free of earth. Now she was soaring, now gliding.

As his fingers reached for the buttons of her gown she struggled to settle her feet on steady ground. But then his lips grazed her throat and she was helpless once more, held powerless by the sensations that ripped through her.

Her gown drifted to the floor about her feet and lay forgotten. Now the only barrier between them was a thin ivory chemise. With deft movements he untied the ribbons of her garment and slid it from her shoulders.

For long moments he studied her. The sight of her beauty left him breathless. In the light of the fire her skin was as white as alabaster, her eyes as green and shimmering as a Highland glen. With a sense of reverence he ran his fingertips lightly across the slope of her shoulders. She quivered beneath his gentle touch. With a sigh he brought his lips to her throat. Arching her neck she moved in his arms and thrilled to the sensations that skittered along her spine.

Never, never had she known such feelings.

He brought his lips lower to the soft swell of her breast. As his mouth closed over her nipple she heard a low, guttural moan. Hers? Or his? It no longer mattered. They were caught up in such waves of passion they could no longer think, only feel.

Her knees trembled and she feared she could no longer stand. It was as if he was in perfect harmony to all her senses. In one swift movement Brice scooped her up into his arms and carried her to the bed, settling her among the snowy linens. His clothes joined hers on the floor and he lay beside her, gathering her into his arms.

His hands, his lips, moved over her, leaving her body a mass of nerve endings.

The heat between them rose up in shimmering waves. A weakness seemed to invade her, leaving her limbs heavy, her mind blank. She drifted on clouds of sensation that sapped her strength, stole her will.

She was helpless, caught up in feelings that she had never even known existed. She was once again kidnapped and held hostage. This time to passion.

As his hands and mouth worked their magic, she moved in his arms, loving the feel of his work-worn fingertips against her soft flesh. How agile his mouth. How clever his hands.

She longed to touch him as he was touching her. And yet, in her fear and innocence, she was afraid. Would he think her a wicked, wanton woman?

Tentatively she reached a hand to his cheek. He moved against her palm slowly and she saw his eyes narrow fractionally.

Growing bolder she brought her hand to his chest and allowed her fingers to skim along the mat of hair. His nipples hardened as her fingers grazed them and she lingered, stroking until she heard his sigh of pleasure.

As her fingers moved lower she encountered a series of raised scars on his flat abdomen.

At her arched look he murmured, "So many old battles. So many old wounds."

Without thinking she pressed her lips to the flat plane of his stomach, tracing her lips across the scars. "I cannot bear to think of you being wounded."

Instantly she felt his stomach muscles contract violently. She experienced a wild thrill at the realization that it was her touch that had caused such a reaction.

She had the power to make this strong warrior flinch. One touch of her hand could leave him as weak as she had been just moments ago. Drunk with her new power she grew even bolder, pressing her lips to his throat while her hands roamed his muscular shoulders, his hair-roughened chest, his stomach.

His chuckle of delight turned into a moan of impatience as her hands moved lower, exploring, arousing.

"Witch."

He rolled on top of her and began an exploration of his own, allowing his lips, his fingertips, to move seductively over her until she writhed and moaned and gasped his name. It took all of his willpower to keep from taking her. This was her first time, he cautioned himself. He wanted it to be everything and more.

"I love you, little firebrand," he growled against her lips.

His fingers found her, moist and ready, and before she could realize what was happening, he took her to the first shuddering crest.

"And I want you more than I have ever wanted anyone, anything."

Her breath was coming so fast she could hardly get the words out. But her hands clutched at his shoulders as she felt herself tumbling out of control. Madness. She had slipped over the edge of madness.

"Oh, Brice. I—love—you." The words were breathy, barely coherent. She arched her body to meet him, needing him with an urgency that matched his. "Please. I—want you."

Her plea ripped through him, shattering his careful control. He slipped inside her, struggling to be gentle. But the moment they came together, he threw caution to the wind. With a savageness that surprised him she moved with him, matching his rhythm, mirroring his strength, until together they gave in to the madness and soared to the moon.

He was enveloped in the scent of wildflowers, and he recalled that she'd had wildflowers entwined in her hair that first day he'd seen her at the altar of the cathedral. Their fragrance filled him until all he could smell was Meredith lying in a meadow of wildflowers.

Higher they climbed, then higher still, until they reached the velvet heavens. A wild, primitive cry was torn from Brice's lips. And a million stars exploded and shattered into shiny silver fragments.

In that moment she gave him her heart. Her honor. Her innocence.

They lay, still locked together, unwilling to break the fragile, intimate contact. Levering himself on his elbows Brice studied the way she looked, her face damp with sheen, her eyes moist.

"Tears, firebrand? God in heaven." With his thumbs he wiped the tears from her cheeks. "I've hurt you."

"Nay." She turned her head to hide her weakness. "It was just—so wonderful."

He rolled to his side and drew her gently into the circle of his arms. "Aye. It was beautiful." He pressed his lips to her eyes and tasted her salty tears. "And it is perfectly natural to cry at something so dazzlingly beautiful."

"You do not think me a foolish child?"

"Nothing you do or say would seem foolish to me. And," he added with a tender smile, "you are far from a child. You are the most beautiful, desirable woman I have ever met."

She sniffed. "More beautiful than the women you met at the Court in France?"

He bit back a laugh at her artless attempt to be reassured. "No woman at Court could match your beauty, my lady, including the queen herself."

"Her ladies-in-waiting thought I resembled Queen Mary."

He caught a strand of her hair and watched as it sifted through his fingers, catching and reflecting the light of the fire. "Your coloring, perhaps. And the fact that you are both small and slender. But you are a rare beauty, Meredith. And far more lovely than our queen."

She grew silent for a moment, gathering her courage for the next question. With a swallow she asked haltingly, "Is it always like this?"

"Loving?"

She seemed relieved that he understood. "Aye."

With his index finger he traced the line of her brow, the curve of her cheek. His voice was low with feeling. "I fear that many people are never blessed with what we have just discovered."

"Why?"

His finger moved over her lips, still swollen from his kisses. Though it seemed impossible, his desire for this beguiling, bewitching creature was beginning to build once again. "They are afraid to give themselves completely to another."

"What is it they fear?"

"Losing control, I suppose. Or perhaps it is the fear of letting another witness their needs, their weaknesses."

"Have you any weaknesses, my lord?" she asked with a smile.

"I have discovered one." His tone was grave, although his lips curved into a hint of a smile. "One very beautiful, very obstinate firebrand that can make me weak with a single touch."

"Like this?" With her finger she traced a pattern across his chest, then lower to his stomach.

He felt the heat as he became aroused. Before he could reach for her she surprised him by rolling on top of him.

Her hair swirled about him, tickling his chest, brushing over his fingers. Her eyes burned brightly, reflecting the light of the fire. She smiled as she began to move over him. Every touch, every movement, aroused him further.

"Firebrand, I am a man still recovering from battle wounds. You will be the death of me."

"Then I shall simply have to leave you alone to rest and recover."

As she made a move to roll away he caught her and dragged her against him. His hands, his lips, began weaving their magic.

Against her throat he growled, "You are the only medicine I need. Stay with me, firebrand. Love me."

With murmured words of endearment they slipped into a world of endless delight. A world where only lovers can go.

Meredith lay in the midnight blackness and listened to Brice's steady, even breathing.

Did he know what he had given her? Did he have any idea how much she'd needed his quiet strength, his calm assurance of his love?

So much had happened in her young life. So much chaos. The murder of her father. Desmond's shocking death at the altar. Her kidnapping.

There had been little time for reflection. Certainly no time for love. Until now.

Brice's arms tightened about her and she felt a quiver of apprehension at the strength in him. Did he have any idea what power he wielded? It was not physical power she feared. Despite his strength, she would have found a way to escape him in time. The power he wielded was emotional. She needed his approval, desired his love forever. Without this Highland warrior, her life would be as before. Empty. Waiting. Yearning for something she could not even give a name to. Until now. Love. That was what she had been waiting a lifetime to share.

With a sigh Brice drew her close and pressed his lips to her temple. She sighed and snuggled close, then was startled by his deep voice.

"Awake again, firebrand?"

"Aye. This is all so new to me. So exciting. I fear I will never be able to sleep."

"Nor I." He nibbled the corner of her lips until she turned her head and gave him full access to her mouth.

His lips were warm and firm and with one easy movement he drew her fully into the kiss.

"Oh, Brice," she breathed against his mouth. "Will you some day grow weary of me and tire of our lovemaking?"

He chuckled, low and deep in his throat, and the sound sent tremors along her spine. "Never, my lady. It would take an eternity and beyond to even dim the love that shines within me for you."

She relaxed against him and lost herself in the kiss.

"But I have a better way to prove my love," he muttered, shifting until he hovered over her. "Far better than words."

Brice lay very still, unwilling to disturb the woman who slept so peacefully in his arms.

All night they had loved, slept, then loved again until they were sated. And still he had not had enough of her. Nothing would ever be enough. A hundred times. A thousand years. He loved her. Body and soul. Completely.

He thought of the beautiful young woman he had watched from the tower of the cathedral. Clothed all in white, her spine rigid, her head held high. Even then he had sensed the strength in her, the determination. And when he had first looked into her eyes he had read the goodness there.

He dared not lose. He wanted the love they shared to be sanctified and blessed by the kirk. He wanted the entire country to know that the Highland Barbarian was loved by this beautiful Lowlands woman. He wanted to shout of their love from the highest mountain.

He glanced at Meredith and saw the slight flicker of her eyes. Sleep was leaving her now. Within moments she would awaken. His woman.

The decision was made instantly. He would send a messenger to the Lowlands to learn the fate of her people. He would wed her now, as soon as it was possible to prepare a wedding feast. And then, with the might of his Highland warriors behind her, she would return triumphant to her people. With the combined strength of her armies and his, Gareth MacKenzie would not dare to continue his litany of murder and lies.

They could bring a renewed sense of peace between the Highlanders and Lowlanders. Perhaps, because of their love, the Scots lairds could cease their endless fighting and join forces to combat their true foe, the English invaders.

Meredith's eyes opened and she found Brice watching her. On his face was a smile of such contentment, she answered with a smile of her own.

"You look rather pleased this morn, my lord."

"Aye. How could I be less than pleased with the woman I love lying in my arms?"

She sighed and drew her arms around his neck. "I feared I would awake and discover it was all a dream."

"It was no dream, my love," he murmured against her lips. "Nor is this."

His kiss was hot, hungry. His lips persuasive. And because he had spent the night learning all the secret, intimate places of her body, he was able to arouse her instantly.

"If it be a dream," she breathed inside his mouth, "pray do not wake me till it is over."

Chapter Fifteen

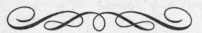

Locked in the arms of her love, Meredith drifted on a cloud of contentment. For days now they had closeted themselves in Brice's chambers, leaving their private haven only occasionally to inspect the work being done on the great hall.

Though everyone at Kinloch House, servants and soldiers alike, whispered about the lovers, Brice and Meredith remained blissfully unaware of anything except each other. Wrapped in a safe cocoon of love, it mattered not to them that they were the object of much speculation.

When Mistress Snow realized what was happening, she instructed the servants to respect the privacy of the laird of the manor and his lady. Their meals were announced, then set up quickly in the sitting chamber. Fires were laid, tapers lit in sconces, linens replaced with as much haste as possible.

Even Angus conspired to keep young Jamie so busy with the carpentry work that the lad had almost no time to visit with Brice and Meredith. Or to disturb their bliss.

Through it all the young couple was so absorbed in their newly discovered love for each other, they never noticed what went on around them.

* * *

In the great hall Brice moved among his men, stopping often to admire the work being done. In the doorway Meredith paused to watch. It was so good to see Brice move without the stiffness that had marked his movements immediately after the battle with the MacKenzies. At last his health was completely restored. His full strength had returned.

At the clatter of arriving horses in the courtyard she turned and made her way to the door. Alston, the red-bearded warrior who had long fought beside Brice, dismounted and handed over his mount to a stable boy before striding across the courtyard.

Glancing at the lathered steed Meredith remarked, "You have ridden far, Alston."

"Aye, my lady." He shook the dust from his plumed hat and paused. "I come from the Lowlands."

Home. The thought was poignant, fleeting. She quickly dismissed it.

"Was there a reason you rode so far from your Highlands?"

"Brice set for me the task of gathering information about the MacAlpins and the MacKenzies, my lady."

She was oddly touched by Brice's concern. "And how do my people fare without me?"

"They continue to be plagued by night riders and highwaymen who steal their sheep and cattle, and even murder those unfortunate enough to be out after dark."

Her smile faded. "And Gareth MacKenzie?"

He seemed to hesitate for a fraction before saying softly, "Gareth MacKenzie rides to Holyroodhouse to have the queen declare you dead."

"Dead!" Her eyes widened in shock. "But why would he do such a thing?"

"Since you have not been seen, he and his men are convinced that you perished in the Highland forests." His voice softened when he saw the pain that crossed her features. "By declaring you officially dead, your next of kin will become the leader of your people."

"My next of kin."

Alston stepped past her with a bow. "My pardon, my lady. I must report my findings to Brice."

As he strode down the long hall, Meredith suddenly leaned against the heavy door as the realization sank in. Her next of kin was her sister, sixteen-year-old Brenna. Sweet, shy Brenna. She would be no match against the charms of Gareth MacKenzie. He would convince her, as he had once convinced Meredith, that they must combine their land and forces if they would stand against the unseen Highland monsters who attacked in the night. The MacAlpins, old Duncan and his wife Mary, as well as all the others, would be so weary of the killings, they would urge poor Brenna to accept Gareth's offer and unite their people against a common enemy. And once wed, Gareth would claim Brenna's land and easily dispose of her, should she prove to be a burden.

And what of the youngest, Megan? Impulsive, headstrong Megan. Would the same fate befall her in time?

Meredith felt a sense of horror and revulsion. She shivered and realized that her hands were as cold as ice. While she was safely ensconced in the Highlands, secure in Brice's love, her little sisters were in grave peril.

Her first thought was to run tearfully to Brice and plead with him to go to their assistance. Then she recalled the extreme hatred Gareth nurtured for Brice. For now, Brice was safe only because Gareth thought him dead. As long as Brice stayed in his Highland forest, he could not be harmed.

The same was true for her. But there was a difference. This was her personal battle. She could not possibly stay here, safe and warm, while her family was in grave danger.

She must show herself to her people. And she must unmask Gareth MacKenzie as the lying murderer she knew him to be.

The MacAlpins would rally round her. Though it would be a bloody battle, they were warriors. Had they not held back the English invaders along the Border for centuries?

The decision was made instantly, with no thought to her own peril. She would return to the Lowlands. She would assemble her people. They would drive Gareth MacKenzie from their land and wrest back control of their own destinies.

With quick strides she hurried to Brice's chambers. Before he returned from his inspection of the great hall, she had much to prepare.

Brice was in a festive mood. The work in the great hall was moving swiftly. In no time it would be restored to its former elegance. Even now, as the charred beams were replaced, and the windows scrubbed of smoke and soot, carpenters labored to make new settles, tables and chairs. Hunters returned with animal hides to replace the ones that had gone up in smoke. And although many of the tapestries had been burned beyond repair, the women of the clan had already begun work on new ones, depicting the Campbell ancestors, their victories, their lineage. These new ones, Mistress Snow had informed him, would also include his own life history, and any wife and children to follow.

So they knew, he thought with a smile. The entire household knew that he and Meredith were lovers. And if the household staff knew, and his men knew, then the entire clan, sequestered in the surrounding forests, had been informed as well.

That thought pleased him. He wanted everyone to know that he loved Meredith MacAlpin. He wanted his friends to

rejoice with him. And as soon as the work on the great hall
was completed, they would join him in a feast to celebrate
his marriage to the beautiful Meredith.

He was also pleased by the news Alston had brought this
day. If Gareth MacKenzie believed that Meredith was dead,
she would be safe from any further attempts on her life. At
least, he reasoned, until such time as she proved to the
Lowlanders that she was indeed alive. It would take time for
Gareth to travel to Holyroodhouse and seek an audience
with the queen. By that time Brice and Meredith would be
wed. Together they would lead his men to the Lowlands to
secure Meredith's birthright. By the sheer numbers of
MacAlpin and Campbell soldiers, they would thwart any
further attempt by Gareth MacKenzie to take by force what
was not his.

Peace. Love. Brice had never dared hope that either
would be experienced in his lifetime. And now both were
within his grasp.

He gave Mistress Snow his request for a very special meal,
then made his way to his chambers. Tonight, if the time
proved right, he would reveal his plans to her. And he would
ask her hand in marriage.

Meredith looked up from the wardrobe. On her cheeks
were two bright spots of color. When she saw him she gave
a little cry and ran to his arms.

The kiss she gave him sent his pulse rate soaring.

"Firebrand," he murmured against her lips. "Have you
missed me so much?"

"Aye."

He marveled at the way she clung to him, as if they had
been apart for days instead of mere hours.

Leading him to a long covered bench pulled up in front of
the fire, she curled up beside him, still clinging to him as if
to a lifeline.

"Do you know how much I love you?"

"Not nearly as much as I love you, my lady. I would die for you," he murmured against her temple.

Instantly she touched a finger to his lips to silence him. "Never say that again. I do not wish you dead, my lord. Not even for me."

"But what good would it do to live if you were not here to live with me?"

"You are important to your people," she said, pulling away slightly. "So many people depend upon you. You have a duty to be here for them."

"And so I shall, little firebrand." He pulled her into his arms and rained kisses across her forehead. "We shall both be here for them." He kissed the tip of her nose. "And we will spend our days having wee bairns and taking them for picnics in the forest." He pressed a kiss to her lips.

His words tormented her. She allowed herself to savor the kiss for long moments before whispering, "Such a lovely dream, my lord."

"It is no dream. We shall live it. We shall have it all."

"Oh, Brice. If only it could be." With tears burning her eyes she wound her arms around his neck and clung to him, burying her face against his throat.

"Trust me," he murmured against her temple. "There is so much I want to tell you. So much I want to share with you."

"Hush, my lord." She blinked away the tears and drew his face down for her kiss. "Not now. I cannot bear to hear mere words. Show me."

With a tenderness he had never known before, he lifted her in his arms and set her on the fur throw spread before the fire.

As he reached for the buttons of her gown, she caught his hand and stared up into his eyes.

"I want you to know this," she said, her voice trembling with emotion. "No matter what happens, I love you, Brice Campbell. For all time. And wherever I am, you are there with me."

He was moved, as much by the intensity of her words as the words themselves. Though this serious little woman often made him laugh, there was now no hint of laughter in his words.

"And I love you, little one. I will love you for a lifetime and beyond."

Bathed in the glow of the fire, they lost themselves in the wonder of their love. Brice marveled at the depth of her passion. Never before had she shown her love so intensely. Never had their love burned brighter, or ignited such fire between them.

Meredith looked down at the sleeping form of her love. It took all her willpower to keep from crying. She must not weep. She must be strong, not only for Brice, but for her sisters who needed her.

"Please understand," she whispered as she scrawled a message on a parchment scroll and set it on a table near the bed.

From his wardrobe she withdrew the things she had prepared earlier. Shedding her delicately embroidered night shift, she pulled on a pair of Brice's breeches, tucking them into tall boots. Over the saffron shirt, a symbol of the Highlander, and dark tunic, she secured a heavy cape. At her waist dangled a sword. Tucked into her waistband was a small, sharp dirk. She tucked her hair beneath a plumed hat and draped a fur throw over her arm. In a small pouch she had stuffed the remains of their supper.

She paused beside Brice's bed and cast a last loving glance at him as he slept. He had whispered love words to her all the while they had savored Mistress Snow's wonderful meal. And while they had sipped wine, he had smiled and hinted that he had important plans to share with her. Plans that would change both their lives.

How she loved him. How she would miss him in the days and weeks to come.

But her home beckoned her. Her clan needed her. She had no choice.

In the doorway to the sitting chamber she paused and peered through the dim light. No one stirred. Satisfied, she closed the door and strode quickly down the stairs.

She avoided the courtyard, choosing instead to leave by a rear door in the scullery. Crossing around to the stables, she chose a great black stallion. Ignoring the sidesaddles, she tossed a man's saddle over the animal's back and rolled and tied the fur behind it.

Because she knew Brice's men patrolled the paths leading to the castle, she led the horse through brambles and dense undergrowth. When she was certain she was far enough away to ride undetected, she pulled herself into the saddle and spurred her mount on. By the time Brice awoke and alerted his men to what she had done, she promised herself, she would be miles away.

Brice drifted on a misty cloud, half awake, half asleep.

What a beautiful night he and Meredith had shared. What a wonderful surprise she was. That fiery, innocent lass he had brought to Kinloch House was a constant delight. Each time he peeled away a layer he discovered an even more exciting creature beneath.

The child in her brought out all his fierce protective instincts. The imp in her made him laugh. The woman in her made him ache.

He rolled to his side and reached for her. He had been too distracted last night by her beauty, by her almost desperate lovemaking, to share his plans with her. Today he would officially ask for her hand in marriage. And then, when she accepted, he would tell her of his plans for their future.

The rest of the bed was empty.

From beneath half-closed lids he noted that the sun was already streaming through the windows. Why did she have to be up and about when he was feeling lazy, and more than a little eager to hold her, to love her as he had last night?

With a sigh he moved to her side of the bed and breathed in her fragrance. Within minutes she would return, mayhaps with a tray laden with Mistress Snow's warm biscuits. They would have a lazy morning of lovemaking, and then he would take her into his confidence.

The bed was cold where she had lain.

Suddenly alarmed, Brice sat up and looked around. The fire had long ago burned to ashes. No one had tended it. Few remains of their supper lay on a tray near the fireplace.

Meredith's night shift lay on the floor. In the open wardrobe her gowns could be seen, hanging neatly on pegs beside his tunics. None of the gowns appeared to be missing.

Crossing the room Brice lifted her night shift. It was unlike Meredith to leave it there. Draping it over his arm he turned and spotted the scroll. In quick strides he walked to the small table and read the message.

Dearest Brice, I go to my sisters who need me. You must not follow. Gareth thinks you dead. Your secret is safe with me. Know always that I love you. M.

A cry of anguish was torn from Brice's lips. Slumping on the edge of the bed he buried his face in Meredith's night shift. It still bore her scent. Inhaling deeply he sat there for long minutes filling himself with her.

Then he stood and tossed the garment aside. There was no time to waste. She was somewhere deep in the Highland forests. There were many dangers out there. Not all of them wild animals.

He must find her before the wrong people did. Or she would be lost to him forever.

Chapter Sixteen

It had been raining steadily for hours. The raindrops filtered through the leaves of the trees, drenching horse and rider as they plodded through the forest.

Across a ridge of the mountain a mist rose up, eerie, ghostlike. Almost hidden below the mist Meredith recognized a lake they had crossed on her journey to Brice's fortress. At least she was heading in the right direction, she consoled herself. But if the weather continued to work against her, the journey would take twice as long as she had anticipated.

On a high rocky crag she brought her mount to a halt and turned to study the trail she had just taken. There was no sign that anyone was following her. Still, she felt a tingling sensation at the back of her neck, as though someone was watching. Brice? Though the day was shrouded in darkness, she guessed that Brice would have awakened less than an hour ago. It would be impossible for him to have come this far in so short a time. Also, she had implored him in her note to stay where he was safe. She prayed that he would listen to the voice of reason and remain in the safety of his Highland home.

If Brice was watching, he would show himself. She felt a tremor of fear and looked over her shoulder. If she was truly being watched, it was not Brice, but a stranger. The thought brought a quick, jolting rush of fear in the pit of her stomach.

She drew the hood of the cloak over her head and tried to shake off the feeling of gloom. She was merely lonely, she consoled herself. She had never dreamed she would feel so lonely. All her life, growing up with loving parents, she and her sisters had known only love and security. And hard work. Growing up in a clan of warriors along the Border, she had been groomed in the art of battle. She knew what it was to take up a sword at a moment's notice when the English soldiers attacked.

Her gentle mother had encouraged all her daughters in the art of nurturing their people. And when they engaged in battle, the entire MacAlpin clan was taken into the manor house for safekeeping until the battle was over. The families, along with their animals, stayed within the compound until it was safe to return to their outlying homes. Always they had stood together, a proud, strong family.

Now, with her parents gone and her sisters' lives in grave peril, the burden of responsibility lay with her alone. Though she felt equal to the task, she sorely missed her parents' quiet strength.

"If only Brice could share this burden with me." To stave off loneliness she talked to her horse.

Why was she torturing herself with such thoughts? Venting her frustration, she nudged her mount with more energy than necessary, sensing its reluctance to plod onward through the mist. But her mind would not give her any rest.

"How did it come to pass that one Highland warrior could mean so much to me? When did I stop thinking only of myself and begin thinking of the two of us as one? When did I begin to put his well-being ahead of my own?"

The horse whinnied in response. Despite her discomfort she smiled.

"It had happened long before we came together in love," she whispered.

During her earliest days of captivity she had discovered that the man who held her hostage was not the man she had thought him to be. The cruel barbarian was a myth, created by legend and the acts of those who would besmirch his good name.

Rain pelted her face and ran in little rivers from her eyelashes to her cheeks. She blinked as she thought of her own father, known throughout Scotland as a fair and honorable man. That thought brought a sense of pride to her. What if someone had blamed him for the acts of another, sullying his good name? Her hand tightened on the cold leather reins. She would search to the ends of the earth for those responsible, and she would give her life if necessary to clear her father's name.

Though she detested war, she realized that Brice had that same right. Gareth MacKenzie must be made to recant his lies and restore Brice's good name to him. Even if it took a war to force his hand. The thought caused her to tremble.

As horse and rider plunged deeper into the forest the tingling began anew. Someone—or something—was watching her. Although the trail was treacherous she dug in her heels and urged her horse into a trot. As the rain-shrouded branches closed in around her she pushed away all thoughts of fear. She was being foolish. How could anyone find her in this dense forest?

Like any true warrior, Brice often had to face down his fears. He had always known that he had as much chance to survive as his opponent.

This time it was different. It was not his life hanging in the balance, but Meredith's. The thought left him terrified.

His first moments of panic had been replaced with rage. Wild, seething rage. He tore through the castle shouting orders at Angus and the others, sending all the inhabitants of Kinloch House and the surrounding forest into a frenzy of activity.

Within an hour the men had prepared their battle gear and were saddling their horses in the courtyard. Mistress Snow and the servants had prepared enough food to allow them to ride without stopping for several days. After that the men should be safely back in the Highlands. If not, they would be forced to hunt for their food.

"What is our plan?" Angus worked feverishly beside Brice, saddling his mount.

"I have none."

"No plan?" Angus turned to study his friend. Always Brice Campbell had been the cool warrior, prepared for any event during battle. But this was a new Brice, a Brice Campbell paralyzed by love.

Brice's first wild, frenzied feelings were now carefully banked. But beneath the icy calm Angus sensed a slow, simmering rage. A rage that still clouded his thinking. The man was spoiling for a fight. Woe to any enemy who crossed his path this day.

"We ride until we find Meredith." Brice pulled himself into the saddle and glanced around at the dozen or so men who followed suit. They were skilled warriors who had ridden at his side in countless battles. He could count on them to come through for him. And this time, more than ever, he would depend on them. "We will ride on to the Borders and rescue Meredith MacAlpin's sisters from MacKenzie's clutches. And we will bring them all back to the Highlands, where they will remain safe."

''That sounds simple enough,'' Alston shouted, fighting to subdue a headstrong mount.

''Aye.''

As Brice led the way into the forest, his mind was awhirl. So simple that it must be flawed. But at the moment he could think of nothing except Meredith. Sweet, beautiful Meredith. Would that God keep his woman safe until she was back in his arms.

Hunched inside the warm woolen cloak, Meredith searched for a familiar landmark. Though she possessed a keen sense of direction, she had ridden this trail only once. And then much of it had been traversed in the dark.

For hours the feeling persisted that she was being followed. But though Meredith stopped often and scanned the surrounding woods, she saw no trace of another human. Had not her mother often accused her of having a vivid imagination? Though at the time it had seemed a blessing, she now realized it was a curse. She was conjuring up dangers where there were none.

From a nearby wood a bird called, its shrill tone piercing the silence. Her hand flew to the dirk at her waist and she peered about, prepared to do battle. When the bird lifted off from the tree and soared heavenward, Meredith wiped her damp hands on her breeches and felt a wild rush of relief.

Moments later she heard the rustle of leaves as a deer, frightened by her appearance, darted behind a boulder. For long minutes her heart pounded in her chest. She swallowed and, calling herself a timid fool, turned her mount toward a ridge of rock to the east.

The rain had finally stopped, although the ground remained moist and spongy. Meredith allowed her mount to pick its path along the trail, trusting the animal's instincts more than her own. Several times the horse stumbled, but each time managed to regain its footing within seconds.

At last they reached the top of the ridge. Stiff from her long hours in the saddle, Meredith slid to the ground. Grasping the animal's reins she led the stallion to the edge of the ravine and peered below. At the sight, she caught her breath.

The spires of trees gently lifted their limbs to the heavens as if in prayer. But hidden beneath their soft thick canopy, she knew, the mountainous trail below her was a maze of winding rivers and steep mountain crags.

There would be no rest if she were to reach flat land by nightfall. The trail below her was every bit as treacherous as the one she had already traveled.

For a moment she pressed her hands to her back to ease her cramped muscles. Then, tossing the reins over the horse's head, she wearily prepared to pull herself back into the saddle.

A strong, muscled arm closed around her throat, pulling her off balance. As she was about to scream a hand closed over her mouth, cutting off her words.

A voice she recognized sent a ripple of terror through her veins. The voice, unmistakably Holden Mackay's, trembled with the excitement of the hunt.

"So, my lady. How convenient of you to leave the safety of the Campbell's bed and come to me. It seems we will have time after all to finish what we started at Kinloch House."

How could she have forgotten this most mortal of all enemies? She cursed herself for her carelessness. The concern for her sisters had erased all reasonable thought.

She pried at his offending hands but could not budge them. With a laugh he tightened his grip on her throat until dark spots danced before her eyes.

In desperation she gripped the hilt of the sword at her waist. With the pressure at her throat it took all of her strength to pull the sword from the scabbard. But when the blade flashed dully her attacker took a step back, releasing her.

She sucked in several long scalding breaths before turning to face him. "Had I a sword at Kinloch House, Mackay, I would have killed you then."

Though he was startled, he threw back his head and laughed. "Do you think yourself a match for me, my lady?" He laughed again. "Remember, woman, I am a Highland warrior. I was born by the sword."

"Then prepare to die by it as well," Meredith called, lifting the point of her sword to his heart.

He leaped aside, surprised by her boldness. He had expected her to weep and to plead for her life. He had not expected her to fight him.

He reached for his own sword and drew it out. As the blade danced through the air, she lunged, pressed and dodged, with all the skill of a trained swordsman.

Holden Mackay wiped a hand across his forehead to erase the sheen of sweat. His own skill was not with the thin sword designed for thrusting, but with the heavier broadsword. It was unheard of that a woman could best a man at any warlike skill. It was just that she had managed to catch him by surprise, he told himself.

With his sword pointed at her heart he lunged. She stepped aside and brought her sword up, catching him in the shoulder. A scarlet stain bubbled to the surface and spilled across his cloak.

He swore viciously and lunged again. This time he almost caught her, but at the last moment she ducked, bringing the point of her sword singing past his temple.

His eyes narrowed. She was good. Very good. And he was being made to look a fool.

Again he lifted his sword and again she dodged the tip of his blade and watched as the blow meant for her fell harmlessly against the branches of a low bush.

"The forest should fear you, Mackay," she taunted him with a laugh. "With your wild parrying you may cut down a valuable tree."

"It is you I will cut down to size. When I finish with you, wench, you will wish you had never been born."

Meredith didn't bother to respond. With agile steps she backed him against the trunk of a gnarled old tree and brought the tip of her sword to his throat.

"Those are the last words you will ever speak."

"I think not." A smile slowly spread across his features, giving him the sinister look of a deadly snake. He pressed a hand tightly to his wounded shoulder but blood quickly oozed through his fingers, dripping onto the damp earth and staining the rocks at his feet. "You will hand over your sword to my men who stand behind you or they will cut you up in little pieces and feed you to the wild animals that roam these mountains."

"Do you think me foolish enough to turn away from you for even one moment? I know your little trick. You think to render me defenseless while I am distracted."

His smile grew. "Take the lady's sword."

Meredith felt a hand at her shoulder and turned, prepared to do battle with another. Half a dozen men faced her, swords drawn. From the looks on their faces she knew that they would have no qualms about killing her where she stood.

From behind came Holden Mackay's evil laughter. "Drop your sword or my men will run you through."

He watched as her sword slipped from her fingers and dropped on the moist ground.

"Now, my lady, I believe we have a score to settle." To his men he shouted, "Bind her and toss her over my saddle. The lady is mine." He leaned close. His breath was hot on her cheek as he gave a hollow laugh and added for her ears alone, "To do with as I please."

Brice and his men rode in single file along the path worn into the earth by Meredith's mount. When it was raining it had been an easy job to trail her. Now that the rain had stopped, he prayed they would find her before the earth dried up and the trail was lost.

None of the men spoke, and though they were weary, not one of them complained of the long hours in the saddle. They knew how much their leader loved the woman they searched for. They would travel to hell and back for Brice Campbell.

As they topped a ridge Brice suddenly reined in his mount and slid to the ground.

"There were men and horses here." Brice pointed to the churned up earth. "And there was a scuffle."

He walked several paces before stooping. He touched a finger to the small footprint imbedded in the soil. "No man's foot could leave so small a mark."

Angus swallowed, reluctant to agree.

"Do you recognize the horses' marks?" Though Brice studied the other prints, his gaze kept returning to the small print that he knew had been made by Meredith's booted foot.

Angus called to Alston, and together the two men went over every mark on the ground. While they did, Brice walked about, careful not to obliterate any of the prints.

"They were Highlanders," Alston called out. "Six or seven of them."

"They rode from a northerly direction," Angus called. "And when they left, they headed north again."

"Mackays," Alston said softly.

Brice felt as if a dagger had been plunged into his heart. Holden Mackay. In his mind he could still see the scene in his chambers, when Mackay had nearly succeeded in taking Meredith by force. He thought of the bruises he had seen on her throat, and the fear he had read in her eyes.

Angus swallowed, aware of the pain Brice would be enduring at this moment. All the fear, all the rage, at last had a focus. "It had to be the Mackays," he said in a near whisper.

They stood and began to walk to where the others waited with their horses.

"God in heaven."

At Brice's exclamation, Angus and Alston hurried to his side. Brice was kneeling near the trunk of a gnarled old tree. At the base lay a discarded sword. His sword, which had been missing along with his clothes and stallion.

He brushed his hand over the damp earth, over the small boulders at the base of the tree.

"Blood."

Angus and Alston looked at each other before Angus said softly, "Aye. 'Tis blood. But we cannot be certain it was the lass's."

"And we cannot be certain it is not." Brice pulled himself into the saddle. His face was a grim mask. "By all that is holy I swear that if Holden Mackay harms her in any way he is a dead man."

He turned to his men. "We ride north. To confront the devil himself."

Chapter Seventeen

Meredith fought back a wave of panic as she was forced to ride, hands tied, astride Mackay's horse.

It had been humiliating enough to be bound and lifted like a sack of grain. But to be held firmly in his arms, his hands brushing the undersides of her breasts while his horse broke into a trot, was almost more than she could bear. She had to swallow back a rush of nausea.

She must not give in to the panic that threatened to reduce her to weeping and hysteria. It was exactly what this monster would want. Instead, she must appear calm, no matter what he said or did.

His men fell into line behind him, their spirits high. Their little foray into the forests this day had brought them an unexpected bonus. For weeks, since their leader had returned from Brice Campbell's castle, he had been brooding and sullen. Now, with the discovery of this lass, he had come alive again. It was obvious that there was a simmering feud between these two. And though the men had no idea what had occurred earlier, Holden Mackay now had someone on whom he could focus his anger.

When the skies once again opened up, Meredith hunched deep into her cloak. But the cold seemed to seep through to her very bones. It was not only because of the weather, she realized. It was because she was already replaying in her mind the scene in Brice's chambers, when Holden Mackay had come dangerously close to taking her by force. She knew what awaited her at the end of this journey, and though she tried, she could not blot it from her mind.

They rode for nearly three hours, often leaving well-worn paths to plunge into the dense forest. There was little said between the men now, but Meredith sensed that they passed signals among themselves. Could there be someone on their trail? Or did they take these evasive routes routinely to avoid running into anyone along the path?

She thought about shouting for help. But who could hear her in the forest? And to invite Mackay's wrath was to invite pain. It would probably please him to have an excuse to silence her with as much force as possible.

With the surefooted ease of horses heading home, the animals picked their way across a swirling river. Meredith studied the depth of the water, nearly to the horses' bellies. If she managed to break free of Holden's grip, how far and fast could she swim before being caught? Worse, could she swim with her hands bound? Or would she risk being sucked beneath the swirling waters? At the moment, drowning seemed a better fate than the one contemplated by her captor.

As if reading her mind Holden Mackay tightened his grip at her waist and gave a low grunt of laughter.

"Thinking of slipping through my clutches, my lady?" He bent toward her, his voice sending chills along her spine. "My men would spear you like a fish by the time you hit the water."

"At least my death would be quick."

"Aye. But far less satisfying for me."

A tremor passed through her. She bit back the words that threatened to spill from her lips. Now was not the time to goad him. She would wait. And watch. And listen.

Up ahead through the mist loomed the Mackay fortress. Though not as graceful or elegant as Brice's, it was every bit as well fortified. Built into the side of a rocky crag, there was only one way in or out. Its massive twin doors were surrounded by a courtyard. On either side of the doors stood armed guards, their swords at the ready. They saluted their leader as the door was thrown open and servants hurried out to assist the tired men.

The servants did not seem surprised by the presence of an unknown woman, and Meredith found herself wondering whether Holden Mackay often brought other unfortunate females to his fortress.

A sullen-looking woman stepped forward. Her dull gaze, Meredith noted, remained downcast, as though afraid to look directly at her master. How many beatings had she endured at the hands of this man?

"Shall I take the woman to your chambers, my lord?"

"Nay. No one touches the female. She will go with me."

He lifted Meredith effortlessly from the horse and set her on her feet. And though she swayed a moment he made no effort to steady her. Catching her bound hands he led her roughly across the courtyard and up great stone steps to the upper floor. He paused outside a door and threw back a heavy timber that barred it. Opening the door he revealed a small windowless room.

Thrusting her inside he set a taper in a sconce along the wall and growled, "You will stay here until I am ready for you."

She saw the smile that gave him a cruel, feral look. He withdrew a dirk from his waistband and advanced toward her, watching her eyes.

Meredith noted the blood that still oozed from his shoulder. Did he intend to retaliate for the wound she had inflicted? She thought of the dirk at her own waistband. In close hand-to-hand combat, Mackay would have the advantage. He was twice her size and weight. And she had already tasted his strength.

He saw the flicker of fear in her eyes as he moved closer. But though she was bound to be afraid of him, she lifted her chin in a defiant gesture and faced him boldly.

Damn the woman! Why did she not beg, or at least flinch?

He stood before her, the blade of the dirk glinting in the candlelight. Without a word he caught her hands and brought the knife cleanly through the rope that bound them.

Though she felt a rush of relief at his gesture, she prayed that no emotion showed on her face.

"If you are wise you will sleep. For you shall have little of that tonight."

He turned away and strode across the room.

She watched as the door closed. She heard the timber being thrown into place. And with her ear to the door she listened as Mackay's footsteps receded.

She began an immediate search of the chamber. Apparently it had been a storage room of sorts. Though it contained several pallets and mounds of furs, there was little else. The room was cold. There was no fireplace. And except for the door, which was bolted by a heavy timber, there was no other way out.

Wrapping herself in several layers of fur, Meredith fell upon a pallet to fight off the chill that rattled her teeth. Despite her best intentions, she gave in to an overpowering weariness and slept.

* * *

Brice rode at the head of his line of men, setting a brisk pace. Though tree limbs snagged at his sleeves and raked his face, he could not slow down. One thought drummed through his mind. Meredith. His beautiful, beloved Meredith was now in the hands of a brute. A brute who would take delight in causing her pain and humiliation.

"We must not take a direct route to Mackay's fortress," Angus advised.

"And why not? We know who has Meredith."

"Aye, old friend. But has it not occurred to you that Mackay might expect you to follow?"

"I will follow. To the ends of the earth and back to rescue my woman."

"It is what Mackay hopes for. Then he will have it all. Meredith to abuse, and you to kill when you attack him in a blind rage."

"What would you have me do?" Brice slowed his mount as they approached a boulder-strewn ridge. "Leave Meredith to that monster?"

"Nay." Angus put a hand on his friend's shoulder. "All of us know what you are suffering. If it were Mistress Snow who found herself in the clutches of Mackay, I would move heaven and earth to save her."

Brice shot a look at his friend. It was more of an admission than Angus had ever volunteered before.

"But I would hope that you and the others would keep me from doing something foolish."

Brice took a long breath, then nudged his horse into a brisk walk. "How then do you propose to keep me from doing something foolish, old friend?"

"While we ride north we must come up with a plan. 'Twould do no good to ride blindly into a trap."

Brice nodded. "I will think on it."

Angus smiled. "Think with your head, Brice, not with your heart."

Meredith heard the sound of the heavy timber being scraped back. She sat up, instantly alert. The door was pulled open. Holden Mackay strode into the room. He wore clean, dry clothes. At his shoulder was a fresh dressing covering the wound Meredith had inflicted with her sword.

Mackay was followed by a figure in a dark hooded cloak. Upon closer inspection Meredith realized the figure was a woman. A short, stooped woman.

Her cloak was damp, which indicated that she did not live within the walls of this fortress. She had been brought from somewhere outside Mackay's home.

"Well? Is she not a prize?" Holden Mackay's voice bounced about the small room. The stench of ale clung to him.

"I cannot tell, with all those clothes."

"Soon enough you will see her without them." Mackay grasped Meredith's arm and hauled her toward the open doorway. "Come. We will retire to my chambers."

Meredith was led down a long hallway and into a cavernous room. Several servants moved about, stoking the fire in the great stone fireplace, setting out an assortment of beautiful gowns on a fur-covered bed. At Mackay's command the servants hurried from the room and closed the door behind them.

Meredith stared at the huge basin of water in front of the fireplace, then at the array of gowns spread out on the bed. At her arched look, Mackay gave her an evil leer.

"You are here to amuse me, Meredith MacAlpin. I want you to look like a lady when I take you. Not," he added, pointing at her breeches and tunic, "like some muddy stable boy."

"Rowena," he said to the stooped woman. "You will bathe the lady and wash her hair in scented water."

"Aye, my lord." The woman tossed aside her cape and walked toward Meredith.

"Do not touch me," Meredith said sharply. "I am capable of undressing myself."

Instantly the woman paused and glanced at Mackay, awaiting his orders.

"We are not barbarians here." His voice was low with seething anger. "I can give you everything that Brice Campbell gave you. Especially servants to assist you. You would not know it to look at her, but Rowena was once an assistant to royalty."

Meredith studied the woman. Despite her crooked spine there was a look of elegance about her. And the gown she wore beneath the damp cloak was expertly tailored.

What would it hurt to allow her to assist? Meredith wondered. It would certainly buy some time. She was away from that horrid storage room and into a room with doors and windows that afforded some means of escape. That was a first step. But she needed time to formulate a plan.

While Mackay crossed the room Meredith took a moment to peer about. There were two windows, which apparently led to balconies. A possible means of escape. Unless the guards were still posted below in the courtyard.

Mackay peered at the gowns spread out on his bed. He lifted a shimmering white satin gown, encrusted with pearls, and ran his hand suggestively across the bodice. "She will wear this one," he said to Rowena.

Then to Meredith he added, "It will remind me of the bride Brice Campbell abducted from the altar. The woman who will now be my bride." He threw back his head and roared with laughter at his own joke. "At least until I tire of her."

"Surely you do not intend to watch while I undress her and bathe her?"

The laughter was gone. His voice was low and dangerous. "And why not? I am her captor. I will do whatever pleases me."

He sat in a chair stretching his long legs out in front of him. "Remove her cloak."

The woman seemed to hesitate, then stepped forward and slipped the heavy cloak from Meredith's shoulders. It dropped to the floor.

Meredith forced herself to show no emotion as the woman reached for the tunic and removed it. Beneath the tunic Meredith was wearing one of Brice's saffron shirts.

"'Tis a man's shirt." Rowena's voice was low, cultured, reminding Meredith of the women who surrounded the queen.

"Aye. And not fit to cover a woman's body." Mackay pointed a finger. "Remove it."

Before Rowena could reach for the buttons of the shirt, Meredith stopped her. "It is a shame—" she spoke directly to the woman, ignoring Holden "—that your lord Mackay cannot be with his men in the great hall, drinking ale and sharing stories of their exciting hunt this day."

Mackay's eyes narrowed. "What game do you play with me, wench?"

"Game?" Meredith gave him an innocent smile. "I merely thought you would be more comfortable with your men than here with women, sharing women's talk."

To Rowena she said in a conspiratorial tone, "Did you know that my lord Mackay hunts humans in the forest? Female humans are his favorite game. Because most of them are helpless. Most," she said with meaning, "but not all."

Out of the corner of her eye she saw Holden Mackay rub a hand over his stiff shoulder.

"How many females have you captured in the past year, my lord?"

For one long minute Mackay could only stare at her. Then he leaped up with a look of fire in his eyes. "I need some ale." He stepped to the door, intent upon calling to a servant. From below he heard the sound of laughter drifting from the great hall, where his men were gathered before the fire.

Below stairs, his men would not make him feel foolish for having nearly been beaten by a woman. Below stairs, there was the comradeship of men who had gone to battle together and had tales of bravery to share.

As a servant stepped forward, Mackay shook his head and sent her away.

For one long minute he turned and stared at the little female who taunted him, who infuriated him. With a look of menace he hissed, "Much as I would enjoy watching you bathe and dress, I would enjoy a tankard or two with the men more." He strode to the door, then turned with a gleam of laughter in his eyes. "Besides, my lady, I will have the pleasure of undressing you myself in just a very short time. And then we shall see who is the victor and who the vanquished."

He pointed to the white gown on the bed. "Remember, woman, I want her to look like the bride Brice Campbell abducted from the altar. The bride Brice Campbell will never have for himself."

His words brought a terrible shaft of pain. But she must not let him see how easily he could hurt her.

Mackay gave a hollow laugh and turned away.

Through narrowed eyes Meredith watched as the door closed behind him. In that brief moment she had noted the guards, whose presence would make her escape more difficult. But she was not about to despair. There were still the windows. And if that attempt failed, she would find another means of escape.

As Holden Mackay's booming voice rang through the hallway, she vowed that he would never hold her in this prison of horrors.

She touched a hand to the dirk hidden at her waist. And no matter what, she would never again allow him to sully her with his touch.

Chapter Eighteen

Brice and Angus lay on their stomachs on a ridge that afforded them a view of Holden Mackay's fortress. For nearly an hour they had noted every sign of movement outside the castle.

They had watched with great interest as a horse and rider approached the courtyard. The rider, a stooped old crone in a dark, shapeless cloak, had slid from the back of the horse and had been greeted warmly by the guards. A bundle had been removed from behind the saddle. Within minutes the doors to the castle were opened to admit the rider and bundle.

While Angus continued to lie and watch, Brice got to his knees and kneaded the stiffness in his shoulders.

"I tell you the best way to attack is simply to storm the courtyard and kill the guards." Brice's tone was harsh with determination.

Angus grimaced. "The doors will be braced from within. 'Twould take a battering ram to force them open."

"Every minute we wait is another minute of agony for Meredith."

"Aye." Angus noted his friend's drooping shoulders. "Do you think I do not know? But there are only ten and two of us. There could be many more times our number within the castle walls. If we can surprise them, we have a chance. But if the guards have time to shout a warning, all is lost."

"Aye." Brice stood, running a hand through his hair. "But with every passing moment I grow desperate."

"I know."

Just then both men looked up as Alston hurried toward them. "Two riders approach."

"Are they headed for Mackay's fortress?"

"Aye, Brice. They are just below us on that ridge. See?" He pointed and the two men followed his direction.

Brice's eyes narrowed thoughtfully, then he turned to Angus and saw that he was smiling. Both men had come to the same decision.

"They are the perfect foil," Brice said. "At all cost we must intercept them before they reach the fortress."

Alston's lips curved into a smile beneath his bushy red beard. "Leave them to me."

A few moments later, as Brice and Angus watched, the two riders were suddenly knocked from their mounts. There was a brief sound of a scuffle. And then the riders' clothes were being removed.

Within a matter of minutes Brice and Angus had exchanged clothes and horses with the dead men.

"You will watch until you see us enter the doors to the fortress," Brice instructed his men. "Before the doors can be closed, you must disarm the guards and storm the castle. Else, all is lost."

"Aye. Have no fear." Alston looked around at the others who nodded and indicated their eagerness to attack. "It will be done."

Meredith stood facing Rowena. She had managed to get rid of Holden Mackay. Now the only one who stood in the way of her freedom was this hunchbacked woman. She would bide her time and watch and listen. And when the time was right . . .

Rowena dipped a hand in the water. "Disrobe, my lady, and I will wash your hair and see to your bath."

For the moment, Meredith decided to go along with the woman's wishes. Slipping the dirk from her waistband she buried it beneath her folded cloak, then removed her shirt and breeches, carefully folding them as well.

As she crossed the room Rowena studied her with a professional eye. "You have a lovely body, my lady. 'Twould please me to create gowns for you."

"Did you sew all these?" Meredith swept her hand to indicate the gowns that littered the bed.

"Aye. These are a sample of my wares."

"Yours is a fine talent."

Meredith saw the woman beam at her compliment. As Rowena helped her into the water and began lathering Meredith's hair she said, "I was once the royal seamstress."

"You sewed for Queen Mary?"

"Aye." The woman's tone grew dreamy. "I was but ten and three when I accompanied the infant queen to France. Because of my deformity, 'twas determined that I would never marry. So I was taught from childhood how to sew. When the queen mother, Marie de Guise, saw my work, she insisted that I would spend my life dressing her child."

"How wonderful. Did you enjoy your time in France?"

"At first. It was so gay there. There were so many balls and state dinners. I was kept so busy I hardly had time to sleep. I was given a little room filled with bolts of silks and satins and a clean bed of my own. Though it was drafty, and far from the queen and her ladies-in-waiting, it was heaven after the humble cottage I had been born in here in the Highlands."

Meredith leaned back in the water, loving the feel of the woman's strong hands against her scalp.

She had been cold, so cold, on the long journey from Kinloch House to this ancient fortress. The warmth of the bath, the fingers at her scalp, threatened to lull her into a false sense of security. She cautioned herself to stay alert to any chance at escape.

"It all sounds wonderful."

Meredith heard the note of pain that crept into Rowena's tone. "Aye. It was. For a time. But when the young queen married the dauphin, his mother, Catherine de' Medici, stated that I was an embarrassment at Court. She insisted that I be sent back to Scotland at once."

Meredith's sense of fair play overcame her earlier dislike of this woman. "Was the queen not able to use her influence on your behalf?"

"Influence." Rowena gave a hollow laugh. "As long as Catherine de' Medici lives, there is no other influence in France save hers."

"But Queen Mary has returned from France." Meredith sat up as the woman wrapped a linen about her damp hair. "Perhaps you should entreat her to reinstate your position and once again use your talents."

Rowena toweled Meredith's hair vigorously, then picked up a cake of fragrant soap. Her tone was one of resignation. "I am a humble Highlander. The queen is surrounded by important people, her time taken up with matters of state. By now she has forgotten her childhood dressmaker. There is no way I could ever approach her."

"What of your lord Mackay? Could he not use his influence as a Highland chief to intercede with the queen?"

"My lord Mackay," Rowena said with a note of contempt, "would never act as an intermediary for one of his

clan. He is a cruel leader who thinks only of his own pleasures."

"Then why do you assist him in this?"

The woman looked away, unable to meet Meredith's
steady gaze. In a soft voice she whispered, "I must survive,
my lady. To refuse Holden Mackay is to invite death."

Meredith fell silent for a moment. She had not given a
thought to the many people who were at his mercy.

"What made him so?"

Rowena handed the soap to Meredith, then lifted a kettle
of hot water from the fire. As she emptied it into the bath
she said, "It is rumored that when he was born, his father,
Douglas Mackay, was engaged in a terrible battle with
English soldiers who had stormed their Highland fortress.
One of the soldiers ran his sword through the swollen stomach of Douglas's wife, Genevieve, who was close to her birthing. Genevieve died, but a servant delivered the bloody
bairn and placed it in Douglas's arms. He scarce looked at
the babe before turning it over to be suckled by a village
woman who had also recently given birth."

So caught up in the story was Meredith that she barely
took time to appreciate the luxury of her bath. In minutes
she stood and wrapped herself in the linen offered by Rowena. Seated before the fire she listened while Rowena dressed
her hair and continued the tale.

"Douglas Mackay was gone for two years, locked in terrible battle with the English. When he returned, he stopped
at the village and claimed his son, who was still living in the
cottage of the woman who had nursed him. Father and son
were never apart after that. When Douglas Mackay died,
Holden Mackay became obsessed with amassing as much
land and power as he could."

"But the death of his mother at the hands of the English and his own cruel birth should not be sufficient reason to be cruel to his people."

Rowena's voice lowered to a murmur, as though fearing that at any moment the object of their discussion might come through the door and overhear her words.

"There are those who say that Douglas Mackay's son was too frail to live, and that the village wench gave up her own son in order to ensure that he would be laird of the manor. Others even whisper that Douglas Mackay's son was murdered by the woman in order to place her own son in the laird's castle. Whatever the truth, she carried it to her grave. But until the day she died, Holden Mackay was devoted to her. It was she who was his adviser; she who taught him greed and avarice and spurred him on to achieve even greater wealth and power than his father before him."

Meredith was too stunned to speak. That might explain Mackay's cruelty. If he was raised from birth to lie and steal another's inheritance, he would become the kind of man who would stop at nothing to succeed.

"Why did Holden Mackay ride with Brice Campbell?" Meredith asked suddenly.

"My lord Mackay boasted that it was his intention to befriend the Highland Barbarian and discover his weaknesses. In that way, he could overthrow Brice Campbell and claim his land and titles."

"Titles?"

"Aye, my lady. Did you not know that Brice Campbell is also Earl of Kinloch? His father was held in highest esteem by King James, until he fell into disfavor just before his death. Despite the blot on his name the queen considers Brice Campbell to be a noble man." Her voice lowered. "But there are those who would disgrace him and force the queen to award his land and titles to others."

Meredith sensed the hand of another in all this. "Could it be that Gareth MacKenzie and Holden Mackay have joined forces in order to destroy Brice and divide his wealth between them?"

"There are many who covet the land and titles of Brice Campbell, my lady."

Meredith was aware of the warmth in Rowena's tone when she spoke of Brice.

"Do you know my lord Campbell?"

"Oh, aye," Rowena said softly. "He was one of the few at Court in France who treated me with kindness." Her tone betrayed her pain. "There are many who fear those who are different. And many more who are merely offended by my appearance."

Meredith felt a wave of compassion for this woman. If only there were some way to erase her pain.

"When Catherine de' Medici ordered me returned to Scotland, it was Brice Campbell who gallantly offered to accompany me. And when I first returned to the Highlands, Holden Mackay promised Brice Campbell that I would be taken care of as befits a royal seamstress." Rowena's voice hardened. "But when Brice Campbell returned to his own castle, I was told that the only thing I would be given was the humble cottage where I was born. I have been forced to accept whatever scraps my lord Mackay tosses to me. I am no better than a beaten dog. It is the way Holden Mackay keeps all of his people obedient to his every wish."

Meredith's earlier resolve returned. She must escape this madman. At any cost.

"Here, my lady," Rowena said, lifting the white gown in her hands. "You must hurry and prepare for your laird. He will be coming for you soon."

When the woman crossed the room, her eyes widened in surprise. In Meredith's hand was the small, deadly dirk.

"My lady..."

"Be still." Meredith moved closer, lifting the knife in a menacing manner. "Put down the gown and remove your clothes."

"My..."

"Quickly."

When Rowena had removed her clothes, Meredith pointed to the white gown. "Now put it on."

"But my lady, it will never fit."

"Do it."

Meredith watched as the woman, with trembling hands, pulled the gown over her head.

"You will sit there," Meredith ordered, pointing to a bench in front of the fire.

When Rowena was seated, Meredith hurriedly pulled on her shirt, tunic and breeches, then stepped into her boots. "With your cloak to hide beneath, the guards will not stop me."

"Perhaps. But they will know that I am not you," Rowena protested.

"Aye." Meredith paused, then lifted a lacy shawl from the bed and placed it over the woman's head. With her hair covered, and the folds hiding the slight hump on her back, the guards would be fooled if they were given only a glimpse.

"Hold out your hands," Meredith commanded.

"My lady, there is no reason to tie me," Rowena said softly as Meredith tore the ribbons from her chemise to use as cord. "I would gladly take your place in order to help you escape this prison."

Her words came as a surprise.

"I thank you." Meredith looked into the woman's eyes and could read her sincerity. "But think about your own safety. If it looks as though you gave me aid or comfort,

Holden Mackay would have every reason to kill you. If, however, he finds your hands tied and your mouth covered, he will believe that I overpowered you." She smiled. "As I nearly overpowered him in the forest."

The woman nodded at the wisdom of Meredith's words.

"Forgive me," Meredith whispered as she tied Rowena's hands. "And thank you for not fighting me." She smiled then, and Rowena realized how truly lovely she was. "As desperate as I am to escape Holden Mackay, I know that I could not have used this dirk on you."

"Godspeed."

"Thank you." Meredith tied a strip of cloth across Rowena's mouth, then fixed the folds of the shawl until she was satisfied that the bindings could not be seen from the doorway.

She tucked the dirk into her waistband, then bundled up the gowns that were strewn about the bed. When all was in readiness she drew the hood of the cloak about her head, took a deep breath, hunched herself over and pulled open the door.

The guards caught a glimpse of the woman, gowned in white, sitting quietly on a chair before the fire. As Meredith pulled the door shut behind her and started toward the stairs, she could hear the guards laughing and speculating about the fate of the poor wench.

With her heart pounding and her palms damp with sweat Meredith descended the stairs. Just as she reached the bottom she found herself face-to-face with Holden Mackay.

His steps were slightly unsteady as he approached her. In his hand was a tankard. He reeked of ale.

"Have you made the wench ready for me?"

"Aye, my lord."

As she began to move past him his hand snaked out, forcing her to stop. Her heartbeat began hammering so loudly in her chest she was certain he could hear it. He had seen through her disguise. She had not hunched herself over far enough. Perhaps a strand of her hair peeked out from beneath the hood. Something had given her away.

"Ten gold sovereigns," he said. "The sum we agreed upon."

"Aye." Her throat was so constricted with fear that the word came out as barely more than a croak.

She opened her palm and prayed that her hand would not tremble. He dropped the coins with hardly more than a glance, then stalked up the stairs.

It took all her willpower to keep from running. But if she was to fool the guards at the door, she must behave as Rowena would.

With halting steps she approached the huge front doors. A servant removed the bracing timber and pulled the heavy doors open. When the guards outside spotted her, one of them retrieved her horse, and even secured the bundle of gowns behind the saddle.

With the guard's assistance, Meredith pulled herself up and nudged the horse into a trot.

As she rode across the courtyard she spotted two riders approaching. Again her heart began a painful hammering in her chest. If Holden Mackay had already reached his chambers, he would discover Rowena in her place. And if he were to call out now, these two riders would seize her and return her to certain death.

She nudged her horse into a run. As she passed the two riders, she kept her face averted.

The two, intent upon their mission, barely noticed the old hunched crone who passed them in the courtyard.

Chapter Nineteen

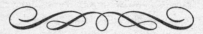

As the hunched woman approached on her horse, Brice felt a prickly feeling at the base of his neck. Something was very wrong. Something he couldn't quite place. Then, as horse and rider drew nearer, a name came into his mind.

Rowena. Of course. The young hunchbacked seamstress who had been cruelly banished by Catherine de' Medici had been from the Mackay clan. He had accompanied her from France to her home in the Highlands, where Holden Mackay had promised to see to her care. Brice felt a momentary stab of regret. He had been too busy to see if Mackay had lived up to his promise.

Rowena had always been an open, friendly woman. That would explain her warm reception by the guards in the courtyard. The soldiers, if they were a decent sort, would take the time to chat with her, assist her.

With hasty movements he pulled the plumed hat low on his head and kept his gaze downcast. If she was familiar with all the soldiers at Mackay's fortress, she might recognize that he and Angus were imposters. Worse, if she were to recognize him from their days at the French Court, she would call out his name. All their carefully laid plans would be for naught.

From the corner of his eye he watched as horse and rider galloped past. She had not even given him so much as a glance.

For another moment he continued to feel that tingling sensation, as though something was not quite right. He shrugged it off. The worst thing a warrior could do before going into battle was to allow himself to be distracted.

He and Angus approached the guards. He experienced the rush of energy he always felt just before battle. Their plan was going to work. He knew it. He felt it.

As their horses drew near, one of the guards called out to a servant inside the house, announcing their arrival. The timber bracing the doors was thrown aside and the doors swung open. Even as a stable boy was reaching for the reins of their horses, Brice and Angus, heads lowered, hats pulled low, were swinging from the saddle and striding toward the open doors.

Once inside they waited as the servant greeted them and began to close the heavy doors. A movement in the shadows of the courtyard alerted Brice and Angus that their men were in place and already overpowering the unsuspecting guards outside.

Drawing a dirk from his waist Angus held the blade to the servant's throat.

"Step away from the door," he ordered.

The wide-eyed servant obeyed.

"Where is your master?" At the man's momentary silence Brice pulled his sword from the scabbard.

The servant stammered, "My lord Mackay has gone to his chambers."

"Where?"

The servant pointed up the wide stone stairs.

"And the woman?"

The servant blinked, then stared transfixed at the sword in Brice's hand. "With my lord Mackay."

Brice's hand tightened about the sword. He would kill Mackay. With his bare hands if necessary. "And where are his men?"

"In the great hall, my lord." The servant pointed again, then trembled in fear as Brice's men poured through the open front doors.

"Go to Meredith," Angus whispered. "We will take Mackay's men."

"Aye." With his sword drawn, Brice started up the stairs.

Just then the door to the great hall opened and several of Mackay's men, obviously drunk, stumbled out. For a moment they simply stared at the dozen strangers who advanced on them. Then, with a shout, they drew their weapons.

Within minutes the rest of Mackay's men spilled through the door of the great hall and joined the battle. Though Brice longed to go to Meredith's aid, he knew that his men were greatly outnumbered.

Without a thought to his own safety, he leaped the several steps that separated them and joined in the fighting.

The air was filled with the sound of sword striking sword as every man fought for his life.

Two men advanced on Brice. With flashing blade he disarmed the first, then traded thrusts with the second soldier, backing him to the wall. As the soldier brought his arm high for the final thrust, Brice was a step quicker, and his blade pierced the man's heart. Clutching his chest the man dropped to the floor. Before Brice could catch his breath the first man, now armed with another sword, took up the fight. Again Brice was forced to defend himself.

This man was a far better swordsman than the other. It took all of Brice's skill to evade his thrusts. But at last he left the man gravely wounded.

Turning away, Brice found himself facing three more opponents. As they fought, Brice felt his energy flagging. The wounds from which he had so recently recovered had left him too drained. Had he possessed less skill with a sword, he would have joined the others who lay on the floor of the great hall, writhing and twisting in pain.

"Behind you," Brice shouted to Angus.

Angus turned to find a swordsman about to land a deadly blow. With agile steps Angus managed to evade the man's blade. With one quick thrust, the man joined his comrades who lay dead and wounded.

"My thanks, old friend." As Angus turned his head he saw two swordsmen behind Brice, about to attack while he fended off a third.

Immediately Angus leaped to Brice's aid. But even while he and Brice fought the three, he could see what a terrible effort this battle was costing his friend. Though Brice's thrusts with the sword were still straight and true, there was a sheen on his forehead and his eyes were glazed with pain.

Two men cut between them, dueling until one of them fell. The other quickly joined in the fight against Angus, and he found himself unable to worry any longer about Brice. It would take all of his concentration and skill just to stay alive.

While Brice continued fighting off the attack of two men, a tall, massive figure filled the doorway. While Brice stood, sword to sword with his opponents, he glanced up and saw Holden Mackay, his sword at the ready, a look of murderous rage in his eyes.

All feeling of weakness vanished. For Brice there was only a wild, churning hatred for this vicious monster. With a few skillful thrusts Brice disposed of his opponents and advanced upon Mackay.

"What have you done to Meredith?"

For a moment Mackay could only stare at Brice with hate-glazed eyes. Could it be that the fool did not know? His lips curled back in a sneer of contempt. "I do not answer to the likes of you, Campbell."

He raised his sword and brought the blade down with a vicious swipe, tearing open the shoulder wound that only days ago had finally mended.

With blood seeping through his tunic Brice stood his ground, exchanging thrust after thrust with Holden Mackay. And although the man was not the swordsman Brice was, he had size on his side, and the wound that was draining Brice of precious strength.

"I warned you that one day you would rue the day you banished me from your castle." Mackay advanced, again and again, until Brice felt the cold stone wall at his back. "You should not have tried to keep the woman for yourself. The spoils of war should be shared by all." He thrust his sword and watched as Brice dodged, and the blade pierced only the fabric of his tunic. He pulled his sword back and advanced again, determined to pin Brice. "Now," he said through gritted teeth, "I will have it all. Your titles, your lands and your woman."

In an unexpectedly agile move, Brice leaped aside and turned, pinning Mackay to the wall. With his sword pointed at Mackay's chest he hissed, "What are you talking about, man? What is this nonsense about titles and lands?"

Holden Mackay's eyes narrowed. "I will tell you, if you promise to let me live."

"I make you no such promise. Now," Brice said, bringing the point of the sword closer, until it pierced Mackay's tunic and shirt and drew a faint thread of blood, "tell me what nonsense you speak."

Mackay began talking quickly, as if hoping to postpone the inevitable. "Gareth MacKenzie offered to share half your land with me, and give me all your titles, if I would but penetrate your castle and discover your weaknesses."

"MacKenzie. So you have been in this with him from the beginning."

"Aye." Mackay's eyes glittered. "I have long coveted the title Earl of Kinloch."

Brice thought of his own disdain for such things. "The title was my father's. He earned it. What good would it do another?"

"It would make me a titled gentleman. I would be as acceptable at Court as you."

"All the titles in the world will not make you what you can never be, Mackay." He ignored the man's look of hatred and pressed the tip of his sword over his opponent's heart. "What has any of this to do with Meredith?"

"Nothing," Mackay snapped. "The woman was a personal prize that I decided to steal from you the way you stole her from MacKenzie."

Brice's eyes narrowed. "You knew all along that I killed the wrong MacKenzie?"

"Aye." Mackay threw back his head and laughed. "You killed the puny brother, Desmond, whose only crime was obeying his eldest brother."

Brice felt a terrible urge to plunge the sword through this monster's heart. But he cautioned himself to hold his famous temper in check. He still did not know the fate of Meredith.

"Is the lady in your chambers?" Brice asked softly.

Mackay's eyes suddenly burned with a feverish light. By the gods, the man did not know. What a wonderful irony.

"The lady is someplace where you will never find her."

"You will tell me or I will make your life a living hell." As Brice shouted, Mackay suddenly brought his hand upward, revealing the razor edge of his sword. He would have severed Brice's head had Angus not stepped in and thrust his blade through Mackay's heart.

A look of shock crossed Holden Mackay's face as he realized he had been mortally wounded. As Angus pulled back his sword, Mackay slumped to the floor. A great gush of blood spilled down Mackay's tunic, the brilliant scarlet spreading in ever-widening circles. His face grew ashen.

With a sense of horror at the turn of events, Brice knelt beside Holden Mackay and whispered, "Before it is too late, tell me what you have done with Meredith."

Mackay's lips curled into a smile. His eyes stared straight ahead. And when Brice touched a hand to the man's throat, he realized there was no pulse.

"May you burn in hell," Brice whispered.

With a growing sense of desperation he raced up the stone steps, Angus just paces behind him. In the great hall, the last of Holden Mackay's men joined his comrades in death.

Rowena sat in the middle of the floor and tasted her own blood. Dazed, she wiped a hand across her mouth and stared for long minutes at her bloodstained hand. Slowly, stiffly, she drew herself to a chair and sat, staring at the flames of the fire, seeing nothing.

The lady Meredith had been correct to tie her and cover her mouth. That alone had probably saved her life. When Holden Mackay had discovered Rowena in place of Meredith, he had demanded an explanation. Once he realized that his prize had eluded him, he had flown into a murderous rage. Never, never had Rowena seen anyone in such a fury. He had picked up a chair and hurled it against the wall where it shattered into a thousand pieces. Still not satisfied he had lifted Rowena from the chair and slapped her, beat her, pummeled her, until she begged for mercy. It was only her plea that she had been overpowered that had saved her from certain death. That, and the sound of battle below stairs. When Holden Mackay left the room to join the fighting, he had been gripped by a lust for blood.

Rowena knew that she should escape while there was yet time. But she seemed gripped by some sort of lethargy. And so she sat, listening to the sounds of battle, staring into the flames of the fire.

That was how Brice found her.

He raced into the chamber, with Angus just a few paces behind. Both men came to an abrupt halt at the sight that greeted them. The room looked more like a battlefield than the laird of the manor's sleeping chamber.

With eyes dulled by pain Rowena glanced up. In a trembling voice she whispered, "My lord Campbell."

He was shocked at finding her here. "Rowena? Did we not pass you some hours ago outside Mackay's fortress?"

She stared in silence, not seeming to comprehend.

Seeing her shocking condition he went to her and knelt before her. He took her hands in his. They were cold. So cold. In her eyes was a glazed look, such as he had often seen in men after battle.

In a tone meant to soothe he said softly, "You are safe now, Rowena. Holden Mackay is dead."

He watched her shoulders slump as she seemed to let go of the terrible tension that had held her in its grip. A sigh rose up from deep within her.

"What has happened here? Where is the lady Meredith?"

Rowena stared into his dark eyes. He had always been so kind to her. She wanted to return the favor. But it was hard to think.

"Holden Mackay sent for me to dress the lady." She stared down at the bloodstained gown she was wearing. "He chose this gown. He said he wanted her to look like the bride you would never have."

Brice's eyes narrowed. In his jaw a little muscle began working.

"Did he touch her?" His hand curled into a fist. "Did he harm her in any way?"

She shook her head.

"You are certain?"

Rowena met his gaze, then slowly nodded.

He felt as if a band around his heart had suddenly been removed. With a rush of relief he asked softly, "Why are you wearing the gown, Rowena?"

Why indeed? She shook her head, as if to erase the pain of Holden Mackay's fists. Slowly, haltingly, her mind cleared.

"When we were alone, the lady Meredith asked me to change clothes with her. I put on her gown."

"Why?"

"So that when she opened the door, the guards outside would think that she was still seated by the fire."

"Why would they not recognize her when she opened the door?"

"The lady Meredith was disguised as me."

Brice could only stare in silence as the meaning sank in.

"The lady wore my cloak and carried my bundle of gowns."

Brice turned to Angus, who stood listening. "The old crone outside the fortress."

Angus let out a moan. "Brice, she is hours ahead of us on the trail."

"Aye." Brice glanced down at Rowena. "And this dazed, bloody creature has taken a beating for her kindness."

"Had it not been for the lady Meredith's thoughtfulness, I feel certain I would not have survived."

Brice's eyes narrowed. "Why do you say that?"

"Because the lady kindly bound my hands and covered my mouth, saying that unless Holden Mackay was convinced that I had been forced into this, he would kill me."

Brice and Angus surveyed the rubble that had once been Holden Mackay's sleeping chamber.

Brice's tone was low with wonder. "From the looks of all this, the lady made a wise decision." He turned to Angus. "Assemble the men. We ride to the Lowlands. And pray we catch up to Meredith before Gareth MacKenzie gets news of what has happened here this day."

Rowena caught Brice's hand. Her eyes brimming with tears she whispered, "Tell the lady Meredith that I send my gratitude. And my love."

Love. Brice felt a sudden shaft of fear that left his blood like ice. Love was what drove him. It was what caused him such pain.

"Pray I do not fail her," he murmured. "Or I may as well join Holden Mackay in the fires of hell."

Chapter Twenty

Meredith was hopelessly lost.

The route from Kinloch House had been difficult enough to follow. But now that she had managed to escape Mackay's fortress, she could locate no familiar landmarks. Plunging blindly through thickets and woods, she urged her mount onward, praying that eventually she would find a river or stream that would point the way homeward.

The only thought that gave her the strength to go on was the knowledge that she had persuaded Brice to remain in his Highland home where he was safe. Whenever she felt the fear begin to engulf her, she would cling to her belief that Brice was out of harm's way. She closed her eyes, trying to picture him as she had so often seen him, lounging in a chair drawn up before the fire, a tankard of ale in his hand, his men clustered about him and Jamie hanging on his every word.

She experienced such a crushing sense of loss, she felt tears mist her eyes.

As she passed beneath a low-hanging branch, it clawed at her cloak and snagged her hair. She ducked low in the saddle, then noted over her shoulder that the bundle of gowns had pried open. Bare branches suddenly bloomed with brilliant scarlet satin, rich ruby velvet and shimmering blue silk.

A breeze caught the rest of the gowns, blowing them into the brush where they were caught and held by jagged stalks and thorns.

"I leave them to you, Mistress Tree." The strange sight gave her sagging spirits a lift. "May you look fetching for years to come."

The sound of her own voice startled her. She had been alone on the trail too long.

Spotting an open area just ahead, she dug in her heels and urged her horse into a run.

Night had long ago fallen and still Meredith continued on. The land had gentled, from steep rocky crags to rolling hills. Though she was not yet asleep, she was no longer alert. The whir and chirp of night creatures and the steady even gait of her mount lulled her until her head bobbed.

When the horse came to the banks of a river, he lowered his head and drank. The sound startled Meredith. She was instantly awake.

For long minutes she merely stared at the narrow ribbon of water glistening in the moonlight. Then she let out a cry of pure delight. Wonder of wonders. They were standing on the banks of the river Tweed. It meandered through gently rolling countryside. Looming in the distance were the Cheviot Hills. Beyond that, England. And there, on the opposite shore of the river, its many turrets shimmering in the silvery moonlight, stood MacAlpin Castle.

Home. There were so many times when she had thought she would never see it again. Now that she was so near, the tears would not stop flowing.

She slid from the saddle and knelt on the bank of the river, drinking her fill. Removing her cloak, she folded it carefully. Then, pulling herself once more into the saddle, she urged her mount into the shallows. Soon the water was deep, and the horse began to swim, while Meredith gamely held on. By the time they had crossed to the far shore, both horse and rider were shivering from the frigid waters. She bundled herself into the cloak and, bending low over the horse's neck, urged him into a trot. The night air danced through her hair as her horse's hooves ate up the final miles.

How Meredith longed to cross the courtyard at breakneck speed and toss the reins to a stable boy as she had done hundreds of times in her young life. How she yearned to hear old Bancroft, the aging doorkeeper, announce her to those assembled. How desperately she desired to throw herself into the outstretched arms of her sisters and hug them to her. But all that must wait.

First she must ascertain that Gareth MacKenzie and his men had not already taken over MacAlpin Castle, hoping to ensnare her in a trap.

Leaving her horse in a stand of trees, she crept toward the rear tower of the castle. Shivering as she crouched behind a row of shrubbery, she studied the darkened windows of the upper floor.

Meredith and her sisters had often horrified their mother by climbing to the upper balconies. They knew every stone, every indentation, along the wall. Now such childhood games would stand her in good stead. Tossing aside her cloak she reached up until she located the jagged edge of a stone with her fingertips. Pulling herself up, she probed with the toe of her boot until she found a foothold. Stretching, she found another rough stone and pulled herself up farther. Again and again she repeated the process until she had reached the upper balcony of her old room. With her last ounce of strength she pulled herself over the edge of the balcony and slumped to the floor, taking in great gulps of air.

As her breathing grew more steady she paused to listen. There was no sound of movement within her old rooms. Crossing the balcony she stepped into the sitting chamber. The room was cold. No fire had been set in the fireplace.

She crossed the room quickly and listened at the door before throwing it open and striding quickly down the hall. She passed several doors before pausing to listen once again.

She pushed open a door and stepped inside. In the sitting chamber a fire crackled invitingly. From the sleeping chamber beyond she could see the movement of shadows. Someone was preparing for sleep.

She crept silently across the room and peered through the open doorway. When she was certain that the persons inside were friendly, she stepped into the light.

Meredith drank in the sight of the slender young woman with coal-black hair that fell in waves to below her waist. Her blue-violet eyes widened for a moment. Then Brenna was racing to her, arms outstretched.

"Meredith. Oh, Meredith."

The two young women fell into each other's arms, laughing and crying.

"They told us you were dead."

"You can see for yourself that I am not."

"Oh. Let me look at you." Brenna held her older sister at arm's length, then drew her close again, trying to swallow the lump that seemed stuck in her throat. "You are so cold. And wet."

"Aye to both. My horse and I swam the river."

"Here." Brenna began removing Meredith's wet clothes, then wrapped her in an ermine-lined cape.

Across the room an old woman stared at Meredith as if seeing a ghost. When at last she was able to gather her wits about her she hurried across the room and began fussing with the cape.

"Ye'll catch the death. Out of those wet boots now."

"Morna." Meredith caught the old woman's hands and held them when she tried to pull away. "There's no need to fuss."

"But I..." Her old nurse found that she could not go on. With tears streaming down her wrinkled cheeks she drew the girl into her arms and clung to her.

"Oh, lass. I thought I'd never see you again."

"There now, Morna. You see, I'm fine. Just fine." Meredith patted her shoulder, then held her a little away.

Brenna, watching the reunion between Meredith and their old nurse, whispered, "I must tell Megan."

Meredith caught her arm and held her when she tried to turn away. In low tones she said, "Only Megan. You must tell no one else that I am here."

Brenna studied her sister for a moment, then nodded. "I will tell no one."

Within minutes Brenna had returned with their youngest sister. At ten and four Megan was already as tall as Meredith and still growing. Her hair the color of ripe wheat and gold-flecked eyes in a small oval face promised a rare beauty when she grew to womanhood.

She pulled her arm free of Brenna's grasp and stamped her foot. "What is it you cannot tell me?"

"This." Brenna stood aside and allowed the youngest to peer into her sleeping chamber.

Megan's eyes grew round before filling with tears. In quick strides she was across the room, locked in her sister's embrace.

"Oh, Meredith. We thought you dead."

"Aye. I have heard the rumors of my death. Though I must confess there were many times when I thought they would be true."

"Why must you keep your presence here a secret?"

"I am here to unmask Gareth MacKenzie as a liar."

Megan turned to stare at sixteen-year-old Brenna, who looked stricken.

Seeing her shock and pain Meredith placed an arm about her sister's shoulders. "What is it, Brenna? What have I said to cause such pain?"

"Gareth has been—courting me." Brenna thought of the uneasy hours she had been forced to spend in the company of Gareth MacKenzie. "Thankfully I have never been alone with him. Old Morna saw to that," Brenna said with a smile. Her smile suddenly faded. "Gareth has already sought the approval of the clan to wed me when he returns from Edinburgh."

"He is not here then?"

"Nay."

At her words, Meredith felt a wave of relief. At least for now she was safe.

"He left only yesterday with a large party of MacKenzie men to seek an audience with the queen. He intends to ask Her Majesty to declare you dead."

"And to declare you the next of kin." Meredith stroked her sister's hair before asking, "Do you love Gareth MacKenzie?"

"Love him?" Brenna trembled and Meredith drew her close. Against her cheek the young woman murmured, "I do not love Gareth. I fear him. But Duncan and the others urged me to accept his offer of marriage in order to secure our borders."

"They said Brenna could do no less than you, Meredith, if she were truly the MacAlpin." Megan's tawny eyes flashed. "We knew that you did not love Desmond. Yet you agreed to wed him for the sake of the clan."

"Aye. Poor Duncan," Meredith said softly. "He was so certain that Gareth would be as good as his word. He is like all the others. Fooled by Gareth's charm, and unable to see what he really is."

"Enough about Gareth MacKenzie. How did you manage to escape from the Highland Barbarian?" Megan asked.

Meredith suddenly realized how much had happened since her abduction at the altar. Her own sisters did not even know about the man who had stolen her heart.

"Come," Meredith said, catching Megan's hand. "Find me a night shift. We will all climb into Brenna's big bed and whisper and giggle as we did when we were children. I will tell you everything."

"I will go below stairs and fetch some biscuits. I've heard those Highlanders eat raw meat." Morna studied the slender girl and added, "It's a wonder you haven't faded away in that barbaric place."

Meredith laughed at her old nurse's words. But as Morna started for the door, Meredith's words stopped her. "Not a word that I am here."

"Not even to Bancroft?"

"Nay. Not even to him. For a little while longer no one must know that I am still alive. Do you understand?"

"Aye."

Morna put her hand on the door but Meredith again stopped her. With the beginnings of a smile she added, "Bring meat and cheese as well. And mayhaps a goblet of ale."

"Ale?" Brenna turned to study her sister.

Meredith laughed. "Aye. Ale. I have learned to like the taste of it. Besides it will warm me."

"I will fetch a night shift," Megan called.

"Hurry back. There is much to tell."

Already the horrors of the past months were slipping from her. How good it was to be home. What a joy to be able to share with her sisters all that had happened since last they were together.

"And he loves you, too?"

"Aye."

"It is all so romantic." Brenna sighed.

"But I do not understand," Megan interrupted. "He is a Highlander. A barbarian. And you are the MacAlpin."

"He is an educated, cultured gentleman," Meredith said. "And a trusted friend of the queen."

"If Brice Campbell loves you, why did he let you come alone to clear his good name?"

"Because now that everyone thinks him dead, he will no longer be hunted. If he shows himself, he will once again have to fear for his life."

"But he is the Highland Barbarian," Megan persisted. "He is the strongest, bravest man alive. All my life I have heard songs sung about him, legends whispered about him. If he is so fearless, why would he be afraid to be hunted?"

Meredith was growing weary of her sisters' questions. Brenna had wanted to know everything, from the moment she had been abducted at the altar, to the moment she climbed the wall of the MacAlpin Castle. Megan, on the other hand, was only interested in the reasons why.

"Do you think he will come for you?" Brenna asked, stifling a yawn.

"Nay." Meredith was annoyed to feel tears spring to her eyes. She tried to blink them away but they continued until they clouded her vision. "I begged him to stay where he would be safe."

"But if he loved you he would care more about your safety than his own."

Megan turned to study her oldest sister. "Are you crying?" In consternation she turned to the middle sister. "Brenna, I have never before seen Meredith cry."

Brenna, the most tenderhearted of the three, shot her youngest sister a warning look. "Our Meredith is merely overwrought. It has been a long and difficult journey for her. She has a right to cry."

"I am not crying." Meredith wiped her eyes with the back of her hand and rolled to one side, pulling the linens over her head. With a sniff she said softly, "Well, perhaps I am. It is just that I am so weary. You are correct. It has been an arduous journey. But it is not yet over."

"What do you mean? You are home now." Brenna yanked the linens aside and peered at her sister.

Meredith sat up. "I mean that on the morrow I must ride to Edinburgh and gain an audience with the queen before Gareth has a chance to have me declared dead."

"But that is not why you are crying," Megan said matter-of-factly.

"Nay." Meredith caught her youngest sister's hands. "I am crying because I miss Brice. And I fear I will never see him again."

Megan's lips curved down into a frown, instantly hating the man who was the cause of Meredith's tears. "If Brice Campbell truly loved you, he would want to know that you were safe."

"But I begged him not to follow me."

"Aye. But how can the man claim to love you and not know if you survived the journey from the Highlands to your home?"

Sixteen-year-old Brenna wrapped an arm about Meredith's shoulder and glared at her younger sister. "Meredith has been through enough. We will not add to her burden."

To Meredith she whispered, "You must sleep now. On the morrow you will feel better about everything."

"Aye. It is sleep that I need."

Meredith kissed her sisters, then lay back against the cushions and closed her eyes. But sleep would not come. Megan's questions echoed in her mind. It was true that she had begged Brice to remain where he was safe. And she truly thought that was what she wanted. But now the nagging thought slipped unbidden to her mind. Did Brice love her enough to risk his own life? Or had he already put her out of his mind, while he and his men filled their hours in the Highlands, rebuilding Kinloch House?

When at last she fell into a restless sleep, she was plagued with dark, sinister dreams, in which a stranger stalked her. At times the stranger had golden hair and tawny skin. She knew that he was truly evil. But at other times the stranger was someone more familiar to her. His hair was dark, burnished, his eyes compelling. There was about him an aura of danger as well, which she strove to ignore. But each time she ran to him he melted into the shadows and disappeared into the Highland mist.

Chapter Twenty-One

Y ou must not go to Edinburgh."

Meredith faced her two sisters. Though it was not yet dawn, the first hint of light could be seen on the horizon.

Over their protests she had pulled on her breeches and tunic and Rowena's heavy hooded cloak. While they begged and pleaded, she had insisted upon hurrying to the wooded place where she had left her horse.

Brenna was close to tears. Megan was indignant.

"Would you rather have me declared dead by the queen and have Brenna forced to wed Gareth MacKenzie?"

"Nay." Megan tried another tactic. "But in Edinburgh you will have to face Gareth MacKenzie alone. If you stay here, we will call all the MacAlpins together and plot to kill him when he returns."

"I must stop Gareth from meeting with the queen. If she declares me dead, how do I prove that I am not?"

Megan shook her head in disgust. In the darkness her blond tresses were a sliver of light.

"Then if you must go, we must ride with you."

"Impossible."

Brenna, who had wisely remained silent during most of this argument, jumped on Megan's suggestion. "Aye. We must go together."

"It is a long and difficult journey," Meredith said as patiently as she could. "If something were to happen to me, it would give me comfort to know that my sisters are here to carry on."

"But it will give us no comfort to wonder what has happened to you, or even whether or not you succeed. We must ride together."

Meredith pulled up her hood and took up the reins. If necessary, she would remind them who was in charge here.

"I am the MacAlpin," she said with quiet authority. "And I declare that I shall ride alone to Edinburgh to gain an audience with the queen. As my sisters, you shall remain here at MacAlpin Castle and carry on in my absence."

"Carry on." Megan sniffed. "We will wilt on the vine while you have all the excitement of Court "

"There is danger and intrigue at Court," Meredith said sternly. "And I will not have my younger sisters exposed to it. You will do as I command."

Brenna and Megan stared at her in sullen silence. Never before had they seen Meredith use such overbearing tactics. It was beneath her.

Suddenly she opened her arms and both sisters flew to her. Against their cheeks she murmured, "Forgive me. I love you both too much to see you harmed. Besides, if I am to arrive in Edinburgh before Gareth MacKenzie and his men I must ride quickly and I must ride alone."

"If any harm comes to you," Brenna worried aloud, "I will never forgive myself for staying behind."

"If you are killed," Megan said menacingly, "I will hate you forever."

At her outburst, Brenna and Meredith stared at her in stunned silence. Then they fell into each other's arms in a fit of laughter. For a moment Megan could only stare at them.

Then, joining in the laughter, she hugged her older sisters when they regained their composure.

"Godspeed," Brenna whispered.

"Hurry home," Megan said.

Meredith pulled herself into the saddle and spurred her horse into a gallop to hide the tears that spilled from her eyes, staining her cheeks. At the crest of a hill she turned and waved. Below her, the two young women, tears blurring their vision, waved until she disappeared from view. And even then, though they could no longer see her, they stood shivering in the predawn chill, unable to tear themselves away.

"Summon a groomsman," Megan said suddenly.

"What?" Brenna stared at her younger sister in surprise. "Why?"

"Because we must hurry if we are to stay close to Meredith on the trail to Edinburgh."

For long minutes Brenna regarded the young girl whose amber eyes glittered with a strange light. Then she did something completely out of character. With a delighted little laugh she lifted her skirts and began running toward the stables. Over her shoulder she called, "We will need travelling clothes. Oh, and our finest gowns for our first meeting with the queen."

Brice had never pushed himself so relentlessly. Though he was near exhaustion from the battle at Holden Mackay's fortress, he gave himself no time to rest.

He and Angus moved among the men, dressing their wounds. Six of their company had suffered wounds severe enough to force them to return to their homes. Brice assigned the other five of his men to return with them, knowing that the wounded could still encounter small groups of Mackay's men in the forest.

That left Brice and Angus to follow the trail left by Meredith.

"We will travel faster alone," he remarked when Angus grumbled about their lack of additional men. "We know where the lady is headed. Now we need only catch her before she can fall into any more danger."

"If there is danger," Angus muttered, saddling both their horses while Brice tended to his own shoulder wound, "you can be certain the lady will find it."

Brice looked up with a frown. "Aye. The lady Meredith does seem to have a gift for getting herself into trouble."

Seeing that his old friend was having trouble with the dressing, Angus dropped the reins and finished tying the strip of cloth about Brice's shoulder.

"Thank you, my friend. Now let us catch the lady. Before she manages to surprise us again."

"MacAlpin Castle?"

Brice and Angus sat astride their horses at the river's edge.

To the east the sky was aflame with the first rosy slashes of dawn light.

"Aye." There was a softness in Brice's tone as he thought of Meredith, asleep in one of the upper chambers. "There is no time to waste. We will surprise her by entering before the household is awake."

Leading the way, he urged his mount into the icy waters, with Angus following. Once on the other bank they dug in their heels and raced across the last miles that separated them from MacAlpin Castle.

At the courtyard they took note of the saddled horses and the packhorses laden with provisions.

"We have arrived not a moment too soon." Before Brice could slide from the saddle the heavy door was opened and two young women, dressed for traveling, emerged.

At the sight of him both of them fell back in alarm.

"I am Brice Campbell," he said, studying them through narrowed eyes. "And from your sister's description of you, I feel as though I already know you." He turned to the sweet, shy beauty whose raven hair had been coiled about her head in a regal style. Her blue-violet eyes were ringed with black lashes. "You are Brenna, whose talents for cooking and sewing are legend. Meredith claims that men from both Scotland and England would beg for a kind look from you. And you," he said, turning to Megan, "are determined to never submit to any man. But with hair the color of gold and eyes like a cat, I suspect you will break many a man's heart."

The sisters' mouths opened in surprise; their eyes widened as he bowed before them.

"I come for Meredith MacAlpin."

How splendid he looked, with his skin tanned and leathery from the sun and his burnished locks tumbling about his forehead. Meredith had boasted about his muscled arms and thighs, his superior strength. And neither girl had forgotten the way he had looked at the cathedral when he had appeared out of the mists to abduct their sister.

Brenna and Megan turned to each other. On Brenna's lovely face was a look of real pleasure. The romantic in her had devoutly prayed that her sister's lover would overcome all obstacles to claim what was his.

"So you are Brice Campbell." She began to take a step forward but Megan caught her arm, holding her back. "We have heard all about you."

At that Brice's brows lifted. "So. Meredith is here. Take me to her at once."

As he slid from the saddle, both young women realized just how tall he was. They had not been prepared for such a fearsome man.

It was Megan who now took charge. "Meredith is not here."

"Do not lie to me, girl." He used his most forceful tone, hoping to intimidate her. "Your sister just admitted that she was here."

"She was. But she is no longer."

His eyes narrowed. "Where has she gone?"

Megan caught Brenna's hand and shot her a warning look.

When they remained silent Brice turned to Angus, who had remained in the saddle, watching with interest. "As you can see, these two do not intend to cooperate with us." He winked. "We shall just have to stay here and watch and wait."

"But you cannot," Megan said, stamping her foot. "If we wait any longer she will get too far ahead . . ."

Brice's eyes crinkled as the smile touched his lips. "So. You intend to follow Meredith. Without her knowledge, apparently. Where does she go?"

Megan and Brenna turned to each other, then clamped their mouths shut.

Brice crossed his arms over his chest and leaned against the packhorse. "A pity you will not need these supplies. I suppose in a few hours it will be too late."

"Tell him," Brenna whispered.

Megan shook her head.

"Tell me." Though Brice kept his tone low, he wanted to throttle the young girl who displayed a cool manner remarkably like her eldest sister's.

"Only if you agree to take us along."

"What?" Brice's hands dropped to his sides, the fists clenched. He took a step closer, his eyes narrowing in sudden anger.

"I will tell you where Meredith is headed. But you must agree to take us along."

"I have had enough." Brice turned to Angus. "Come. We will follow her trail."

"It will take you too long," Megan said. "But if you take us with you, we can save you the trouble of searching for a trail."

"You will slow us down. Your sister's life depends upon finding her before Gareth MacKenzie does."

"We will not slow you. We promise. And as for Gareth." Megan shot a look at her sister, who gave her an encouraging nod. "We know where he is, too."

Brice gave a sigh of impatience. "You are testing me, woman. Tell me. And quickly."

"First you must promise to take us along."

Brice gritted his teeth, then nodded.

With a smile Megan said, "Meredith rides to Edinburgh, to seek an audience with the queen before Gareth has her declared dead."

Reluctantly Brice helped the two girls onto their horses before pulling himself up into the saddle. "Angus, take the reins of that packhorse. We ride to Edinburgh."

"To see the queen." As they urged their horses into a trot, Brenna and Megan shouted the words in unison.

To the two young women, it was to be a grand adventure. To Brice, it was a race against time.

Meredith sat astride her horse and drank in the sights of the capital city of Scotland. She had traveled across High Street, surely the cleanest in the world. Channels had been dug on either side to drain off the rain. There were stone houses with their wooden galleries, and farther on, the grand houses and gardens of the Canongate, which led to Holyroodhouse. In Market Cross, with its stocks and pillories, men and women in somber dress bustled about. People gathered to talk, to shop, to discuss the events at Court. Goldsmith apprentices from Elphinstone Court and tinsmiths from West Bow were here, along with stall holders from Lawnmarket. And while they discoursed about the queen, they also discussed the one who ruled Edinburgh and all of Scotland with even more power and persuasion than the queen. John Knox, leader of the Kirk, had spoken openly about his contempt for petticoat government. He waited and watched and vowed that this Catholic queen would feel the wrath of God, as had her mother, as had her young French husband.

Meredith studied the dark, menacing fortress that was home to the queen. Its towers and battlements were not unlike Brice's Highland fortress. And yet it lacked the warm setting and opulence of a Highland castle.

Brice, she thought as she made her way to Holyroodhouse. If only Brice were here with her. She resented the heat she felt at the mere thought of him. She resented the way her body betrayed her, going all weak and soft when she needed to be strong. She would put aside all thought of Brice Campbell. For now she needed a clear head, a steady heartbeat.

She straightened her spine and urged her mount on, past Tolbooth Prison. How many were incarcerated there, she wondered, whose only crimes were gaiety and laughter? She thought of the love, the laughter, she had discovered at Kinloch House. How far away seemed the Highlands. How far away her love.

With every clatter of her horse's hooves she drew nearer and nearer to Holyroodhouse. And farther away from any chance to escape Gareth MacKenzie. For surely Gareth was already here in the capital city, awaiting an audience with the queen.

With fear and trepidation she approached the gates of the palace. There were perhaps two dozen people milling about, awaiting notification of an appointment with the queen. Many of them grumbled that they had been forced to return each day for more than two weeks.

Meredith's heart fell. Two weeks. She had not thought about where she would stay in Edinburgh if the queen would not see her immediately.

And what of Gareth MacKenzie? Would he not also be here, or one of his men? Unless, she thought with a jolt, he had been granted an audience immediately. Then, of course, she would already have been declared dead.

She studied the faces in the crowd. There were men and women in their finest clothing, looking extremely uncomfortable. There were clan chiefs, noblemen and a few common citizens who had matters of interest to discuss with the queen. But there was no sign of MacKenzie men. Meredith gave a sigh of relief when she did not see Gareth. So far, her luck was holding.

As the gatekeeper approached, she made a sudden decision. With so many important people waiting for an audience, the queen could not be expected to remember one insignificant Highland wench. But there was one whose name would open doors.

As the gatekeeper asked her name and the purpose of her visit she replied in a clear voice, "Meredith MacAlpin to see the queen. At the request of Brice Campbell."

Her words were recorded and the gatekeeper withdrew. Slipping from the saddle she led her horse to a trough where he drank.

Within a matter of minutes the gatekeeper returned and in a loud voice called, "Meredith MacAlpin."

She was aware of the sudden interest of the crowd. Men who had hardly glanced her way now studied her with open curiosity. Women, aghast at the sight of a woman wearing men's breeches and tunic, and flaunting the Highland saffron shirt, watched her with looks that ranged from contempt to amazement.

As she pushed her way to the front of the crowd, the gatekeeper opened the gates and waited until she and her mount were safely inside.

As the heavy gates were closing he bowed slightly and said, "Welcome to Holyroodhouse, my lady. The queen will see you now."

Chapter Twenty-Two

The sky was an angry black cauldron that boiled and bubbled. And when at last the billowing black clouds opened up, the downpour was sudden and drenching.

Seeking shelter for the women, Brice found a small hay barn. Inside they inhaled the sweet moist fragrance of dry hay.

Brenna drew her cape about her and found a spot in the corner where she could sit and observe. From what she had seen, this man who had won her sister's undying love was nothing more than a tough, demanding warrior who drove himself and everyone around him to the point of exhaustion. What was it about him that endeared him to Meredith?

Megan, shaking the raindrops from her cloak, paced about, curiosity causing her to peer into every nook. Satisfied, she perched on a mound of hay in the middle of the room and watched as Brice and Angus led the horses in out of the rain. She was clearly fascinated by this man who had stolen her sister, and then captured her heart.

As was her nature she blurted out what was on her mind, without regard to sensitivities.

"Why did you let Meredith undertake such a dangerous journey alone?"

Brice rubbed a rough cloth over his horse's quivering flank, choosing to remain silent for several minutes while he completed his task. "Your sister gave me no choice. She slipped away after I had fallen asleep."

"It seems to have taken you a good deal of time to catch up with her."

"We had..." He glanced toward Angus. "An unexpected diversion."

"What diversion?" Megan demanded.

If he found her questions impertinent he gave no indication. "Meredith was abducted by a Highland chief."

He saw the girl's mouth drop open. His words were clipped, his description sparse to save Meredith's sisters from undue suffering. "When my men and I went to her aid, we found ourselves badly outnumbered."

"Not for the first time," Angus said dryly.

"Aye." Brice chuckled. "It seems to be a habit with us of late, old friend."

Brenna noted the affection between the two men. It warmed her to know that Brice Campbell could inspire such devotion. Perhaps there was something endearing about him. For her sister's sake she hoped so.

As he worked Brenna noted the way Brice favored one arm. "Could that be where you were wounded, my lord?"

"What wound?" Megan asked.

Surprised, Brice glanced up. "You are very observant, Brenna. I thought I hid it rather well." He touched a hand to the tunic that covered the dressing at his shoulder.

"You were wounded?" Megan studied him a moment, deciding that she liked the idea of a wounded man continuing on, in the face of pain. "But you managed to best your enemy." Megan's eyes danced with the thought of the battle. Like Meredith she would not hesitate to take up a sword.

"If you were fighting to save Meredith, how did she manage to elude you?"

Brice's smile grew. "Your sister seems to have become a master of disguise."

At the incredulous look on the faces of the two young women he added, "She pretended to be a hunchbacked seamstress, and slipped past everyone."

"Even you?" Megan asked.

"Aye. I confess I did not recognize her."

"And now she is ahead of you again," Brenna said thoughtfully.

"Not for long." Brice strode to the door and peered at the darkened sky. "Already the clouds are breaking to the west. Within the hour we will be once more on the road to Edinburgh."

"Do you make haste because you love Meredith?" Megan asked boldly. "Or are you merely angry that a woman has bested you?"

Brice stood by the door, illuminated by a flash of lightning. At that moment he looked as fearsome as any barbarian. "You have the right to know my feelings for your sister. And so I will tell you." He turned toward the quiet, regal Brenna. "Both of you." In a voice that managed to be both tender and fierce he said, "I love Meredith."

"If you love her as you claim," Megan demanded, "why did you not immediately return her to her home?"

"I did not trust Gareth MacKenzie. I feared for her safety here in the Lowlands."

"And so you placed her in even more danger in your Highlands."

"Sometimes, little one," Brice said to Megan, "we are asked to choose between the lesser of evils. I thought that by keeping Meredith with me in the Highlands, I could be close enough to always come to her aid." He turned to study the progress of the storm. His face was ruggedly handsome in profile. His eyes narrowed thoughtfully. "I have learned that I cannot always be beside the woman I love, to protect her from every harm. I pray the Fates are there to guide her hand and her sword."

"You are a patient man," Brenna said with quiet conviction.

"Nay." Brice almost laughed at the thought. "I am far from patient. But I have had to learn a valuable lesson. When we love someone we are sometimes called upon to make terrible decisions. Decisions that cause pain for one while offering great rewards for the other."

"I do not understand," Megan said.

"He means," Brenna said softly, "that by allowing Meredith to return to the Lowlands to clear his name, he risks losing her."

At her words Brice's hands balled into fists by his side.

"My lord," Brenna said softly.

He turned to her.

"Would you pay any price for my sister's happiness?"

"Aye. Any price." His tone was low, vibrating with feeling. "I would even risk losing her if it meant her happiness."

Brenna shivered. The intensity of his words frightened her. She prayed that neither her beloved older sister nor this fierce Highland warrior would be forced to pay the ultimate price.

Dusk was settling over the city when Brice led his tired party through the streets of Edinburgh.

"It is too late to approach Holyroodhouse this evening. We will have to wait until the morrow to arrange an audience with the queen. For now I will see about lodging."

Leading the way down a narrow lane near the Canongate, he stopped before a tidy inn. Leaving the women with Angus, Brice went inside. Within minutes he was back to help the women dismount. Lifting their supplies from the packhorse, he led the way to a suite of comfortable rooms.

"Angus and I have the rooms across the hall," he explained. "The innkeeper will provide us with a meal. As soon as you have refreshed yourselves, you may join us below stairs to sup."

Megan and Brenna were grateful for the chance to wash away the grime of the journey. Running a brush through their tangled curls, they smoothed their gowns and draped shawls of delicate lace about their shoulders. Then they made their way to the dining room.

Brice and Angus were standing before a roaring fire, enjoying tankards of ale. Their conversation was low, muted. They looked up as the two young women entered.

"We will sit here." Brice led them to a table set with fine linen and china.

Under the direction of the innkeeper a serving wench offered goblets of wine to warm them. She passed around whole roasted goose, suet pudding and sweetbreads. With tea there were biscuits warm from the oven, spread with clotted cream and jam.

At last they sat back, content, replete.

"I do not remember when a meal tasted so lovely." Brenna sighed.

"Aye. 'Twas a difficult journey. But you were true to your word," Brice said, emptying his tankard. "You neither complained nor slowed us down."

Megan voiced the fear that none of them had been willing to put into words. "What of Meredith? Do you think she is as fortunate as we are, Brice?"

He glanced at Megan, then at her sister, and read the fear on both their faces. "Aye. Somewhere in Edinburgh she is sitting before a roaring fire, enjoying a fine meal." He could not allow himself to think about the alternative. He would not allow himself to think about his beloved Meredith prowling the darkened streets in search of decent lodging. And in the process, running into Gareth MacKenzie and his men.

Brice escorted the young women to their rooms, then returned to his own suite and reached for his sword and scabbard.

"Where do go you now, old friend?"

Brice turned to Angus. "Stay here and see to the safety of Meredith's sisters."

"And you?"

"I cannot sleep, knowing that Meredith is somewhere here in Edinburgh, possibly in grave danger."

"The city is too large to find one lone woman."

"Mayhaps. But I must try."

Angus watched as his friend stalked across the room. He listened as Brice's footsteps faded on the stairs. There would be no rest for Brice Campbell this night. Or any night until he once again held the woman **he** loved in his arms.

"Now where have you hidden away that rogue Brice Campbell and his beautiful hostage, Meredith Mac-Alpin?"

At the familiar majestic tones Meredith sat up and rubbed her eyes. God in heaven. She had fallen asleep in the queen's own chambers. How she must look with her hair in wild disarray and her clothes soiled from the long journey.

Her clothes. Meredith glanced down at the breeches and tunic and the faded cloak and let out a little gasp. This was not how she had planned on meeting the queen.

As she swung her legs to the floor the door was thrown open and the queen, followed by her ever-present Maries, strode into the room.

"Now where is that rogue?"

"Brice Campbell was not with her," Mary Fleming said gently. "Although the gatekeeper mentioned both names, the young woman was alone."

"It is true then. Brice is dead."

"Majesty." Meredith curtsied and kept her head lowered as she explained, "Brice is not dead."

She did not see the look that crossed the queen's face. A look of relief that slowly became a look of pleasure.

"I used Brice's name because I knew you would not remember me."

"Not remember the woman who pretended to be me at dinner?" The queen gave a musical laugh. "How could I ever forget you, Meredith MacAlpin?"

"I am honored, Majesty." Meredith dared to lift her head and realized that the queen was studying her carefully.

"Such an extraordinary traveling costume, Meredith."

"Aye, Majesty." Meredith blushed clear to her toes. "The breeches and tunic are Brice's. The cloak belonged to a wonderful seamstress who befriended me."

"Surely you have not ridden all the way from the Highlands?"

"I have, Majesty. But first I made a stop at my home on the Border."

"I have been hearing tales of murder along the Border," the queen said, taking a seat and indicating a chair for Meredith.

"There have been many murders, Majesty."

"'Tis said they are committed by the Highland Barbarian."

"You know that cannot be true." Meredith leaned forward, praying that the queen would allow her to speak frankly.

"And how would I know that?"

"You know Brice Campbell to be an honorable man."

"Aye. I do. But I did not think you shared my opinion. The last time I saw you, you were begging to be saved from his clutches."

Meredith saw the gleam of laughter in the queen's eyes and smiled. "So much has changed since last I saw you, Majesty."

"So it would seem." The queen signaled for wine. When it was poured, she lifted a goblet and waited until Meredith and the Maries did the same. "You must tell me everything that has happened between you and Brice since I left." The queen's eyes glittered with a strange light. "And you must leave nothing out."

"Oh, Majesty." Meredith took a sip of the wine, allowing its warmth to soothe. "There is so much to tell."

"We have all the time in the world."

While Meredith began, the servants brought in a sumptuous meal.

"So," the queen said as Meredith recounted the attack by Gareth MacKenzie and the resulting injury to Brice, "you found yourself fighting alongside Brice's men for your very life."

"Aye, Majesty. And when the battle was over, Kinloch House was burned and many of its inhabitants wounded. Among them Brice. We feared he would not live."

"And that is how the rumor of his death came about?"

"Aye. Gareth and his men found no heartbeat. Nor did I upon first examination. But finally I found a pulse, weak, feeble, but a sign of life nevertheless."

"And you bravely brought him through the crisis."

Meredith glanced toward the queen to see if she were jesting. But there was no hint of a smile on her face.

"Aye. He survived. Thanks be to God."

"Why did you leave him?"

"When I heard that Gareth MacKenzie intended to seek an audience with you and have me declared dead, I knew that I had to journey to Edinburgh and fight for my rights."

"Once again you have proven your mettle, Meredith MacAlpin. You make all Scotswomen proud." The queen allowed her gaze to linger a moment on Meredith's face before she turned to Mary Fleming. "Is it not Divine Providence that has sent her to us?"

Fleming nodded and spoke rapidly in French to the others, who began laughing and nodding.

"What is it, Majesty?"

The queen stood, drawing herself up to her full height before staring down at Meredith. "You are privileged to write history, Meredith MacAlpin. Because of your strong resemblance to your queen, and the fact that you have been sent to me at my very hour of need, you will provide a great service to your queen."

Meredith glanced uneasily around the table, puzzled by the tension she could feel.

"Tomorrow at Court, Meredith," the queen said somberly, "you will be me."

"You, Majesty? But where will you be?"

"I will be—indisposed," the queen said enigmatically.

"But why?"

The queen clapped her hands and began to laugh. "I cannot keep this a secret from you, Meredith. Tomorrow I am to be kidnapped by a secret admirer."

"Kidnapped." Meredith was thunderstruck.

"Aye. Is it not the most romantic thing you have ever heard of? Ever since I heard your story, I have yearned to experience such a thing. And now it has come to pass. A certain—nobleman desires to be alone with me. And since the queen can never be alone with a gentleman, I must arrange to be kidnapped. But, of course, if I were not to appear at Court, there would have to be a reasonable explanation. We had thought that I would plead one of my famous headaches. But now that you are here, I need not be absent from Court at all. Is this not truly exciting?"

"But, Majesty, there are affairs of state to be determined each day at Court. How can I handle such issues?"

"Simple. Whatever you decree, it is the decree of the queen."

"Majesty!" Meredith felt a sense of hysteria bubbling dangerously close to the surface. But the queen blithely went on making her plans.

"Flem will help you with names and faces. And Seton and Beaton will sit on either side of you for assistance. Because of you, your queen will experience a day of freedom, Meredith."

Feeling desperately alone, Meredith glanced about the room. Candles flickered in sconces along walls hung with rich French tapestries and gilt-framed mirrors. On the floor were elegant carpets. The table, the chairs, nearly all the furniture in the queen's sitting chamber, had been brought from France. The women seated around the queen giggled and made comments in French, and Mary responded rapidly in the same language.

As she sat in their midst, watching, listening, it occurred to Meredith that they could just as easily have been in the French Court. In fact, she realized with sudden knowledge, that was what Mary had created here in Edinburgh. Dismissing the somber landscape beyond the walls of Holyroodhouse, denying the tension created by John Knox against her, Mary had created a pale imitation of the Court in France, which she so desperately missed. The man she planned to meet secretly would take the place, for a while, of the husband she still mourned. And the women around her, wishing to see to her happiness, were part of the game.

It was all a game, Meredith thought with a sense of panic. The palace, the Court, the petitioners who awaited the verdict of their queen. All a terrible, awe-inspiring game. And on the morrow, she would become a key player in this deadly game. A game that as yet seemed to have no rules.

Chapter Twenty-Three

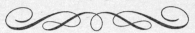

Brenna, Megan and Angus looked up from their early-morning meal as the door to the inn was thrown open. When Brice stepped inside Angus hurried to him. There was no need to ask the question that sprang to his lips. One look at the tight, hard set of Brice's mouth told Angus all he wanted to know.

"You did not find her."

"Not a trace." Brice ran a hand over the stubble of dark beard that covered his chin. "I inquired at every inn and stable. There has been no sign of her."

"Perhaps she was delayed along the way."

Brice's eyes were bleak. "Or ran into Gareth Mac-Kenzie's company."

"Come, old friend," Angus said gently. "Break your fast with us."

"Nay. We must hurry to Holyroodhouse and demand a private audience with the queen." He brushed past Angus. "I will make myself presentable and then we ride."

Brenna and Megan turned to each other with a growing sense of dread. They had not known until this moment that Brice had stayed out all night searching for Meredith. They pushed away from the table, feeling a hard knot of fear in the pit of their stomachs. What had happened to their beloved Meredith?

Within the hour the four were riding through the city to the queen's residence. The keeper of the gate of Holyroodhouse accepted a message from Brice, then withdrew. After what seemed an eternity he returned, along with a soldier who rolled the heavy gate open. The gatekeeper motioned for the four visitors to follow him.

Brice's look was impassive, his fears carefully hidden behind the mask of a proper nobleman. Behind him, Brenna and Megan could hardly contain their excitement. Despite their fears for their sister, one thought was uppermost in their minds. The palace. They were actually inside the palace and were going to meet the queen.

A servant drew open the heavy draperies, allowing the morning sunlight to stream into the room. In the ornate bed Meredith awoke from sleep as one drugged. After her exhausting journey from the Highlands, her body had begged for rest. And despite the fears that plagued her upon the queen's announcement the previous night, sleep had claimed her the moment she had lain her head upon the pillow.

"Meredith. Meredith." A hand tugged at her shoulder. The voice of Mary Fleming sounded urgent. "You must wake and dress quickly. You have visitors."

"Visitors?"

Fleming's mouth curved into a mysterious smile. "I think you will be pleased. Now make haste."

Next door, in the queen's chambers, Meredith could hear the sound of that familiar, haughty voice and the frantic activity of servants as they prepared their monarch.

Like one in a daze Meredith allowed herself to be bundled into one of the queen's own cut-velvet robes. Her hair was quickly brushed. Meredith was led into the queen's sitting chamber, where Mary, surrounded by her Maries, was being hastily prepared to receive visitors.

At least a dozen servants bustled about the room setting up a morning meal that could have fed an entire village.

When the queen was properly coifed and gowned, she nodded to Mary Seton. ''Show our visitors in.''

With a puzzled frown Meredith turned toward the door. For a moment she could only stare at the two young women who stood nervously together clutching each other's hands. Then with a shout, they rushed forward and fell into her arms.

''Oh, Brenna. Megan.'' With tears streaming down her cheeks Meredith caught them to her and hugged them fiercely.

''How in the world did you two get to Edinburgh? And however did you talk your way inside the castle?''

''We had help,'' Brenna said softly.

As she drew aside, Meredith became aware of the tall figure framed in the doorway. For a moment her heart forgot to beat.

''Brice? Oh, is it truly you?'' She started toward him, her arms outstretched. Then, remembering where she was, she stopped and clutched her hands together, drinking in the sight of him.

''You look—fatigued. You should not have attempted so long a journey.''

''I am fatigued because I spent the night searching for you, firebrand. And thinking you dead. Or worse.'' For the first time he allowed himself to smile as he crossed to her in quick strides and brought his hand to her cheek.

He studied the pallor of her skin, the dark circles beneath her eyes. ''Are you truly all right, Meredith?''

''Oh, now that I see you and my sisters—'' she turned and caught their hands ''—I feel wonderful.''

"Would you care to greet your queen now, Brice Campbell, or do you intend to stand there all morn and devour that maiden with your eyes?"

With a laugh Brice broke contact and crossed the room. With a deep bow he caught Mary's hand and brought it to his lips. Then, with a laugh, he lifted her out of her chair, swung her around and kissed her on each cheek before setting her on her feet.

"Rogue." She sighed, touching a hand to her cheek. "You are the only man who would ever dare to do such a thing."

"The only man, Majesty?"

Mary blushed furiously. "What have you heard?"

"Rumors." Brice's voice lowered, for her ears only. "The Border Earl of Bothwell is a virile, amorous man, Mary. But beware. A kingdom is at stake here."

Mary became noticibly agitated. With high color she turned to meet the two beautiful young strangers. "Who are these lovely creatures? Come greet your queen."

Meredith performed the introductions. "Majesty, may I present my sister, Brenna."

The dark-haired beauty curtsied, keeping her gaze lowered.

"And my youngest sister, Megan."

The blond imp curtsied as she had been taught, then boldly studied the queen.

"So there are two more like you. I can see that they will soon be breaking hearts across Scotland. Welcome to Holyroodhouse."

"And you know my old friend, Angus Gordon," Brice said, clapping a hand on Angus's shoulder.

"Of course. Welcome, Angus. Come," Mary said, taking Brice's hand and leading him to the table. "We will break our fast. And you will tell us why you have surprised us with this visit."

Though Brice managed to respond to all the queen's questions, he could not keep his eyes off the beautiful woman who sat across the table. How he longed to carry her away from the noise and babble, away from prying eyes, and share with her all the love that was stored inside his heart. It was not enough to know that she was safe. He needed to touch her, to gather her to him, to hold her.

"... several days?"

Brice tore his gaze from Meredith and turned to find the queen looking at him with a knowing smile.

"I am sorry, Majesty. I was—distracted."

"So you were." She smiled. "If you are not careful, my friend, there will be rumors."

He chuckled. "But there is no kingdom at stake."

"No, my dear rogue. Merely a pair of hearts." The queen stood, and everyone at table got to their feet.

"I have a long and exhausting day ahead of me." She could not stifle the smile that tugged at the corners of her lips. "You will excuse me. Brice," she added, "we will talk again on the morrow."

"As you wish." Brice bowed over her hand, then signaled for Angus and the others to follow him. At the doorway Mary called, "Meredith, you will stay awhile. We have business to attend to."

Meredith kissed her sisters' cheeks, then touched her hand to Brice's. Instantly she felt the heat and yearned for some time alone with him. There was so much she needed to tell him. So much she wanted to ask.

She watched as a servant led Brice and the others to a nearby chamber, where their every comfort would be taken care of.

When the door closed, Meredith turned toward the queen, who was issuing orders to her staff. "For the rest of the morning I shall be indisposed. There will be no exceptions."

The reality of what lay ahead caused Meredith's stomach to churn.

Surely in the light of day the queen would see the folly of her plan. It was unthinkable that Mary would permit herself to be abducted by a nobleman for the sake of a romantic interlude. She must realize the risk to her reputation if her secret was discovered. Further, could not the queen see how impossible it was for an imposter to assume the throne? Even for one day?

Meredith's head swam with questions as she turned to watch the flurry of activity. Several servants were busy laying out a gown of regal scarlet velvet, along with a tiara of diamonds and rubies, and a necklace of ornate gold filigree and matching rubies.

Meredith's mouth rounded in an O of appreciation. "Oh, Majesty, it is breathtakingly beautiful. You will look magnificent."

The queen smiled indulgently while her friends giggled like children.

"I will not be wearing it," Mary said without a trace of regret. "The gown is for you, Meredith."

"Majesty." Meredith drew back. "I could not. It is too fine."

"But you will be presiding over Court this day. You must look every inch the queen."

Meredith crossed her arms over her middle, feeling her stomach churn. "Please, Majesty. I beg you. Forget this foolish dream. You must not do this thing you plan."

"But I shall." The queen stood and walked to her, grasping her cold hands and forcing her to meet her steady gaze.

"For so long now I have dreamed of being, not the queen, but an ordinary woman. I want to experience what other women have, Meredith. I want to be loved like a woman. And you are going to make this dream possible."

"Majesty," Meredith whispered, forcing the words from a throat that had gone suddenly dry. "What will become of the people who come to the queen for solace, and find me instead? What of the pronouncements I make this day in your name? Are they all to be withdrawn on the morrow?"

"Nay, Meredith. Have no fear." Mary brought her arm about the trembling woman and drew her close. "When you sit upon the throne this day, you speak for the queen. You are the queen. Whatever you declare, it is law. And whatever you rescind, it is rescinded for all time. Is that clear?"

A violent tremor rocked the young woman's slender frame. "Oh, Majesty. That makes it even more difficult to bear. I am not worthy to pass judgment on others. I have not the right."

"I give you the right," the queen said sternly. "Am I not your queen?"

"Aye, Majesty."

"Then kneel, Meredith, and accept the edict of your queen."

Meredith knelt and the queen touched a hand to her shoulder. In regal tones she pronounced, "I, Mary Stuart, Queen of Scotland, do declare you, Meredith MacAlpin, the bearer of my name and seal this day. All that you proclaim on this day shall be law. Let no man rescind your orders."

Meredith swallowed down the little knot of fear that rose in her throat. When the queen caught her hands and drew her to her feet, she was startled to see that the Maries were no longer laughing. For the first time they realized what a dangerous scheme had been set in motion.

"Now," the queen said regally, "go to your sisters and the rogue who carries his heart on his sleeve. Confide in no one. And when it is time to dress for Court, you must do so without drawing undue attention to yourself." As Meredith prepared to make further protest, the queen gave her a friendly shove. "Go. I command you to put aside your fears."

Even though it was a royal command, Meredith knew it was impossible to obey. Her fears for what was to come could not be ignored.

The preparations for Court were a blur of activity. Meredith stood in the queen's chambers, staring at her reflection in a looking glass, while servants dressed her hair and helped her into her gown and jewels. When the crown of diamonds and rubies was placed upon her head, she felt as if the weight of the entire world had suddenly been thrust upon her.

She turned to where Mary stood, surrounded by her Maries. Wearing a flowing gossamer gown of palest pink, with her hair loose and falling in soft waves to her waist, the queen looked for the first time like the young girl she was. Her cheeks were flushed with the thrill of her adventure. Her eyes sparkled. With a little laugh she crossed the room and took Meredith's cold hands.

"Meredith MacAlpin. You have earned the undying gratitude of your queen."

"Majesty."

As Meredith began to curtsy Mary stopped her. "You will bow to no one this day. Remember. You are the queen."

As tears misted Meredith's eyes Mary called, "Flem, take Her Majesty to meet with Lord Aston." To Meredith she said softly, "He will go over your appointments this day, which have already been scheduled. If there is time he will ask you to read the list of petitioners."

So that the others could not hear, Meredith whispered, "Majesty, there is still time to end this charade."

"Look at me," the queen commanded.

Meredith stared into her eyes.

"Would you ask me to give up this one chance to live as others do?"

Meredith slowly shook her head. "I am unworthy to ask anything of you, Majesty."

"God bless you," the queen said with feeling. Then, hugging Meredith to her, she turned away.

Mary Fleming took Meredith's arm and led her to a small council chamber where the queen met daily with her advisers.

The keeper of the gate at Holyroodhouse strode toward the crowd of elegantly dressed men and women who gathered at the entrance of the castle. Unrolling his scroll, he began to read the list of names who would be granted an audience.

From their position in an upper window, Brenna and Megan watched the spectacle with avid interest. When Meredith had told them that they would be permitted to attend Court this day, they nearly fainted. Had it not been for the strong arms of the men who accompanied them, they would not have been brave enough to walk through the hallowed halls and follow the gnarled old man who led the procession to the throne room.

As they were ushered into the elegant great hall, they stared at lush tapestries depicting the royal lineage from the time of the first great Scottish king. The floors were covered with rich carpets bearing the royal seal. Around the room were chairs covered in regal red velvet. And on a raised dais stood a throne, covered in rich scarlet brocade. Slightly behind the throne to either side were chairs for the queen's advisers.

The petitioners were escorted to chairs in a gallery section set on either side of the throne. Brenna and Megan had hoped to find chairs in front, but most of the gallery was already filled. They were forced to take seats in the far corner of the gallery behind rows of spectators. Brice and Angus stood behind them.

A flurry of trumpets heralded the arrival of the queen. Brenna and Megan strained to see over the heads of the spectators, but all they caught was a glimpse of scarlet velvet and the glint of rubies and diamonds that adorned the royal crown.

For his part, Brice was completely disinterested in the pomp of the royal Court. He had had his fill of such things in his youth. His thoughts centered on only one. Meredith. To know that she was safe, and spending the day in the security of the queen's palace, filled his heart with peace.

Their brief meeting after morning meal had been unsatisfying. Though they had talked about her journey from the Highlands, and the perils they had both faced, there had been no time alone.

Tonight, he thought with a rush of heat. Tonight he would go to Meredith's chambers. And at last they would be reunited.

When the queen ascended the throne, Brice glanced at the two young women who actually trembled with excitement. For all his disenchantment with royalty, he realized he would enjoy watching the proceedings through the eyes of Brenna and Megan. If only Meredith could have joined him. Or better, if they could have slipped away during these long hours. But she had insisted that there were pressing matters that she must attend for the sake of the queen.

Brice's eyes narrowed. When he and Mary Stuart were alone on the morrow, he would confide his fears about Meredith's safety. And he would officially ask the queen to look into the mysterious murders taking place along the Border. It had never mattered to him before. Let others think what they wanted about him. But now it was time to clear his name. So that he could ask Meredith MacAlpin to share it.

Meredith's heart swelled as she walked up the aisle and lifted her hand to the masses of people who bowed and curtsied as she passed. She was experiencing her first taste of what it was like to be loved and revered by so many. And yet the nagging thought persisted. How could it be that none of them noticed that she was an imposter? Even Lord Aston, the queen's aide, had gone over the list of activities without so much as a pause to glance directly into her face. Did she dare to hope that she could get through the entire day without being found out?

As she took her seat upon the throne, she cast a benevolent smile over the crowd.

Lord Aston began reading the first petition. As he read from the scroll, Meredith allowed her gaze to scan the spectators. They were staring at her with such awe, she felt her throat go dry. What was she doing here? God in heaven. This was not some silly game being played out so that the queen could experience romance. This was, for many of the people seated before her, a matter of life and death.

As Lord Aston's voice droned on she lost her sense of concentration. It no longer mattered what the petitioner was requesting of his queen. She was an imposter. An ordinary woman who was being asked to make decisions that would affect the lives of the people she loved.

As Lord Aston finished his speech, Meredith waited for the voice of doom. Surely God would strike her down for such arrogance. She waited for the sound of thunder. Instead there was an ominous silence.

Meredith felt Flem's hand upon her arm and gave a guilty start, bringing her out of her reverie. What had just been requested of her? She couldn't think. Could not even recall the words that had just been spoken.

The crowd shifted uneasily as Lord Aston repeated the petition a second time. Forcing herself to pay attention, Meredith spoke in halting tones.

"I shall take the petitioner's request under advisement. Proceed with the next, Lord Aston."

The crowd gave a murmur of disapproval. They had come here to watch the high- and lowborn among them spar with the queen. They did not wish to have any controversial topics set aside.

Her aide seemed perplexed as he uncurled the second scroll and began to read. This one was easier. A petitioner requested that his neighbor's land be given to him because the neighbor had allowed the land to go fallow.

"What would you do with the land if I were to give it to you?" Meredith asked.

The portly man stood and bowed his head respectfully. Beside him, his wife beamed with pride at her husband's moment of glory.

"I would plant it with crops, Majesty. I have a fine, healthy herd and they have need of more food."

"And who would do this planting?"

"I have four strapping sons."

"You are truly blessed," Meredith said. She looked into the crowd. "Who owns this land?"

A plump woman, her gray hair pulled into an untidy knot, stood. "I do, Majesty."

"Do you have a husband?" Meredith asked.

"He died a year ago." The woman fingered a sash at her waist, too humble to look at the regal figure on the throne.

"Are there any sons who can work the land?"

"I have a son, Majesty. A bonnie lad he is. But he is off fighting the English who raided our Border."

"No other children?"

"There is a daughter, Majesty. Her husband was killed by the English, and she and her three bairns are now living with me. She and I have tried to till the soil but it is more than we can manage."

Meredith studied the woman, then glanced at the neighbor who desired her land. If only, she thought, life could always be equitable. But some were born with health, or acquired wealth, while others seemed always beaten down by the trials of this life.

"Until this woman's son returns and is able to work the land I will grant you permission to plant your crops on her land."

The man smiled, enormously pleased at his good fortune.

"Provided you give half your crops to your neighbor in payment for the use of such land."

The man's mouth dropped open. "But it is my labor, Majesty, that produces the crops."

"Aye. And her land. Furthermore, when her son returns, the land reverts to him and his mother."

"But, Majesty..."

"That is the judgment of your queen."

During this entire exchange, the crowd had grown very quiet. It was obvious, from the smiles on many of the faces, that they were pleased with the queen's decision.

At the queen's first words, Brenna and Megan stared at each other in shock. Though the clothes and jewels were those of a queen, the voice was Meredith's. There was no mistaking it. But though both girls craned to see over the crowd, they could not see their queen's face.

As distracted as Brice was, he, too, knew that the voice he was hearing was not that of Mary. From his position at the back of the gallery he studied the regal figure upon the throne.

By all that was holy. Meredith. Disguised as the queen.

A smile touched his lips and crinkled the corners of his eyes. So that was why she had been so unnerved this morrow. The rumors about the queen's tryst with Lord Bothwell were the truth. And once again his little firebrand was being shamelessly used by Mary.

Brenna and Megan tugged at his sleeve, eager to share their secret. But he put a finger to his lips and nodded. Puzzled, they turned around and continued to watch as this amazing charade was played out.

The petitions dragged on and Meredith handled those that were within her realm. Any that seemed too complicated, or too politically explosive, were "taken under advisement." Each time Meredith made a decision her voice grew stronger, her mannerisms more regal, until she found herself thinking and acting like the queen.

When a nervous old woman in a shabby dress petitioned to force a nobleman to pay her for the clothes she had made him, Meredith turned to study the finely attired man.

"Did the lady make the clothes you are wearing?"

He bowed slightly before his queen. "Aye, Majesty. But one of my own servants had to strengthen the seam here," he said pointing, "or I would not have been able to wear it."

"Has she made other clothes as well?"

"Some, Majesty. But all of them needed additional work."

"And you have paid this woman nothing?"

"Her work was shoddy."

"Yet you continue to wear the clothes she made."

The man fell silent.

"You will pay her the sum you promised her, and ten gold sovereigns more."

"More! Why, Majesty?"

"Because you did not live up to the terms of your agreement. If the clothes needed further sewing, they should have been returned immediately for repairs. The fact that you accepted them, and wore them, proves that they were adequate."

The look on the man's face told the spectators that he was not happy with the judgment. But the dressmaker saw the smiles on the faces of the crowd as she passed.

"I would take a moment," the queen said to Lord Aston as he prepared to read the next petition.

He paused.

Seeing the dressmaker's dilemma had reminded her of a debt she owed. This may be her only chance to repay it.

In regal tones Meredith said, "I decree that the official dressmaker to the queen shall be Rowena, a woman from the Highland clan Mackay. See that she is brought to Edinburgh this day in the queen's own carriage."

Lord Aston recorded the edict on a scroll, then stood and cleared his throat before proceeding with the next petition.

In the back of the gallery, Brice watched the woman he loved with a mixture of humor and awe. What an amazing woman she was. She was handling affairs of state as if she had been born for this task alone. He chuckled. Mary Stuart would feel the results of her charade for many years to come.

Lord Aston's voice rang through the chambers.

"Gareth MacKenzie of the Borders, in the matter of the death of Meredith MacAlpin."

At his words Meredith felt her throat go dry. At the sudden movement in the gallery, she turned to watch as the figures parted and one stepped forward. As she sat on the throne, she found herself face-to-face with the man she most feared and hated. Gareth MacKenzie.

Chapter Twenty-Four

Gareth was feeling supremely confident. Standing in the presence of the queen, with his men around him, he intended to paint a heroic picture of himself. He was aware, of course, that his golden hair and handsome face endeared him to most people. And in front of this young queen he would be the most charming man in all of Scotland.

He had rehearsed his speech until he was certain there was nothing he had forgotten. With characteristic boldness he began.

"My younger brother, Desmond, was to have wed the lady Meredith MacAlpin. On his wedding day Desmond was brutally murdered by the Highland Barbarian, Brice Campbell. His young bride was carried off to Campbell's Highland castle."

Meredith was aware of the gasps from many in the crowd. Scant months ago she, too, would have feared for the life of anyone abducted by Brice Campbell. His reputation as a scoundrel and murderer had been carefully established throughout the land.

In the back of the gallery Brice listened with a look of intense concentration to this man who had set out to destroy his reputation and who had nearly succeeded in ending his life as well.

"To avenge my brother's death and to save the young innocent from this savage, my men and I attacked Campbell's Highland home, Kinloch House, and though we were outnumbered, managed to kill Brice Campbell. But the lady, probably fearing for her life at the hands of that barbarian, fled into the Highland forests. My men and I searched for days but found no trace of her. It is our belief that the lady perished in the Highlands."

"Could she not have taken refuge in a cottage?"

"We inquired of many Highlanders, Majesty. No one has seen her."

"But if you have no proof of her death, why do you wish to have her declared dead?"

"Her clan is left without leadership or protection, Majesty. There are but two helpless maidens left to lead the MacAlpin clan." Gareth puffed up his chest and stood straighter. "I would be willing to wed the next eldest, Brenna, and offer the protection of my men."

"How very gracious of you." Meredith's tone frosted over. "If I grant your request, and you wed Brenna MacAlpin, you will claim her land as your own?"

"'Twould be my right, Majesty. But in return I would pledge my armies to the protection of her people."

"So, if you were to acquire the MacAlpin properties there would be no more lads murdered in the night, my lord MacKenzie? There would be no mysterious visits from this Highland Barbarian, who has been blamed for the deaths of every man, woman, child and sheep in Scotland?"

At the queen's sarcastic outburst Gareth felt the first tremor of alarm.

"The Highland Barbarian is dead, Majesty. Have you forgotten that I killed him?"

"I have forgotten nothing. This occurred during your attack upon his home, I believe."

When Gareth nodded she asked innocently, "With this Brice Campbell dead, why would the MacAlpins need your protection?"

He paused. He had not expected this question. "There are others who would prowl the darkness in search of those weaker than they. It has always been thus."

"Others? Are you suggesting that some of the murders along the Border may not have been committed by Brice Campbell?"

He was taken aback by that. "I—would suppose that is true."

"Some murders of Borderers may even have been committed by Borderers?"

Where was the queen leading him? "I do not know, Majesty."

"Come now, my lord MacKenzie. Have you no idea who might have gone about murdering innocent lads?"

"Nay. I know not."

"But I know." She got to her feet and stood facing him, small, elegant, regal. Her voice rang with authority. "Your queen must care about all the people in her realm. Even an insignificant Border lad who dares not walk about a darkened lane lest he be put upon by those bent upon destruction."

Gareth shivered. She knew about Duncan's grandson. His mind raced. "Young MacAlpin was murdered by the Highland Barbarian. I myself witnessed it."

"What an amazing man this barbarian is," Meredith said, her voice like ice. "He can be in two places at once."

Gareth began to protest, but her next words stopped him.

"When you were witnessing this murder, Brice Campbell was entertaining your queen at his Highland castle."

A loud murmur rippled through the crowd.

Gareth's mouth opened but no words could come out.

"Do you still wish to state that you were there when the lad was murdered?"

"Perhaps I was mistaken." Gareth, feeling a sheen of moisture on his forehead, stumbled about for some explanation to smooth over his awkward situation. "Perhaps I came upon him moments after."

"And you did not actually witness his murder?"

"I . . ." He stared at a spot on the floor. "Nay, Majesty."

"But it was your knife that was found bloodied. A knife you said was taken from you and plunged into the lad's heart. You told all who would listen that the blame lay with the Highland Barbarian."

Gareth was stung by her harshness. The woman was publicly humiliating him.

"I—did not recognize the men who murdered the lad, Majesty. But I thought one of them to be the Highland Barbarian."

"As you thought many times, my lord MacKenzie. Have you not accused Brice Campbell of every Border incident for the past two years?"

There was a long pause, and Gareth felt the monarch's gaze leveled on him. He chose not to respond to her attack.

"Now about this matter of Meredith MacAlpin."

Gareth stiffened at the dark mood of the queen. "I request that your Majesty declare her dead."

Meredith pointed a bejeweled finger at the man who stood trembling before her. "I declare that Meredith MacAlpin is alive."

The crowd leaned forward, their murmured words nearly drowning out her voice.

In the back of the gallery, Brice tensed, wishing he could inch his way through the crowd and get closer to Meredith.

MacKenzie had many men here with him. Backed into a corner, he would be like a vicious dog.

"Why would you declare her alive, Majesty?" Gareth's voice rose in anger.

"Your queen has seen her."

"That—that is splendid news," Gareth said in halting tones, trying vainly to salvage his image.

"Aye. Splendid." Meredith was beginning to enjoy herself. "In fact, the lass visited your queen here in Holyroodhouse this very day."

"She is here?" Gareth's eyes narrowed. Without realizing it, his hand went to the sword at his waist.

"She had me spellbound with her stories." Meredith paused for dramatic effect, then said in a voice that carried through the hall, "Meredith MacAlpin overheard you plotting her murder."

For a moment the crowd fell silent, then many stood and began craning their necks for a better view of this unexpected confrontation.

"The woman lies, Majesty."

"Why would she lie about this, my lord?"

"Perhaps she took a blow to the head during her abduction by the Barbarian." Gareth was now sweating profusely, and he wiped a hand across his brow. "I would ask to be allowed to confront the woman who spreads such lies about me."

"You are confronting the woman..." Meredith began, then caught herself. How could she have forgotten who she was supposed to be? "Who speaks for her." She prayed her attempt at a regal tone would cover her lapse. "This day I declare that all lands now held by you, Gareth MacKenzie, shall be equally divided among those clans who have suffered the loss of loved ones by your hands. You will be stripped of all titles. And you shall be banished forever from

Scotland. If you return, you will face imprisonment in Tolbooth."

The crowd came to its feet in a frenzy of excitement. How
could they have known that an audience this day with the
queen would offer such an adventure?

Gareth, standing in front of the queen's throne, appeared stricken. Then, taking advantage of the confusion,
he darted past the throne and disappeared through an open
doorway.

"Seize him," Meredith shouted to the guards who stood
on either side of the throne.

Before the guards took a single step, Brice had vaulted
over the railing that separated the gallery from the throne.
Sword in hand he followed Gareth in hot pursuit.

Still wearing the queen's gown, Meredith sat in the guest
chambers with her two sisters and Mary Fleming.

The crowds of spectators had been disbursed. Soldiers
were busy combing every inch of the palace. Angus had
gone off in search of Brice.

"We are safe here," Fleming said softly. "That horrid
man will soon be found and punished."

"I fear for Brice." Meredith paced, unable to sit.

"Brice Campbell is the most dangerous warrior in all of
Scotland. Why should you fear for his safety?"

"He is weary from his long journey. He may grow careless."

"Aye. And he is drained, having suffered a wound at the
hands of a Highland enemy, Holden Mackay." Brenna's soft
voice trembled.

"Mackay?" Meredith whirled on her sister. "What are
you saying?"

"Brice told us that he and his men attacked Mackay's fortress searching for you. But you had already escaped in disguise."

"God in heaven." Meredith slumped into a chair. "And what of Mackay?"

"Mackay is dead. But in the battle, Brice was wounded."

Meredith pressed her fingers to her temples to ease the terrible throbbing that had been building throughout the day.

"You should rest," Fleming said softly.

"I will rest when this is over."

They looked up expectantly at the sound of hurried footsteps. At the sight of the queen, Meredith could hardly hide her disappointment. She had hoped it would be Brice.

"Oh, my darlings, you must gather around me and hear about my wonderful day." Mary gave Meredith a quick appraisal, and noting her obvious distress, murmured, "So now you have had a taste of what it is like to be ruler. Was she a good queen, Flem?"

"She was most fair, Majesty. And very quick of mind. You will be receiving congratulations on your wise decisions of today for many weeks to come."

"Ah. That only adds to an already perfect adventure."

"You were happy with your—abductor?"

The queen blushed. "The Earl of Bothwell is an exciting suitor. And a wicked rogue, much like your Brice Campbell," she said to Meredith.

"Will you tell us everything?" Flem asked.

Mary laughed. "You know I will, Flem. Now let me begin with the very first moment my lover arrived at my chambers."

Brenna glanced at Meredith's pale face. With calm assurance, she surprised the queen and her Maries by taking

Meredith by the hand. "Please excuse us, Majesty. Meredith must rest or she will make herself ill."

Though she protested, Meredith allowed herself to be led to the sleeping chamber.

"I will help you change into something comfortable." Brenna reached for the buttons of the scarlet gown.

"Nay." Meredith stopped her. "Until the queen gives her permission, I must continue the charade."

"Aye." Brenna removed the crown and unpinned Meredith's hair. "But at least you can be comfortable."

"I will not sleep. I will merely rest for a few minutes."

"Rest then," Brenna whispered, helping her into bed. "We will be just outside the door in the sitting chamber."

Meredith's weak smile revealed her exhaustion. "I am so glad you are here."

"Then you do not mind that we disobeyed your orders?"

"Nay." Meredith opened her arms and embraced her sister.

"Rest now. Soon enough we will be home."

Home. Meredith watched as the door closed. It had been such a long time since she had enjoyed the simple pleasures of home.

Her lids fluttered. With a sigh she gave in to the overwhelming feelings that swamped her. Within minutes she was fast asleep.

The sun had made its arc to the western sky. Evening shadows drifted across the grounds of Holyroodhouse. Meredith heard the door to the outer chamber open, and heard, from the sitting chamber, the sounds of her sisters chatting with the queen. The servants had apparently brought an evening meal. From the peals of laughter that could be heard, it was obvious that the queen was still regaling them with tales of her adventure. What a delightful surprise to know that her sisters were here to share this.

At the muted sound of footsteps Meredith sat up, a bright expectant smile on her face. "Brice..."

The man who appeared beside her bed was not Brice. His golden hair and evil, dangerous smile made her heart stop.

"So, my lady. At last I find you."

As she opened her mouth to scream, he covered her mouth with his hand. In his other hand was a small, deadly knife. "If you summon the others, they will die as well. The choice is yours."

Meredith thought about the two sisters she adored. She would rather die at the hands of this monster than give him the chance to harm Brenna or Megan. She nodded her agreement. When he removed his hand she sucked in several deep breaths and fought to control her terror.

Roughly he threw back the bed covers and dragged her to her feet. The moment the bed linens fell away, he stared in openmouthed surprise.

"That gown... You..." His eyes narrowed. "You! It was not the queen who publicly humiliated me this day. It was you."

"Aye. And it was nearly as satisfying as seeing you dead." She tossed her head, striving for courage she did not really feel. "You cannot hope to kill me and escape this palace. There are guards everywhere."

"I have evaded them for hours," he scoffed. "When darkness covers the land I will join my men who wait for me beyond the city."

"But where can you go? You cannot hide forever. You have been banished from Scotland."

"By you. Not by the queen."

"I speak for the queen." With her hands at her hips she met his level look. "The words I spoke this day are already law."

"There are ways around the law." He spoke quickly, as though he had already given this some thought. "There are many countries that would welcome a man who can command armies."

"You would ask your men to leave their homes and follow you?"

"They will go where I lead them." He moved closer. "The French queen hates Mary Stuart. She would pay me handsomely to fight for her cause."

"That would make you a traitor as well as a murderer."

"You are a fool." He studied the firm young body beneath the elegant gown. "Together we could have owned all of the Borderland."

"Then you are the bigger fool. I would have rather died than permitted you to touch me."

His hand snaked out, catching her roughly by the shoulder. "Then you shall have your wish." His gaze pinned her. "From the beginning you were the problem. But you will be a problem no more."

"What do you intend to do with me?"

His breath was hot against her temple as he dragged her toward the door. "I had hoped to kill you. But now you will be my assurance that I leave this prison. If any of the queen's guards stop us, you will be as convincing as you were this day. You, little witch, will help me reach my men safely. And," he added with a cruel laugh, "if you prove useful enough, I may even take you all the way to France with me."

As he dragged her toward the outer door, the inner door between the sitting chamber and sleeping chamber was suddenly thrown open. Brice stood framed in the doorway. Beyond him stood the queen, her face aglow, her Maries surrounding her like fluttering birds.

At the sight of Meredith being held at knife point, Brice's blood froze.

Gareth found himself staring at a ghost.

"You are dead. I killed you."

"And I have come back to haunt you," Brice said through gritted teeth.

"Nay. It cannot be. I plunged my sword through your heart. I watched the lifeblood spill from you. As my father did before me with your father."

At his words everyone went deathly quiet.

It was Brice who broke the silence. "Was it also your father who spread lies about my father?"

Gareth gave an evil smile. "Aye. He coveted his wealth and titles. And he taught his sons well. Once a man's name is muddied, it is never clean again."

"And the lies spread about me in the French Court?"

Meredith suddenly realized what heartache Brice must have suffered in a foreign land, with enemies such as the MacKenzies.

"Aye." Gareth laughed. "The queen mother felt that you were exerting too much influence on the young queen. It was my task to see that you were—encouraged to leave."

"Release the woman." Brice's words were deadly soft. "This fight is between the two of us."

Gareth tightened his grip on Meredith's throat. "You will drop your weapon or my dirk will find the woman's heart."

The other women stood in stunned silence in the doorway. Their faces mirrored their shock as they watched and listened.

For a long moment Brice's gaze held Meredith's. He thought of all the battles he had fought, the victories he had savored. How simple life had been when he'd had nothing to lose except his own life. But it was Meredith's life that hung in the balance. And he would gladly pay any price, even death, to save her.

He made a move to toss aside his sword.

As his hand moved to his scabbard Meredith gave a cry. "No, Brice. I cannot let him kill you."

In a panic Gareth pressed the blade tightly to Meredith's throat. She gave a sudden cry of pain. Blood spilled down her bodice.

At the sight of her blood Brice lost all reason. Like a man possessed he lunged, catching Meredith by the arm and yanking her free of Gareth's grasp. With one fluid movement he plunged his sword through Gareth's heart.

For a moment Gareth stared at his assailant, his eyes round and unblinking. Then, with a cry bubbling in his throat, he dropped to the floor.

As Meredith slumped to her knees Brice caught her and lifted her in his strong arms. With blood streaming from her wound she clung to him and whispered, "Oh, Brice, hold me."

Before he could respond she sank into a sea of darkness.

Meredith drifted in and out of consciousness.

Through a blur of voices she heard Brice's voice, low and troubled. "She should have responded to your physician's potion by now."

She thought she heard Brenna calmly stating, "It is exhaustion. She has been through too much these past months. She must be returned to MacAlpin Castle. There she will rest and grow strong."

There was another voice, regal, haughty. "You will take my carriage and a company of my soldiers. She can be home by morning light."

And Megan's voice, high-pitched in agitation. "If anything will give her the will to live it is home."

"Home." Though Meredith's mouth formed the word, no sound came out.

She felt Brice's arms around her, cradling her against his chest. She breathed in the familiar scent of him and sighed as sleep once more overtook her.

Meredith lay very still, listening to the sound of birds on the sloping lawns of MacAlpin Castle. She snuggled deeper into the furs surrounding her and breathed in the fragrance of roses that wafted from the cultivated gardens below her window.

Opening her eyes she saw the figure in the chair beside her bed. Brice, his chin rough and unshaven, his eyes red rimmed from lack of sleep, sat watching her.

"At last you are awake." He sat forward and caught her hand.

"Have I slept long?" Her words were wrenched from a throat that felt raw.

He nodded. "I feared you would never wake." He smiled, causing her heart to tumble wildly. "I remembered that other world that once held me in its spell, and thought it had claimed you instead."

"How long have I been home?"

Home. The word caused a terrible pain around his heart. How long had he denied her the comfort of her home?

"For three days now you have slept in your own bed. But you were not here. You were somewhere else. I could not reach you. No one could."

Meredith remembered the way she had suffered when Brice had lingered near death's door. Seeking to comfort him she placed her hand over his. "You need worry no longer, my lord. I am home now. And I am here to stay."

A look of pain crossed his handsome features and she longed to draw him close and ease his suffering. Instead she asked, "Why is my throat so constricted?"

"You do not remember?"

At her arched brow he said softly, "Gareth MacKenzie cut your throat."

She touched a hand to the dressing that covered the wound. "And Gareth?"

"Dead."

She seemed to take a long time to let that fact sink in. She remembered the horrified look on Brice's face as he yanked her free of Gareth's grasp. But nothing more. Neither the pain nor the panic. In a voice still softened by sleep she whispered, "Leave me, Brice, and take your rest. 'Tis over at last. Now we can all live in peace."

Peace. He watched, tormented, as her lids fluttered, then closed. How could he have forgotten her position as leader of her clan? He had foolishly nurtured the dream of making her his bride and uniting their clans. But she was a Borderer, whose gentle, rolling countryside was a battleground that divided Scotland and England. And he was a Highlander, whose people depended upon his leadership for their very survival in a harsh environment. His father had been brutally taken from them. It would not be fair to leave them without a leader again.

Neither of them could go with the other and leave their people leaderless.

Brenna, who had paused in the doorway, reluctant to intrude, now walked to the bedside and touched a hand to her sister's forehead.

"Already the healing has begun. With rest she will soon be as strong as before."

She was surprised to see the stricken look on Brice's face. "I thought that would make you happy, my lord Campbell."

"Aye. I am delighted that Meredith is regaining her strength." He stood wearily. "But now that I know she will survive, I must leave."

"Rest here a few days, my lord, until Meredith is strong enough to speak with you. From what I know of your time together in the Highlands, you have much to talk over."

So she had confided in her sisters.

He shook his head and ran a hand over the beard that darkened his chin. "She has already spoken. She desires to live in her home in peace."

"I heard her words," Brenna said softly. "But when she is stronger..."

"When she is stronger," Brice said firmly, "she will unite her people and rebuild that which Gareth MacKenzie sought to destroy. And I," he said, strapping on his sword and tossing a cape over his shoulder, "have a clan depending upon me as well. I have left them leaderless long enough."

"Meredith will wish to thank you, Brice."

He took Brenna's hands in his and kissed her cheek. "Thanks are not necessary. It is my fault that she has been denied her home for so long now. Tell her only that I..." He stopped abruptly as Angus and Megan walked into the room. With a wry smile he said, "Tell Meredith that I wish her every happiness."

In a low voice the others could not hear Brenna asked, "Do you love her, Brice?"

"Aye. With all my heart. And for that reason I must leave her. She has a duty. As do I."

"You once said that you would even risk losing her if it meant her happiness."

He said nothing.

Brenna and Megan watched as Brice strode quickly from the room without a backward glance. Within minutes he and Angus could be seen urging their mounts into a gallop toward the river Tweed.

With a heavy heart Brenna draped an arm about her sister's shoulder. The two sisters stood at the balcony window and watched until both figures disappeared into the Highland mists.

Chapter Twenty-Five

Brice leaned a hip against the window of his balcony and watched as a falcon slowly circled, searching for prey.

From below stairs came the sad, sorrowful sounds of Jamie's lute. For days now the lad's music seemed to mirror Brice's feelings.

What had he once told Meredith? That he had never felt lonely in his Highland fortress. He gave a bitter laugh and lifted his face to the sky, seeing the falcon's mate suddenly appear. The two birds soared together, looking as though they could touch the sun. Then they suddenly swooped, skimming low to the ground before once more lifting, soaring, until they were lost from view.

He felt a terrible, aching sense of loss.

Ever since he had returned to Kinloch House he had felt restless and irritable. In his absence the great hall had been restored. The women had completed the new tapestries, relating the proud history of the Campbells. Tradesmen in the villages had made new chairs, tables, and settles. Weavers had provided fresh linens. The castle sparkled under the loving care of Mistress Snow and the servants, who filled it with the fresh scents of mint and evergreen.

It was so empty.

Though it resounded with the voices of the serving girls and the laughter of Brice's men, it no longer brought him joy to walk the halls of Kinloch House.

In every room he saw her. In the refectory, sitting beside Jamie, listening to the booming voices of his men while she quietly ate. In the great hall, warming herself before the fire. In his sleeping chamber, lying beside him. Thoughts of Meredith tormented him.

He had never dreamed it would be so painful to let go.

He had waged terrible, bitter arguments with himself. If he were half a man he would ride to the Borders and take her. It had always been the Highlanders' way. But her plea, in her moment of pain, had touched him deeply. Home. For too long she had been denied the comfort of her home. Because of him. If he truly loved her, he had to give her what she most craved. And in that moment he had seen with perfect clarity. Meredith needed her home. He had no right to deny her her heart's desire.

If she loved him, he thought with growing resentment, she would come to him. She would leave her people without a leader, without protection from the invaders to the south, and come to him. She would leave her gentle rolling hills behind and make her home with him. He studied the land, trying to see it from her eyes. Where he saw shady glens and waterfalls, she would see dark forests where the sun never penetrated. Where he saw wide, peaceful vistas she would see a harsh, primitive wilderness.

What foolishness. She had a duty to her people. And he had a duty to his.

He frowned, cursing the day he had seen her standing at the altar, looking like an angel from heaven. If he had never met her, had never allowed himself to love her, he would not now have this terrible aching void in his life.

He cursed himself for wallowing in self-pity like some lovesick lad. Pulling on his tunic he strode down the stairs and picked up an axe. There were trees to be felled. He would feel better after a day of punishing physical labor.

Darkness spread over the land. In his chambers Brice turned away from the balcony window and sprawled upon a low bench pulled in front of the fire. Below he could hear the sound of his men's voices, low, muted, as they discussed the events of the day. He had no desire to join them.

He heard the sad, haunting notes of Jamie's lute and felt a wave of regret. The lad missed her. Almost as much as Brice did. Jamie had blurted the truth earlier today while they had worked together in the forest. He'd admitted that when Brice returned without Meredith, he had felt as if he'd lost his mother again.

It had been a blow to Brice. But he vowed to spend more time with the lad to ease him through this sense of loss. In time the pain would cease. For both of them.

He lifted a half-filled tankard and drank. At a knock on the door he called, "Enter."

Angus entered, then beckoned for Mistress Snow to follow.

"Do we disturb you, old friend?"

"Nay."

Brice stood and indicated the settle. The housekeeper took a seat but Angus preferred to stand.

Brice glanced from his friend to the woman. Both of them were grinning and looked as if they would burst if they did not soon share their news.

"Mistress Snow has consented to marry me," Angus said.

Brice caught his friend in a great bear hug. "I am happy for you." He turned to embrace the blushing woman. "For both of you."

"Thank you, my lord."

Brice turned to Angus. "When will you wed?"

"We will speak to the rector on the morrow. I would prefer it yesterday." He and Brice shared a laugh. "But my bride would like a fortnight to return to her cottage in yonder forest and prepare it properly for our dwelling."

"The cottage." Brice turned to Mistress Snow, then clapped a hand on his old friend's shoulder. "I do not think a humble cottage would be the proper dwelling for the leader of the Mackay clan."

Angus stared at him without comprehending.

"With Holden Mackay dead, we must find a way to unite his clan with ours. I have been thinking that you would be the perfect clan leader, my friend. Though I was loath to send you away when I knew that your heart was here with Mistress Snow." Brice gave them both a knowing smile. "But now that you are to be wed, you have solved my dilemma. Would you and your bride be willing to live in the Mackay fortress and help me bring peace to these Highlands?"

Angus stared at Brice for long minutes, then turned and lifted Mistress Snow into his arms. "What say you, lass? Would you be willing to give up your duties here at Kinloch House and live like the lady of the manor?"

"Oh, Angus." As he lifted her high in the air she laughed in delight. "I cannot believe it."

"Nor can I." He set her on her feet and, keeping one arm draped about her, extended his other arm toward his old friend. "I would like Alston as my right hand. He is good with people. Mackay's men will take to him."

"He is yours."

"We must go below stairs and tell the others." Angus turned to Brice. "Will you join us?"

"In a while."

When they had left, Brice turned to stare thoughtfully into the flames of the fire. He would miss the company of Angus and Alston, the red-bearded giant. And the loss of Mistress Snow would surely be felt in Kinloch House. But he was happy for his friends.

If only he could shake off this heaviness around his heart.

The hounds set off a wild frenzy of barking. He heard the babble of voices and the sound of Jamie's lute. They would no doubt celebrate long into the night. This sad place badly needed a celebration.

Picking up his tankard he drained it and set it on the mantel. At a sound from the doorway he turned.

His mind was playing tricks on him. He was seeing her again, looking far lovelier than she had ever looked before.

She wore a hooded cape of lush green velvet, lined with ermine. Her cheeks were flushed, and her green eyes sparkled with a light that he had seen before, on that first night they had loved. She slid the hood back to reveal a mane of mahogany hair that tumbled down her back in a riot of curls. Entwined in her hair were ivy and wildflowers, their sweet perfume filling the air.

He blinked. The vision did not vanish. Instead she took a step closer. Her lips parted in the sweetest smile.

"Meredith." His heart stopped.

"Aye."

He felt his throat go dry. "You are not a vision?"

"Nay, my lord." She laughed and crossed the room until she was standing in front of him. "Touch me. I will not vanish."

Touch her? He wanted to crush her to him. Instead he reached a hand to her and felt his fingertips gently brush her cheek.

"How did you get here?"

"I rode."

"Alone?" His eyes narrowed.

"Nay, my lord. I brought a company of my men."

"Ah." At last his senses were returning. The floor, which for a moment had tilted dangerously, was now steady once more. He brought his other hand to her face and stared down into her eyes. "Why have you come, Meredith?"

"To invite you to a wedding."

"A wedding?" His heart tumbled. His brows drew together in a frown.

"Aye."

"Whose wedding?"

She smiled. "Mine."

His frown became a scowl. She felt his battle for control as he dropped his hands to his sides, where they curled into fists. "You did not wait long to wed."

"I have waited long enough." When she saw the look of pain that crossed his features she could no longer carry on the charade. "Oh, Brice. If you could but see your face." She reached up to touch him and the cape slid from her shoulders, revealing a white gossamer gown that skimmed her breasts and fell in soft folds to the tips of kid slippers.

His hands grasped her shoulders so tightly that she gasped. "You look," he whispered, "as beautiful as you did on that morn when first I saw you in the cathedral."

"This time," she said, looking up at him with love shining in her eyes, "I dressed for you."

"For me." He allowed his gaze to travel slowly over her, devouring her.

And then he knew.

"You've come to stay?"

"Aye. If you'll have me."

"Oh, Meredith." He drew her into the circle of his arms and kissed her with a savageness that left them both dazed and reeling.

He lifted his head and touched a fingertip to the tear that squeezed from her eye and coursed down her cheek. "Tears, firebrand?"

"I was so afraid, Brice."

"Of what?"

"Afraid this was all a terrible mistake. Afraid that when I reached your beloved Highlands you would not want me."

"Oh, my love. You are all I want."

"Then why did you leave me without a word?"

"I had no right to ask you to give up your title, your power, your home, for me."

Another tear spilled over, and then another while she wrapped her arms about his neck and clung to him. So Brenna had been right. She would be forever thankful to her sister for urging her to take the risk.

Against his throat she whispered, "You are all I want, Brice. Without you it is empty."

"Oh, little firebrand." He buried his lips in a tangle of her hair and crushed her to him. "What arrangements have you made for your clan?"

"Brenna will be the MacAlpin." She smiled. "Without Gareth MacKenzie to divide them, the Borderers have united to stand against any English attack. Though I fear Brenna's greatest challenge will not be with the English, but with our sister, Megan."

Brice laughed. "Aye. The lass is like another I know." He kissed the tip of her nose.

"Be very careful, my lord. We are not yet wed."

"Nay. But Angus and Mistress Snow are below stairs now planning their wedding. And if we are wise, we will ask to share their ceremony on the morrow."

"Oh, Brice. Could we?" She caught his hand. "Let us go below and speak to them."

She was surprised when he resisted. Before she could tug again on his hand he dragged her roughly against him and covered her lips with his. Instantly she felt the rush of desire that begged for release.

"We will talk with them later." The words were ground against her lips.

They sank to their knees on the fur throw. His fingers moved to the buttons of her gown.

"My men..."

"Will be invited to a wedding on the morrow. But for tonight, my beloved, just let me love you."

Love. "Oh, Brice," she breathed against his lips. "I love you so."

"And I love you, Meredith. So much." His fingers began to weave their magic. His lips moved over her, igniting little fires wherever they touched. "Welcome home, little firebrand."

Home. Aye. These Highlands were now home. This man, this Highland Barbarian, held her heart.

She felt a welling of so much love. A love that would endure even beyond this lifetime. A love to last an eternity.

Author's Note

A quotation from John Fordun's "Chronicles" in Skene's *Celtic Scotland*, from 1363 to 1384, states:

> The highlanders...are a savage and untamed nation, rude and independent...comely in person but unsightly in dress, hostile to the English people and language...and exceedingly cruel. They are, however, faithful and obedient to their crown and country....

That quotation fascinated me. And as I researched, I discovered some who could have been my ancestors. I admit that I fell in love with these highland barbarians.

* * * * *

COMING NEXT MONTH

#43 THE GENTLEMAN—Kristin James

In the eyes of St. Louis society, Stephen Ferguson was the
picture of gentility and elegance. But when he arrived in
Nora Springs, Montana, valet in tow, Jessie Randall
thought him a rarefied fop. She soon found out just how
much of a man Stephen was....

#44 SUMMER'S PROMISE—Lucy Elliot

Everyone whispered about Caroline Fielding, the sadder-
but-wiser girl who'd sailed to the Colonies to avoid
scandal. Her only dream was for a life of peaceful
seclusion in the New England wilderness. French trapper
Daniel Ledet shared the same need for solitude—until he
met Caroline.

AVAILALBLE NOW:

#41 HIGHLAND
BARBARIAN
Ruth Langan

#42 PASSION'S EMBRACE
Cassie Edwards

**In April, Harlequin brings you the
world's most popular romance author**

JANET DAILEY

No Quarter Asked

Out of print since 1974!

After the tragic death of her father, Stacy's world is shattered. She needs to get away by herself to sort things out. She leaves behind her boyfriend, Carter Price, who wants to marry her. However, as soon as she arrives at her rented cabin in Texas, Cord Harris, owner of a large ranch, seems determined to get her to leave. When Stacy has a fall and is injured, Cord reluctantly takes her to his own ranch. Unknown to Stacy, Carter's father has written to Cord and asked him to keep an eye on Stacy and try to convince her to return home. After a few weeks there, in spite of Cord's hateful treatment that involves her working as a ranch hand and the return of Lydia, his ex-fiancée, by the time Carter comes to escort her back, Stacy knows that she is in love with Cord and doesn't want to go.

**Watch for *Fiesta San Antonio* in July and
For Bitter or Worse in September.**

JDA-1